NEXT GIRL TO DIE

NEXT GIRL TO DIE

DEA POIRIER

THOMAS & MERCER

Published by Thomas & Mercer, Seattle
www.apub.com

ISBN-13: 9781503959200
ISBN-10: 1503959201

Cover design by Caroline Teagle Johnson

Printed in the United States of America

For my grandmother

CHAPTER 1

At some point, as you get older, you stop counting things—how many times you've been on an airplane, driven across the country, or solved a murder. No matter how many murders I solve, it won't fix me.

I close the file in front of me. It hits me close to home; memories of another murder strain against the box in the back of my mind, where I've hidden them. The teenage girl in the file was killed in a hit-and-run. Vehicular homicide is still homicide, and that means it falls to me to solve it. I lean back in a chair at a borrowed desk, and it squeaks in protest. Normally, I sit out in the station bull pen with the other detectives, but I needed to concentrate on my final notes for this case. Though seeing it through should feel like a load off, it doesn't. Death is a cloud that will never lift. Footsteps in the hall draw my attention, and I sit up a little straighter, just in case Sergeant Gomez is about to pop her head in.

Instead Roxie's face appears, her dark fauxhawk swept up, her usual curls smoothed away. In this light, her medium-brown complexion has an undertone of ocher, thanks to old lights flickering above us. She offers me a half grin, the kind she always dons when she's testing my mood. I push the file away from me like a plate of food that's been picked at for too long—if only someone would show up to whisk it away.

"How's it coming?" she asks.

"Done." I shove up from the desk and stalk over to the windows, looking down over the busy street beneath us. Traffic, the city—it's something that I can always use to distract myself. Maybe it's still a wonder because I grew up without it.

"You want to get out of here? Maybe catch a movie tonight?" she asks.

It would be nice to get away, to take a step back. In the middle of a case, it's impossible for me to pull myself away, for me to get any distance from it. But until another case falls in my lap—and another will; it always does—I'll take this reprieve while I can. "Yeah, let's do it," I say, but before I even have the words all the way out, my phone vibrates in my pocket. The number on the screen isn't familiar, but the area code sure is—it's the area code of my hometown. Seeing it, even just thinking of Vinalhaven, is like being punched in the gut. My finger hovers over the accept button, but I look to Roxie. "Could you give me a minute?"

Her brows furrow, and the look she gives me makes me wonder what my own face must look like. "Sure. I'll be at my desk. Take as long as you need," she says before pulling the door closed.

I hold my breath and accept the call. Normally I answer my phone as *Detective*, but for this call—who am I? So I settle for "Hello?"

"Claire Calderwood?" A man's voice—low and gruff—cuts through the silence in the office.

"Yes," I say, and I clench the hand that isn't holding my phone into a fist. "Who is this?"

"Sergeant Michaels," he says. "Of the Vinalhaven Police Department." He tacks on the next statement like it only just occurred to him to say it, as if he's unfamiliar with introducing himself.

"What do you need?" I ask, my words clipped. Normally I'd give a sergeant the respect they deserve, but I'm so caught off guard that he's lucky I'm talking at all. It takes a few seconds for my mind to dredge up memories of him; the last time I saw him, I was in high school.

"We've got a situation that I was hoping you could help with. Some people in town mentioned that when you left Vinalhaven, you went to work in Detroit as a homicide detective." Papers shuffle in the background while he speaks. I can imagine him sifting through the paperwork.

I know what's coming next before he says a word. Another girl is dead. *Another* girl. My sister was the first. Emotion tightens around my chest, like I've got my vest on too tight. The memories threaten to breach the wall I've built around them. I clench my fist tighter, my fingernails cutting half moons into my palm, as I try to push past it.

"Emma Carver—I'm not sure if you knew her; she would have been five or so when you moved—she was—" He stops so suddenly that I check the screen to see if the call dropped.

"She was killed," I say, finishing the sentence for him. The words don't hold the weight they should. But when you've been saying words like *murder*, *homicide*, and *dead* since you were fifteen, they lose their luster.

"Yes," he says finally.

There's a long pause, and I decide to take the reins, saving me from the memories threatening to slither back to the surface. "When was she murdered?"

"Three days ago," he says. "Strangled. Her body was found in Grimes Park."

The park that sits on the southernmost tip of the island, next to the marina, the same park my sister's body was found in. A shiver traces down my spine, though it's stifling in the office. Six months after Rachel died, I stood in that park hoping it would reveal the secrets of what happened to my sister. It never did.

"I know you're working in Detroit, but we're in over our heads. We could really use the help," he says, his voice strained.

When Rachel died, I had no choice but to stick around until I was eighteen—until I could flee the island that took my sister. And since, not once have I considered going back. I left that life behind, shedding it like an old skin. A few times over the years, usually around the anniversary of Rachel's death, guilt got the best of me, and I considered opening up her cold case to try and solve it. But I couldn't; it would have been like picking a scab, opening up that wound all over again.

When I say nothing, he continues. "I know this could be painful for you—given your history. But maybe this could help you get some closure."

I want to laugh at that. Closure is a goddamn fairy tale. There's no closure when your sister is murdered.

"Claire—I mean, Detective Calderwood—please. If you can't help, if we can't find who did this—" He stops, as if he knows he's gone too far.

My nails dig into my palm so sharply I wince. The pain keeps me present, though; I can't let my emotions surge forward again. "I need to think about it. Send me what you have in her file, at the least. I'll take a look and see what I can do."

"I'll send it, but really, Claire, we need someone like you here. You know this island better than an outsider. You think like us. You know that people here don't want to talk to mainlanders. More importantly, they don't want to help them."

"I know," I say. Because he's right. If they bring in anyone else, no one on the island will trust that person. I finish my call with Sergeant Michaels. Instead of finding Roxie, I stare back out the window, oblivious to the people below. It's not the city I see now; it's my sister reflected in the window.

CHAPTER 2

A cold, salty wind sweeps across the bay; I lean over the railing of the ferry into it, letting the mist kiss my face until my skin tingles. My long blonde hair whips against my neck, my cheeks, and I wish I'd put it up. The sun is dying on the horizon, setting the world ablaze in a blanket of orange and red. I can't deny that I missed this. Above me, a seagull caws, and it drags me back to my childhood, days spent on the pebbled beach while the cold water tickled my toes. The waves hiss as they crest against the side of the ferry. In Detroit, I missed nature, being able to go outdoors, being able to breathe air that wasn't thick with exhaust and smoke. I didn't go there to breathe; I went there to bury my problems beneath the crime and crowded streets—and at the very least, it served that purpose well.

There, I didn't think I'd be the girl who escaped her dead sister and abandoned her grieving family. There, I was supposed to be free. I thought beneath the towering skyscrapers and the crumbling Motor City, I'd be just another no one. And most days, I'd much rather be no one than the sister of Rachel Calderwood. It hasn't gone as I planned, though. Now the whole world feels like hers, not just the island we grew up on. I guess that's what happens when someone dies. It's impossible to see the world without wondering what it'd look like if she were still in it.

It doesn't take long to spot Vinalhaven growing out of the bay in front of us. From this far away, it doesn't look like the place that took my sister from me; the small wood-frame houses among the rolling hills make it look like a postcard. The houses rise behind the marina; it's thick with boats, more than I remember. I left here thinking the town would die right along with Rachel. Because how could it recover if I couldn't? Here it is, though, like nothing ever happened. Its life went on, while mine seemed to end.

I squint against the sun as the fading light shimmers across the water. I try to see beyond the marina, to downtown, but I'm too far away. The reds, whites, and grays are broken and blurred like in a kaleidoscope. Downtown means I'm close to the house I've rented. It's two minutes from Main Street, thankfully as far from my parents' house as I could get—and the best I could do on three weeks' notice. Unfortunately, that also means I'm as far from my grandmother's house as I can get as well. My heart aches when I think of her. I haven't seen her since before Rachel died, before there was a falling-out between her and my mother.

The ferry's horn echoes across the bay, a low tune, a lament. With each roar of the engine, we press closer to the island, and my stomach creeps into my throat, bringing regret along for the ride. What the hell was I thinking coming back here? I should have stayed in Detroit. I was stupid to think coming here wouldn't dredge up all the feelings I locked inside when I left, because here they are, burning all the way up my esophagus.

As the dock comes into view, my heart hammers like it's trying to get out. It's too late to run now, too late to back out. I need to pull on my big-girl britches and get my shit together.

I can do this, I tell myself over and over, until I almost believe it.

Until I see *them*.

My mom's long blonde hair is swept up on top of her head; every strand is strangled in hair spray, plastered into place. Her arm is latched on to my dad, like if she doesn't hold on for dear life, he might take off. I've always felt like he meant to leave but never got around to it. Now he just hides in the house and spends most of his time avoiding my mother. I don't blame him; that's what I've been trying to do for the last fifteen years.

A thin smile causes the sides of her mouth to crease heavily. I force a smile on my face and hope it hides every single thing I'm feeling. If my mother senses anything, she'll pounce, trying desperately to fix whatever she feels is wrong. While Rachel was alive, all the energy was focused on her. But the moment she was gone, it shifted to me. She needed to *fix* me, to make sure I didn't end up like Rachel. It's like someone crossbred a shark and a shrink.

The ferry bounces to a stop against the dock. For a few minutes the workers tie us in, then finally drop the ramp. My mother's eyes are on me the entire time, like she's afraid if she looks away, I'll disappear. Like maybe I'm a mirage. As soon as I'm able to step off the boat, I close the distance between us, and my mother gives me a stiff hug. "I am *so* glad you're home," she says in a voice flatter than usual, as if me being home might be an inconvenience.

As soon as she lets me go, my father folds me into his arms. "I've missed you, kiddo," he says in his low voice.

"Me too," I force myself to say. Things with them have been difficult since Rachel died. My mother became an overbearing control freak, while my father retreated. He may as well have been a ghost. Maybe that will be the one good part of coming back: maybe there will be some way to repair our relationship. Granted, they don't see the splinters. They probably never will—or maybe they just don't want to.

"I really wish you'd stay with us," she says, glancing over her shoulder back toward Main Street.

"Mom, it's a fifteen-minute drive. At least I'm not still in Detroit," I say, trying not to let frustration reach my voice.

She purses her lips like she's going to say something else but thinks better of it. "Did you have a good flight?" she finally asks.

"The flight was fine," I say, because I have no desire to relive the account of the guy who snored next to me the whole time.

"You know what would be wonderful?" she starts, and the brakes in my mind squeal, because whatever follows those words will not be wonderful, not in the least. "You should have dinner with us tonight."

"I wish I could; I need to settle in, dig into my case."

"Your things aren't even here. You can't settle in. That's exactly why you should have stayed with us. Everything is still in your room."

The memories are hard enough, never mind staying with my parents in my old room, where everything is exactly where it was thirteen years ago. Like it's some kind of museum. Rachel's room hasn't changed since the day she died either. Two untouched rooms, two monuments to my mother's lost daughters. It took years for me to realize my unchanging room had nothing to do with me and everything to do with my mother. I guess it was her way of keeping us close after she lost us both—or maybe it's the only thing about us she ended up being able to control.

We walk along the sidewalk through downtown; it looks almost exactly like it did the last time I was here. A few stores have updated their signs, repainted. The wooden signs still hang on brackets, creaking in the wind. We pass the small hotel right off the bay, several restaurants, and a small post office set inside an old house. I steer us toward the small Victorian I'm renting, and I'm surprised to find the house across the street has been turned into a bed-and-breakfast. Mrs. Peterson described this house to me as small, but *small* on this island is a relative term. Most of the houses on the island are enormous old wood-frame houses. They're not grand by any means; they're the usual houses that sprout out of most of New England. The *fancy* houses are reserved for the northern parts of the island, where the air reeks of old money.

The two-story yellow Victorian sits just off the street. A splintered walkway leads to the wraparound porch. At three bedrooms and 2,500 square feet, my rental was the smallest on the island I could find. It's way too much house for me, especially after living in a one-bedroom apartment for years, but the pickings were slim. And if there's one thing I remember well about island life, it's that you take what you can get.

"You should get a dog," my mom says when she grimaces at the house. The statement stops me in my tracks. She hates animals, always has. Rachel and I must have asked for a dog a thousand times. When we couldn't get a dog, Rachel asked for a horse, a cat, a parakeet, a hamster, and finally a rabbit. I was convinced we wouldn't even be allowed to have a fish. I can't imagine what would change her mind now.

"I don't have time for a dog. I'll be working," I argue. Detective work means long strange hours that aren't conducive to animal care—or to a life at all, actually. Despite the fact that I would love a cat or a dog, it'd be cruel.

"You can't live in this big house by yourself. It's not safe."

Being a beat cop and a detective has taught me that *no one* is really safe no matter what. If I'm not safe at home with a gun on my nightstand, I'm not safe anywhere.

I brush off the comment and walk up the path to the house. It should count for something that I've kept myself alive for the last thirteen years, but that's not how things work with my mother. The nervous energy still radiates off her as I unlock the door.

My dad follows me into the house, floorboards creaking beneath our feet. "Nice place," he says as he deposits my bags in the living room.

Before moving in, I arranged with Mrs. Peterson to have rental furniture delivered. So at the very least, I'll have a bed and a couch until the rest of my things arrive. There's no way I'd make it a week on these hardwood floors with just a sleeping bag. The walls are stark white, and the room still smells sharply like fresh paint. I walk through the living room to the dining room and large kitchen. My mother trails behind me as I inspect it. And though I expect her to voice her disappointment, for once, she bites her tongue.

"We should all go get dinner at the Haven or some other restaurant, just like we used to for your birthday," Dad says as he lingers behind me.

I turn, ready to say no, but the look on his face is almost enough to make me cave. Dad's been super reclusive for the past fifteen years, and it's obvious from his pallor that that hasn't changed since I left.

"You know I'm not eating anywhere with fishermen," Mom snaps before I get a chance to say a word.

He deflates, and his shoulders sag. "We should get out of your hair," my dad says and squeezes my shoulder.

My mom nods, though she clearly doesn't agree. The downward curve of her lips and the flare of her nostrils, like she's smelled something foul, say everything her words don't. "Consider the dog, please."

"Fine," I say, though I have no intention of doing so.

This isn't the first time she's tried to force something on me in the name of *safety*. In my teens, she screwed my windows shut. After I left, I got regular care packages of pepper sprays, knives disguised as cosmetics, and Tasers, and even now I occasionally get gift certificates for self-defense classes.

The front door slams behind them. My mother's shrill voice echoes outside, but I try not to eavesdrop—knowing her, she's got nothing nice to say. To distract myself, I grab my suitcases and drag them upstairs, where the rooms are all filled with cigarette-stained striped wallpaper that's probably been around since the New Deal. If I bought the place, that'd be the first thing to go. But it's going to be a long time before I convince myself to buy something here. *Temporary.* That's what this is. Because if it's not, it's like I've backslid. All those years of progress I made on my own—gone.

A simple full-size bed stands against the back wall in the master. It's the only thing in here, but it's obvious it hasn't always been. There are outlines along the wall of where the previous tenants' furniture used to be. I stare at them, and they remind me of footprints in the snow—a shadow of a life that came before me. I try to push it from my mind, to not think about how long they were here or how long I might be. I shove my suitcases under the window and glance out over the yard and beyond. A lump as hard as a pebble lodges in my throat. I should have been more careful when I found this house; my desire to stay as far away from my parents as possible blurred my memory of the town. I yank the curtains closed as if that will erase what I saw. My bedroom window overlooks the park where Rachel's and Emma's bodies were dumped. It never did make sense to me. Rachel would sneak out, yes—but she always went to the park near our house, a park five minutes away. She'd never have come so close to downtown while she was supposed to be in bed. No one knows how her body got there. Then again, I'm not sure how hard they looked.

A chill snakes down my spine and doesn't stop until even my bones are cold. I'll have to face her eventually. But for now, I'll shut her out like I always do.

CHAPTER 3

Outside the small police station, a low conversation carries on the breeze through the open windows. I can't make out the words, but I stand and listen anyway. The noise is calming, compared to the stark silence that settles over the island most of the time. With the constant hush, I've barely been able to sit still all morning, my nerves gnawing at me. Everything is so familiar yet so foreign at the same time. Years ago, I knew this island and everyone on it like they were part of me, for better or for worse. Now it's like I'm looking in on them all from the other side of a mirror.

I take a deep breath and steady myself before I open the front door. A reception desk stands in the middle of the small room, taking up most of it. Four plastic chairs are shoved up against the walls, covered in a thin layer of dust. Behind the desk, a woman peeks up from behind her monitors and clears her throat. She appraises me carefully. I straighten my shirt and smooth a few strands that have come loose from my ponytail.

"Detective Calderwood?" she asks in a high voice, and I'm not sure if it's because she recognizes me or because Sergeant Michaels told her I was coming.

I nod and close the few steps between me and the desk. I stare at her for too long. She's got a tiny triangular nose and a wide face. But I determine quickly that she's too young to be someone I knew well.

"I'm Mindy," she says with a smile and sweeps her short brown hair behind her ear. She's got brown eyes that look small, but it may just be the glasses she's wearing.

Relief washes over me at her name. I don't remember a single Mindy. "Nice to meet you." I shake her hand.

"So you're the hotshot detective from Detroit, right?" she asks, and I swear her eyes triple in size. I wasn't aware that living in Detroit qualified me for hotshot status.

I nod. "Guess so. Where are you from?"

"Bangor," she says with a half smile. "I've never been to Detroit, or anywhere else." She chews her lip.

She can't be older than twenty. She may be even younger than that. "Don't worry. You've got plenty of time." I want to tell her to leave now and never look back, the advice I wish someone would give me right now. Instead, I push my fingernails into the palm of my hand.

She grins like that's exactly what she needed to hear.

"Where can I find the sergeant?" I ask, because I won't be able to keep up this small talk for much longer.

She points toward the door to her left. "Straight ahead and to the right."

"Thanks. It was good meeting you," I say as I slip away to the sergeant's office. I pass several desks lining the walls; the tops are piled with papers, legal pads, and family photos. Each desk has someone swiveling in an office chair. The conversations rumbling through the room stop as I walk by. From the looks of it, there are four patrol officers. One of the officers, Jason, went to my high school and dated one of my good friends, Kyle, for a while. Two of the others, Vince and Marshall, have worked at the station since I was in middle school, at least. The fourth guy's got long, greasy, mousy-brown hair and a pretty impressive beard.

It's a typical look for many of the fishermen here. He sits by himself in the corner, and all the other guys are angled away from him. I'm not sure who he is, but after a few moments it clicks into place: Allen Warren. I went to high school with him.

The sergeant's office is only a few feet beyond the bull pen, down a short hallway. This whole place is stark, decorated about as well as a hospital. The Detroit office was sleek, modern. Sergeant Michaels is hunched behind his desk when I knock on the open door. Gray hair dusts his temples and the sides of his head. His glasses have slipped down, the bulb at the end of his nose the only thing holding them up. His cheeks are pink, like they always have been—as a kid I imagined he was some descendant of Santa Claus. It's not that he's built like old Saint Nick—not at all, actually. He's tall and broad, like he was born to play football.

He stands from behind the overflowing desk, and I'm reminded of how large he is. "Claire!" his voice booms, and there's an authority to it that nearly makes me jump. "How was your flight?"

I reach across the desk and shake his hand. "It was fine. It's good to see you again." I haven't seen Sergeant Michaels since I was in high school, and back then he was a beat cop.

"Do you want to have a seat and catch up for a bit?" He motions to the two chairs in front of his desk, both of which are stacked high with folders.

"I'd actually prefer to dive right in, if you don't mind." The good thing about police work is that there's always plenty of it to distract me from my problems.

He chuckles and waves me toward the door. "Ha! You haven't changed a bit—always got your nose to the grindstone," he says in a tone that makes me half expect to have my cheeks squeezed.

That's not how I've ever seen myself. Not that I'm about to argue with him. He moves past me through the door, and I follow. He leads me into a small office not far from his. The desk is stacked with folders and paperwork, but it's not in anywhere near as bad shape as his—at least I can see the keyboard.

"This'll be your office. Hope it's all right. I'm not sure what you had in Detroit," he says like he expects me to take off at the sight of it.

This isn't exactly a promotion, but I sure as hell didn't get an office at the old station. "This will be fine. Thank you."

"Feel free to introduce yourself to the guys when you have time. I'm sure you know them already, though."

"What do you have so far on Emma?" He sent me some of the interviews for her case a few days ago. From what I've seen, they've got less than nothing to go on. It's been over a month since they found her body. In Detroit, we would be close to bringing someone in. But things work at a different pace on the island. Things are slower; the resources here don't compare to a big city's.

"Just what we've sent you. The initial autopsy, the interviews we've done of her close friends and family. Her parents have been ruled out as suspects. Any of the other officers can catch you up if you have questions. Is there anything else you need?"

I shake my head. "No, I can take it from here." Though a few more questions might help me, I've gone on less before. With the way he keeps inching toward the door, I must be keeping him from something. He's obviously got plenty on his plate without babysitting me.

He stops at the door. "The top folder has everything we've found so far," he says before striding back to his office.

I sling my purse onto the back of the chair. It groans as I sit and scoot closer to the desk. Though I press the space bar a few times, it takes a long time for the computer to whir to life; once it does, I type in the password scrawled on a sticky note taped to the screen. For nearly two hours, I scour the information on the computer and in the file. The files on Emma aren't organized well. The interviews are mixed in with details I already know about the case—strangled with a cloth over her face, flannel fibers found in her lungs, flesh removed from her back.

She was found in the middle of the night in Grimes Park. There are no signs that Emma was taken from her house, and the lack of evidence of a struggle in the park leads me to believe she was killed elsewhere.

A few things about all the details stick out to me. Why would someone cover her face while strangling her? Where did they take her to kill her? Obviously somewhere private where they wouldn't be seen. The park is too wide open and exposed to strangle someone, and since there was no blood found in the park, they'd have had to cut the flesh off her elsewhere. Even if Rachel hadn't also been found there, my assumption would be that Emma isn't the first murder by this killer.

The phone on my desk rings, and I jump.

"Hello," I say, then catch myself. "Detective Calderwood."

"It's Mindy. There's someone here to see you."

"You can send them back," I say automatically, sure it's my mom dropping in to check on me. Quickly I sweep back any strands that may have come loose from my ponytail and sit back in my chair. The last thing I want is for her to sense how stressed I am.

A light knock at the door catches me off guard; my mom isn't the knocking type. "Come in."

A tall man stands at my door. His dirty-blond hair dusts his earlobes. His strong jaw is covered by a five-o'clock shadow. A slight smile curves his full lips. For a long moment after he opens the door, we appraise one another, as if we're sizing each other up. His blue eyes are piercing and beautiful at the same time. He clears his throat and adjusts the laptop bag hanging from his shoulder.

"Claire Calderwood?" he asks, like I'm not quite who he was expecting. He's got a slow drawl, the kind I've only heard in the movies. *Maybe he's from Texas.*

"That's me," I say just as he moves a stack of files from the chair across from my desk and takes a seat. I raise a brow at that: how presumptuous.

He leans back and squares his shoulders.

"And you are?" I ask when he doesn't introduce himself.

"I need to talk to you about your sister," he says, and my stomach bottoms out. "Rachel," he clarifies, as if I wouldn't know. I've only got one sister. *Had* one sister. And despite the distraction of my sister's name, it's not lost on me that he avoided telling me who he is.

My mouth and throat are bone dry. I start to say something—anything—but my words are lost beneath a whirlwind of thoughts. Who the hell is this guy to walk in here and ask to talk about my sister? I knew the questions about Rachel would catch up to me back here, but right now—it's jarring. I wasn't expecting it so soon. For thirteen years I've managed to keep questions about her at bay.

"I really can't talk about her right now." It's not just that I don't have time to. I *can't*. I turn my attention back to my computer, hoping he'll get the hint.

"I'm sorry," he says, breaking the awkward silence building between us. I glance at him, eyebrow raised. "I shouldn't have just come at you like that. I've been looking for you for weeks," he says, excitement lifting his voice. I cock my head at that. "No, no," he says with his hands raised in surrender. "Not in like a creepy, stalker, *I've been looking for you* kind of way."

There's a heavy lump in my throat that showed up the second this guy got here. Maybe once I ditch him, the lump will disappear, and I'll be able to focus on my caseload.

"Can we start over?" There's an edge to his voice, and for the first time, his full lips curve into a frown. "I'm Noah Washington. I'm a journalist," he says as he extends his hand to shake mine. "With the fifteenth anniversary of Rachel's death coming up, I was really hoping to dig into new details, shine a light on it. And then cover it all on a cold case podcast."

For a long moment, I look at his hand, unsure if I want to shake it. The intensity behind his big blue eyes softens. Years of experience have taught me not to trust journalists.

"Will you *please* answer some questions about Rachel?"

Anger flares inside me. I don't have time for this. There's a homicide investigation that needs my attention.

"I wish you luck with your research, but I need you to go. I'm very busy." I turn my attention back to the computer.

"I just need a few minutes of your time." He leans close to me, his eyes pleading.

"Not today, Mr. Washington. Please go." I use the best tone of dismissal that I can.

When he doesn't move, I glance toward him, hoping my expression will mirror my words.

The look on his face is resigned, like it's what he expected me to say. "I'll keep digging. I'm going to find out the truth. I'm going to find out what happened to her."

What the hell does he think he's going to find that the police couldn't?

I do a quick Google search to see if Noah is who he says he is, because something about him rubs me the wrong way. The page fills with article after article written by Noah covering everything from politics to true crime. I shake my head as I consider that. I hope he moves on, because if he keeps digging, I know what he'll find.

He'll figure out that I'm the reason Rachel's dead.

CHAPTER 4

After kicking Noah out of my office, I head out onto Main Street in search of answers. I've gone over all the interviews of Emma's family and friends several times, and one keeps sticking out to me. Maybe it's my gut, or maybe it's my experience keeping secrets as a teen. But there are quite a few holes in the questioning of Madeline Clark, the mayor's daughter and Emma's best friend. To make matters worse, Madeline was questioned with her father present. Any teen is going to clam up—or lie—under those circumstances.

It's a short walk to the mayor's house, but I measure my steps, letting the questions build in my mind. I've been a detective for three years, but I still have to watch my tone, the way I ask questions. When I was a beat cop, my sergeant told me over and over again that I was too blunt and brash to climb the ladder. Six months later, I proved the asshole wrong. I've become a master at biting my tongue. *Most of the time.*

On the sidewalk, I stand staring at the mayor's house—a white wood-frame house off Clamshell Alley. This is the kind of town with cutesy names like Clamshell Alley and Frog Hollow Road. Since I last saw the house, they've added bright-blue shutters that don't suit it. I try not to gawk and instead sip my coffee to settle my nerves. It's like preparing for war, but the enemy is my emotions. The boards groan beneath my feet as I walk across the wide porch. I knock slowly and listen for movement inside the house.

There's a rustling to the left, where the living room is. I know that's where it is because one of my best friends in high school, Ashley, lived in this house when it was in much better condition. I know its secrets, its stories. When we were twelve, we carved our names into the rafters of the attic. She buried a time capsule in the backyard the same year. Rachel and I used to play here—that is, until I realized my friend liked Rachel better than she liked me. It wasn't the first time one of my friends ended up liking her better, and it wasn't the last. Being here, seeing this house again, it's enough to tug my memories straight back there.

I'm able to trace footsteps through the house before the door opens. A balding man stands before me, the mayor. Time has worn on him. He's tall and lanky, and his body doesn't match his face. His brown eyes have dimmed from chocolate brown to hazelnut. Deep lines are etched on either side of his mouth, framing jowls.

With the way he's got the door cracked only a few inches, it's like he thinks I'm going to slip in without permission.

"Mayor Clark?"

He nods and narrows his eyes. There's a flicker of recognition. "Claire?"

I nod. "I'm sure that Sergeant Michaels mentioned I was coming on as the new detective?" I *know* Sergeant Michaels told him.

"Yeah, he did mention that. With everything going on, it slipped my mind."

"I was hoping for a few minutes with Madeline, if you don't mind." I take a step toward the door. I'm not going to force my way inside, but seeing as he hasn't invited me in, I'm not sure he's going to let me talk to her at all. It's been nearly a month since Madeline was last questioned. Sometimes people remember new details after the cloud of grief lifts.

It's important that I talk to her sooner rather than later. She could be the key to solving this case.

He glances back over his shoulder, deep into the house. To his left, back in the living room, a TV is droning on.

"I'll just be a minute, really," I say when he still hasn't budged. "It's important to make sure she hasn't thought of anything else that could help with the investigation into Emma's murder."

He hesitates, and for a moment, I think I'm going to have to press him harder, but he waves me in. "I'll go get her," he says as he heads for the stairs.

"Actually, I think it might be easier if I talk to her in her room, if you don't mind." If there's anything about Madeline's life—or Emma's—that she doesn't want her father to know, those details aren't going to come out in an interview if he's there. I'd just have her come to the station, but that tends to spook witnesses. And seeing as she's the daughter of the mayor, that would go over like a fart in church.

He shows me up the stairs and knocks, and once Madeline has given a mumbled agreement to the interview, I slip inside. Mayor Clark stands on the landing for a moment, peering in the room. I offer him a smile before saying, "It'll be fine, really. I'm sure if she needs you, she'll call you up."

Madeline's room is quite large, big enough to house her queen-size bed, a small sofa near the bay window, and three dressers. Each dresser is topped with cheerleading trophies and pictures of her with friends. The walls are a soft lavender that seems to glow, even with the gray light streaming in from outside. Between two windows on the far wall, an ornate wooden cross hangs. The bed isn't made, and there's a pile of clothes sitting on the end, like I caught her in the middle of doing laundry.

Madeline sweeps her long blonde hair over her shoulder and flashes me a half smile. She's around five foot three, an inch or two shorter than me. Her blue eyes are piercing, an almost cerulean blue. It unnerves me how much this girl looks like Rachel, but I can't let it show.

I start to introduce myself, but halfway through *Detective*, she interrupts me.

"You're investigating Emma's . . ." She stops and looks at the floor, digging her toes into the carpet.

"Yeah, I am. Do you mind if I ask you a few questions? I know you've already been interviewed, but I'm hoping that maybe you've thought of something else since you spoke with the other officer."

"I don't mind," she says, finally looking back at me.

"You okay, Maddy?" her dad calls up the stairs.

She rolls her eyes. "Yeah, Dad, fine," she yells back. Once his footsteps trail off downstairs, she shuts the door and slumps on the edge of her bed. "He's been so overprotective lately."

I brush off the comment about her father. I can see why he'd be overprotective. "When did you and Emma become friends? I heard that you were really close."

She digs her thumbnail into her quilt. "Yeah, we were best friends. But we really only became friends like a year ago."

"A year ago?"

"Before that we just weren't really friends with the same people."

"Is there a reason for that?" I ask as I take notes.

She chews her lip and looks toward the door, like her dad might be standing outside listening. I wonder if he does that often.

"Madeline, I'm not going to tell your dad anything you say. You don't need to worry about that. But we need to figure out who did this to Emma, and you might know something that could help," I urge, but I'm careful to keep my words from being too forceful.

"I don't want it to sound like I'm talking shit about her, because I'm not."

"I understand," I say, and I really do. I struggled with the same balance after Rachel died. Everyone always wanted to remember the best of Rachel. Some days, all I could remember was the bad, and no one else seemed to know that Rachel existed.

"Emma and I weren't super close until she started coming to church. She joined up with the choir group. I'm in it too. She had a really good voice. She was trying to keep herself occupied. So she didn't slip up again."

I remember the file mentioning that Emma was in the choir. "Slip up?"

"Emma did drugs. She didn't want anyone to know about it." She looks down at her comforter again.

I think back to the autopsy. There wasn't anything on her toxicology to suggest that she'd been high in the few weeks preceding her death. "What drugs was she using?"

"Speed, mostly. Meth if she had to. Adderall. Anything she could get that would keep her up. She hated sleeping, hated being tired. She just wanted to be going all the time." Her lips twist and her jaw quivers, like she might be on the verge of crying. Though I offer to give her a break, she refuses. I jot down notes as she talks. While the words flow, she doesn't look at me once.

"She wanted to change, though; that's why she started coming to church," she explains.

"So that was about a year ago?"

She nods and picks at her nails. "Yeah, and that's when we started to get close."

"Do you have any idea what she was doing out the night that she was killed?"

"I can guess that she was trying to get drugs at the docks again. But I don't know for sure." She hangs her head, and I can see the war waging in her mind. Would things be different if she'd known?

"Had she relapsed before?"

"Three or four times. But it usually just took a week or two for her to get back on track." She presses her lips together and sniffles. Grief wells in her eyes, threatening to spill over. Her gaze shifts from me to the wall, and it's as if she's lost completely behind her tears. My heart seizes as my mind flashes to Rachel. I won't let it drag me back down, though. I can't.

"I just wish I'd done something, you know?"

I don't answer. But I do know.

"Was there anyone at school she had problems with? Anyone who bullied her or anyone who showed unusual interest in her?"

She shrugs. "Not really. There are a couple of girls who are bitches to everyone. The Arey sisters. But they wouldn't hurt anyone. They just want everyone to be as miserable as they are."

"Was she seeing anyone?"

"Nope."

"Are you sure about that?" I ask.

"She wouldn't have kept that a secret from me." Her eyes darken as she says the words, like maybe she isn't so sure she believes them.

"Can you think of any reason that Emma might have been in the park the night she died?" I ask, switching gears.

"She usually went to the docks if she was having a hard time—that's where she got drugs. Maybe someone asked her to go to the park? Or she went there after she got what she wanted?" Her voice is high in pitch and nearly breaks. She wraps her arms tightly around her chest like she's close to crying. I give her a minute before asking anything else.

"Did she say anything else to you the night she died? Is there anywhere else she might have gone other than the docks?"

"She just said the normal stuff. She was stressed about a chemistry test. I don't think she'd go anywhere else. I'm surprised she went to the park at all."

"Did Emma have a scar or anything on her left shoulder blade?" I ask, hoping to get an idea of why the flesh was cut from her back. There's a note about the flesh, but her parents didn't know why it had been cut.

"She had a tattoo there of an angel. I have one too. We got them together." A sad smile quirks her lips. Her eyes shoot toward the door. "Don't tell my dad, though. Our parents didn't know we got them."

I don't ask how they both managed to get tattoos underage. So the tattoo was removed from her body. As a trophy? Or something else?

"Is there anything else about her that you think I should know?"

She crosses her arms and shakes her head. "I didn't want anyone to know about the drugs, because she wasn't some burnout druggie, you know? She was just doing what she had to do. She didn't deserve this."

"I know, Madeline. I'm not going to take this any less seriously because she was involved with drugs. Whatever she might have done, she didn't deserve this."

I finish up with Madeline. She doesn't have much else of importance to say, but I listen anyway. It's clear that she needs to talk. After I leave the Clarks', I interview a few other friends of Emma's, who give me more of the same details. Emma was a good girl, she didn't get into much trouble, and other than maybe going to the docks, there was no reason for her to be out that night. After I've finished with the interviews, I pick up a rental car downtown that I'll need until my car arrives and head back to the station. I type up my notes and add them to each of the files.

Because of Emma's likely visit to the docks the night she died, one detail in the file sticks out to me—a missing boat. Four days after Emma's death, Paul Clark, the mayor's brother, reported his boat missing.

I head out of the station, climb into my rental car, and turn onto Main Street, hoping that there may be some connection between the missing boat and Emma's murder. Paul's house is on the nicest part of the island, where the houses are nearly the size of mansions. It's where I feel the most out of place. Old money, the founding families: it's where they all reside. Where I *should* reside—if you ask my mother. Everyone in these houses has roots that go back hundreds of years. Technically

I do, too, but I like to think I snapped those roots thirteen years ago. This island has always felt like an intermission, a stopping point before I get to where I should really be.

I throw open the car door and walk the brick pathway to the three-story wood-frame house. The house is as old as the settlement here, though it's had additions, like nearly all the other houses at the north end of the island. This was one of the founding houses, one of thirteen total on the island. They aren't marked or anything, but the teachers were sure to tell us about them in school. Some of the other kids were filled with pride at the idea that their ancestors had always lived on the island. Me, however—I wanted to see what the rest of the world held. As more and more of the families settled here, the number of houses grew. Each year only a few new houses are built.

The large oak door looms in front of me. I eye the griffin knocker with its rusting edges. This close to the ocean, the constant salt in the air eats away at anything metal. It takes me a few moments of staring at the knocker to finally use it. I have to knock four more times before he finally answers.

I vaguely remember Paul from my childhood. Seeing him here is almost startling. His features are sharp, so much so that it's jarring. He's rail thin, with wide shoulders. Though he's got an oversize sweater, it does nothing to hide that fact. He might be the brother of the mayor, but I can't find a familiar feature between the two of them.

"Hello," he says as he eyes me up and down. The way his eyes crawl my body makes my fingers twitch against my thigh. I'm not sure if he's checking me out or sizing me up, but either way, if he keeps it up, I'm going to mace him. There's always been something off about him, but I didn't spend enough time around him to ever put my finger on it.

"I'm Detective Calderwood," I say. "I was hoping we could talk for a few minutes about your boat."

"Calderwood," he says in a tone that's almost a purr. "Claire?" he asks, as if there are any other Calderwoods on the island my age.

Everyone on my father's side ended up with boys, and they were all smart enough to leave and stay gone.

"Yeah. Can I come in for a few minutes?" The idea of being alone with this guy makes my skin squirm, but I've been alone with much worse.

He offers me what appears to be an attempt at a smile, but it comes off as more of a grimace. A look warning me of the lie he's about to tell. "Of course, come in." He waves me past. He guides me through the historic home, and the hollow echo of our footsteps on the wooden floors resonates around me. The house is sparsely decorated. What is here I'd guess was decorated by his mother before she passed.

"Can I get you anything?" he offers.

I shake my head. "No, thank you, though."

Paul ushers me into a formal sitting room that looks like it's never been used. The walls are lined with bookshelves. The only part of the room that isn't wood is a fireplace covered in slate. An antique red velvet sofa and a few chairs sit in the middle of the room on top of an ornate rug. From what I can see, the house is decorated like a dollhouse—an old, stuffy dollhouse.

"Please, take a seat." He gestures a little too broadly at the sofa.

When I sit on the ugly, grimy sofa, a puff of dust billows out that smells like stale baby powder.

"Sorry, we don't use the room much," he says, and I wonder who *we* is. As far as I know, he lives here alone. "So you had some questions about my boat. Did you find it?"

"No, not yet. I was hoping you might have some information that would point me in the right direction."

"I'll help however I can," he says dryly.

"Great." I pull my notepad from my jacket. "When was the last time you saw the boat?"

He looks away and furrows his brows. "It was sometime in late July." He scratches his chin.

I flip through my notepad. "I see here that you didn't report that the boat was missing until October seventeenth, is that correct?"

He rubs the back of his neck and looks at the window behind me. "Yes, that's right," he mumbles.

"Why did you wait so long before reporting that the boat was missing?" I ask, sure to keep my tone even so it doesn't sound accusatory. But it strikes me as really odd that it took him so long to report it missing.

He wipes his hands together, then picks at one of his fingernails. "I wasn't sure if it was missing. I didn't use it a lot, so I didn't notice for a while that it was gone." I can smell the bullshit on his breath. How could anyone not realize their boat was missing for *months*?

"How often would you say that you used your boat?"

"It really depends. If the weather is great, every weekend. I'd been busy with work, though, so I didn't have as many chances to use it this year."

"Is there anyone you've been in an argument with recently? Anyone you think might take the boat to get back at you? Maybe an ex-girlfriend?"

He shrugs. "No one comes to mind."

"Anyone from work?"

"I do tutoring and teach driver's ed. I don't think any of them did it." He laces his fingers together, resting his hands on his knees. And I swear for a moment a hint of a smirk twists his lips.

"What do you tutor?"

"Bio, anatomy, any of the sciences, really."

"Has anyone failed recently? Someone might blame that on you." A lot of times, it's someone they know who does this. Someone they wouldn't suspect of doing something like this. There has to be a trigger. He may not remember it now, but some event precipitated this.

He presses his lips together but shakes his head. There's only so much I can ask without him thinking I'm here to question him. The last thing I need right now is to get on the bad side of the mayor's brother my first week back on the island.

"Okay, well, thank you so much for your time. Hopefully we'll track down who did this soon. If you need anything for making an insurance claim, just let me know," I say as I push off the sofa. I walk toward the door, Paul trailing behind me. I stop when his hand touches my shoulder. I move away from him, out of his reach.

"If it looks like one of the kids did it, I don't want to press charges," he says, and I look back.

"Oh?"

"It's just a boat. I'll get another one. It's not worth ruining one of the kids' futures." His words lack conviction.

"Did you ever have issues with teens on the island *borrowing* your boat?" I ask.

He shakes his head weakly. "No, nothing like that."

"Were you ever worried they were hanging out near your boat? Or maybe considering taking it?" If he's mentioning not wanting to go after the kids for possibly taking his boat, he's got to have a reason for it.

"I didn't mean anything by it. I don't think they took it," he says, his tone firm. Clearly he's done with this conversation.

I nod. "I'll let you know as soon as we have any leads."

I'm still trying to process the conversation with Paul as I reach the walkway, but that's when I see *him.* Noah leans against my rental, his arms crossed, head cocked. His hair is slicked back slightly, but it's still rough enough to make me wonder if it's on purpose.

"Mr. Washington," I say, nodding to him.

"Detective." He whips a small notebook from his pocket and takes a few steps toward me.

I grind my teeth and continue to my car.

"Is Paul Clark a person of interest in Emma's death?"

"No, he's not. I'm here about an unrelated case." Normally I wouldn't comment at all. But sometimes not commenting leads to wild speculation, and in this case, I don't want that. The last thing I need is the mayor pissed off because I didn't shoot down the idea that his brother is a suspect in a murder investigation.

"And what case might that be?"

I stop walking and cross my arms. "A missing boat."

He raises a brow at that. "And a missing boat takes precedence over a murder investigation?"

I bite my tongue. "I have no comment on that."

"You have no comment on the fact that the mayor seems to be extending his reach to find a missing boat for his brother instead of finding Emma's killer?"

I prop my car door open, and before shutting it, I say, "As I said, no comment."

I shove the key into the ignition and throw the car into drive, and halfway down the street I swear I can still feel Noah's eyes nearly burning a hole in the back of my skull. With the frustration and questioning behind me, I head back to the station and dig back into the interviews of Emma's friends, family, and classmates.

CHAPTER 5

Minutes or maybe hours after falling asleep, I bolt upright in bed. The house is cold. Frigid air seeps in with every breath of wind. It doesn't help that this place doesn't feel like home. I'm cast adrift here. Being on this island feels like I'm intruding on someone else's life. It's like staying in a house you'll never quite feel welcome in. To be honest, I felt this way about Detroit at first too. It wasn't mine; it didn't belong to me. It took a long time for me to become accustomed to the sights, the smells. On this island, the sound of the waves, the chatter of the gulls, and the low billowing of the boats move through my veins like blood. In Detroit, at first my teeth were on edge with every car horn, every shout, and every single siren that split the air. I thought I'd grind my teeth to dust in a month. Eventually, though, I was folded into Detroit, enveloped into the madness like I belonged.

One thing keeps echoing in my mind. *You don't belong here.*

Temporary, I tell myself again. I want to get that word tattooed on my arm. It's the constant reminder I need. As if future me is whispering in my ear, *It gets better; hang on*. I'll solve this, and I can get out of here.

On the windowsill, my phone buzzes, the sound cutting through the night. My toes curl against the cold wood floors as I shuffle to answer it. The blue glow from the screen illuminates the dark room, and I squint against it.

"Yeah?" My voice is rough, as gravely as the old roads winding through the island like rocky veins.

"Claire?" Sergeant Michaels's voice booms from the phone, loud enough that I flinch.

"Yes, it's Claire," I confirm. I don't know who the hell else he thinks is going to be answering my phone.

"I need you over at Grimes Park, ASAP," he says, and I realize he doesn't sound as tired as he should for this time of night. His voice is clear, firm, like he's been awake for hours. I try to wish away the adrenaline-laced, feverish beats of my heart. My mind drowns in thoughts that try to convince me that it's *nothing*. Of course being dragged from bed at five a.m. by your boss can't mean *nothing*. Especially not in *that* park. The park where Rachel and Emma were both found.

My stomach pitches, and my heart thrums as I drag my suitcase on top of the bed and unpack an outfit. "Of course. What's wrong?"

He clears his throat. "There's another body in the park," he says and then ends the call.

Every horrible scene that could wait for me slithers from the recesses of my mind. Automatically, I think of Rachel, but I can't do that. I can't let my emotions drag me back there.

I throw on slacks and a T-shirt. It takes a few minutes, but I snap out of my exhaustion by brushing my teeth and then my hair. Dark circles hang beneath my gray eyes, but I know I had them long before I got here. Detective work is just time spent counting down to my next sleepless night. I throw on my coat and head out the front door. A burst of cold air hits me the moment I step outside, forcing me to suck in a sharp breath. Fat gray clouds, illuminated softly by the dying moonlight, are so low in the sky that they look like they're feet from dragging across the building tops.

I drive down Main Street, my window open, the cold air hitting my face, serving to wake me up. I roll through the abandoned streets downtown. Another death in this park makes my skin crawl, and a bad feeling makes my stomach roil. I'm not stupid enough to believe in curses, but if I did, that's the kind of word I'd use to describe Grimes Park. They should bulldoze it and build a gas station in its place.

For a while after they found Rachel there, no one called the park by its name; it was just *that* park. Then, by the time I turned eighteen, people would say its name, but only in hushed tones, like if they said it too loud, more horrible things would befall the island.

I wonder if they ever started saying it without whispering.

I'm the first officer to arrive, which isn't all that surprising. Sergeant Michaels lives at the northernmost edge of the island. It'll take him about twenty minutes to get here. I draw my flashlight and click it on to survey the scene. The park is a wide-open space, lots of grass, room for dogs to roam. On the right side, near the tree line, there's abandoned, rusting playground equipment with a small pavilion next to it. Thick evergreens ring the whole park, cutting it off from the rocky shore that surrounds us. Though the trees keep me from seeing the beach, they don't stop the sound of lapping waves.

In the middle of the park, amid the sprawl of yellow-brown grass and pockets of snow, there's a young girl's body. I pull out my phone to snap pictures, first from a distance, then more as I step closer. Long blonde hair is splayed out on the ground. The grass and snow around her aren't disturbed, and it strikes me immediately that there isn't a single blade out of place, no footprints. There's no dirt around her, on her. This girl wasn't killed here. She was placed here. I focus the camera on her face, and that's when it hits me—that's when I see her for the first time. Madeline Clark. Emma's friend, the girl I interviewed less than twelve hours ago. It crushes me like a ton of bricks. My chest is heavy, and my mind screams, *Why? How?*

Purple polka-dot Chuck Taylors point toward the sky. Her outfit, a tank top and jeans, tells me either that she wasn't planning on being outside for long or that she left her coat somewhere. Her skinny jeans are still belted into place. Other than mud on the knees and sand around her ankles, the pants are in good condition. She wasn't sexually assaulted, or it's not likely, anyway. Neither was Emma. I'm not sure about Rachel; no one ever told me. I've never looked at her file, and I could barely get my parents to say a word about her after she died. A dark smudge on Madeline's shoulder sticks out against her pale flesh—blood, but there's no blood around her. A gold necklace with a calligraphy *M* hangs loose from her bruised neck, the chain cascading across the hollow of her throat. The tip of the *M* dusts a pocket of snow under her shoulder and head. Other than the bruise on her neck, she doesn't look injured. Emma was also strangled, though, a detail that's making a warning take root in the back of my mind.

Madeline's young enough that she's still got a cherub's face, a bow of a mouth. Her big blue eyes stare toward the sky. Purple marks circle her neck—hands much larger than mine snuffed the life out of Madeline. That tells me this was personal. Someone angry, someone focused on *her*. It takes a long time to strangle someone, longer than you'd think. Four to six minutes at least of staring someone in the eye while you kill them. Someone had to hate her to do that.

As I secure the crime scene, Jason pulls up and nods at me as he climbs out of his cruiser. Mrs. Holt, the woman who found the body, is still lingering in the parking lot. Thankfully Sergeant Michaels told her to stick around. I give Jason a quick update, and he takes over securing the crime scene so that I can question the woman.

"Thank you for your patience," I say.

Mrs. Holt starts to say something, but it just comes out as a strangled squeak. She's got short brown hair, a nose that reminds me of a bird's beak, and a pointy chin. All her features are very angular. A small dog prances at her feet, desperate for my attention. She picks the dog up and makes a shushing sound as she clutches it to her chest.

"Do you mind answering a few questions?"

She's bundled up in a thick coat and pants that look like they were made for skiing. While the cold is already creeping up my sleeves, it hasn't even pinkened her cheeks. "Gotta make it quick. Markey gets cold," Mrs. Holt says as she gestures to the dog.

"What time did you head down here?"

"Around four thirty. That's when Markey usually wakes me up for his walks."

"Did you see anyone here when you got to the park?"

"In the park? No. I saw fishermen downtown as I was coming, though. But they're always at the café around four."

"So no one going to or from the park? Did you notice any cars on Main Street as you walked?"

She shakes her head and glances toward the body. "No, I don't remember seeing any." I sidestep a bit, hoping to block her view some. In a town this size, there's no chance that she didn't know Madeline. Everyone knows everyone here, whether they like it or not.

I think she's too distracted to give me much else, if she even saw anything at all, that is. "If you think of anything else, please call me at the station. And if you would, try not to mention this to anyone in town yet. Not until we've notified the family."

The flash of a camera catches my eye. My gaze snaps to the photographer, and anger rises inside me so swiftly I barely have time to process it.

What the fuck is he doing at my crime scene?

Noah stands a few feet from the body with a large camera clutched in his hands. I need to get him away from here before he contaminates the scene. Jason turns toward me, then to Noah, but he's too far away to get to him before I do. There's another flash as I stalk after him. I have half a mind to tackle him and make him eat that camera.

As I close in, I growl, "You take one more goddamn picture, and you're going to have to drag that camera up from the bottom of the bay."

"Freedom of the press—ever heard of it?" He throws the words at me like daggers.

"Contaminating a crime scene—ever heard of it?" I snap back through gritted teeth.

"I didn't contaminate your crime scene by taking a few pictures." He snaps another picture. "I'm not about to let another small-town police department mess up another murder investigation."

"What exactly is that supposed to mean? And you don't think you're going to contaminate it? Silly me, I thought your business card said *journalist*, not *crime scene investigator*. I'm glad you're so sure you didn't compromise my investigation."

"I would never do anything to jeopardize any investigation."

"Well, thank God, I'll keep that in mind as my perp walks free because you *didn't mean to*."

He furrows his brow. "I'm not trying to get in your way. I'm not trying to mess this up."

"You've got a funny way of showing it," I say as I look down and shake my head. "I need you to go. The least you can do is email me those pictures. I need to enter them into evidence."

"Sure, if you give me that interview." He clicks the cap on his lens.

"Extortion and crime scene contamination before six a.m.? I hope you put that on your résumé." I fire the words off at him like bullets.

"I'll send you the pictures."

"Thanks," I say, the hard edge still clipping my words.

He nods, slings his camera strap over his shoulder, and starts to walk away.

"Hey, Noah," I say before he gets too far.

He stops and looks over his shoulder at me, his eyes gleaming in the low light.

"If you show up at one of my crime scenes again, you'll end up in cuffs."

He says nothing and gives no indication that he heard me before he stalks off.

"What else do you need me to do?" Jason asks as I approach.

"Scan the park and the coast. Bag anything that could be potential evidence."

It takes a long time for my rage to simmer. Seeing Madeline like this, knowing that another girl lay here a month ago, and Rachel fifteen years before that—it makes a bad feeling coil in my gut. A thought circles in the back of my mind: Could it be a serial killer? A copycat? Jason clicks on his flashlight and heads toward the edge of the park.

As he goes to check for other evidence, I put in calls to the CSI team and medical examiner. But there's nothing they can do until the ferries start running. Frustration needles me. Everything is going to take ten times longer than it would in Detroit.

Sergeant Michaels rolls up a little after five thirty, half an hour since he called me out here, parking his car beside mine. He's got on a bulky coat thrown over a button-up. I'm pretty sure he was wearing the same one in the office yesterday. He pulls a cigarette from between his lips, stomps it out, and strides over. I catch him up and let him know when the CSI and ME teams will arrive.

"Thanks for handling this," he says as he nods toward me. He glances at the body and shakes his head. I can tell the moment his eyes spot the bruising ringing her neck, and his fist clenches at his side. "Did you call the mayor?"

"No, we need to get the body out of here first. In Detroit we usually have the family identify after the evidence has been processed, preferably at the morgue. But we may run into some trouble with that anyway. That journalist was here taking pictures of the body."

"The mayor already knows about the murder. I didn't realize it was Maddie. Vince called him after it was called in to the station. It's protocol." He scratches his jaw. "That journalist better stay out of our way."

Another car pulls up beside Sergeant Michaels's in the small parking lot, but I don't recognize it. Maybe it's Allen's or Vince's. I eye the car, waiting for one of the guys from the station to climb out. But when Mayor Clark throws the door open, my stomach leaps. He jogs forward and freezes, his eyes locked on the body behind me.

"Is it Maddie? Is it her?" he shouts so loudly his voice cracks. My heart nearly shatters for him, but I have to hold it together. My mind keeps skipping back to Rachel, but I can't let it. He jogs toward us, and I hold my hands up automatically.

"Mayor Clark, this is a crime scene. You cannot come any closer."

Tears stream down his red cheeks. His eyes are glassy, grief and terror swimming in them. "She's not home. Maddie's not there." He looks around me—the cloth over her face shields her, but there's nothing I can do about the shoes poking out the bottom.

The passenger door opens, and a tiny girl with brown hair slips from Mayor Clark's car. She jogs toward us; the girl can't be any older than fourteen. She's got the same nose and chin as Madeline, but her hair and her eyes are like her father's. Mayor Clark drops to his knees, sobbing, and the girl freezes, staring at him. "Oh God," she chokes out and covers her mouth to stifle her sobs.

My heart aches with a fresh wave of grief. I know their pain; that very same agony is etched on my soul. I glance at Sergeant Michaels and gesture at Mayor Clark, trying to wordlessly urge him to help me get him off the ground. Together, we each put an arm under his and help him up. We steer him back toward the edge of the park, to his car. The girl follows us, her trail of sniffles letting us know she's close.

"Mayor Clark, I'm so sorry for your loss. I really am. I need to keep this crime scene secure, though, so we can catch who did this," I explain as gently as I can manage.

He glances at me, and the light has gone out of his eyes. That gaze—I know it well. I saw it in the mirror for years. It's what teaches you that while some losses you can rebuild from, with others, no matter what you do, you'll never be the same. Some impacts are too great to heal from.

Jason calls behind us, and I leave Sergeant Michaels to the Clarks when he waves me off. In his hands, Jason's got several bags, each marked with scribbles.

"What'd you find?" I ask as I take the bags.

"Gloves and a pillowcase in the water. At the edge of the woods over there"—he points toward the tree line—"I found that gold cross."

"She was wearing that yesterday." She had it on while I interviewed her. I know it has to be the same cross because it's unlike any I've ever seen. It's got gold ivy growing around it.

"What do you make of it?" He glances toward the sheet.

"She wasn't killed here. There's no sign of struggle. If she'd been strangled here, there'd be marks on the ground around her. She was killed elsewhere and placed here." My guess would be that the body was brought through the trees surrounding the park, which back up to the beach; otherwise, the killer would have had to bring the body through downtown to get here. But I stay silent about this fact since I have no evidence to back up my theory yet. I think back to all the conversations I had with Roxie about intent and psychology as it related to murder. "Putting her here means they wanted her to be found. They wanted someone to know what they did. The method makes me think this was personal, though. Whoever did this knew Madeline well." My mind rushes to try and connect the dots between the deaths. These three girls look nearly identical, all found in this park, all strangled.

I don't want to say it. Hell, I don't even want to think it, but I'm afraid if we don't figure this out fast, more girls will die.

He shakes his head. "This isn't the kind of thing that happens here."

I want to tell him it is, but I can't. Once is a fluke. Twice, three times: that means it *does* happen here. Copycats can be dangerous. If they're committed enough, that is. This might only be the beginning, or it could be my imagination desperately searching for a connection to Rachel.

I look back into the night, toward the heart of the island. This is the last thing I wanted for my homecoming.

I know deep down that I brought this darkness back with me.

CHAPTER 6

The sun edges above the horizon, and finally I let out the breath I feel I've been holding for hours. It's been a long night, made longer still by waiting in the cold for the team from Augusta and the fear that Noah might sneak back onto my crime scene to take more pictures. Around eight, the CSI team comes and combs the scene. I stick around to see if I can gather any information from them, but CSI guys don't like to speculate or point fingers. They only talk when they've got facts.

I steel myself inside the station. I've got to question Mayor Clark. This fresh—straight after her death—I might not get anything other than sniffles and sobs, but this is the most vital time. It can make or break an investigation. After I inform the sergeant of my intentions, the stress and fatigue of the morning really start to take their toll. I'm going to need some caffeine to make it through the questioning.

On my way to the mayor's, I make a quick pit stop at the coffee shop. It's a tiny place, a storefront sandwiched between a cleaners and a small butcher shop. The brick facade and simple café sign make it look like it's old world. In reality, it opened while I was in high school. Before that, it was a bakery. I can picture myself here fifteen years ago with Rachel at my side. Dad would bring us for cupcakes. The memory makes my heart ache, and I fall back on my training to distance myself from it. Compartmentalization is the most useful skill I've ever learned.

I glance up and notice a security camera pointing down Main Street. That'll give me a hint of what was happening downtown around the time of Madeline's death. I need to get a copy of that video. A bell, as delicate as one on a cat collar, jingles as I walk through the door.

Large glass windows, partly frosted over, partly fogged with cold, line the front of the café. The interior looks exactly the same, save for a new paint color, which is a much better choice. Tables are packed tight in the front of the café, like they anticipated everyone in the island hanging out here at once. Right now, though, it's empty. I can't imagine Vinalhaven ever being the kind of place where people pack into the café to use Wi-Fi.

Behind the counter, a woman with large gauges in her ears and purple eyeliner smiles at me. She's got dark hair pulled up, revealing star tattoos trailing to the collar of her shirt. When I look closer, I realize there's turquoise strewn throughout her bun. She looks out of place here. I wouldn't bat an eye if I saw her on the streets of Detroit, but I can't help but wonder what my mother thinks of this woman.

"Claire?" she calls a little too loudly.

"Hi," I say as I approach the counter and search her face. If she knows my name, I must have known her.

"Morgan," she says when it's clear I don't recognize her.

The name strikes a chord, but it doesn't match my memory. Morgan was a small girl, a band geek. She didn't do a single thing to stand out.

"How are you?" I ask, trying my best to sound like I remember her or like I've even considered her existence at some point since I left. The truth is once I left the island, the only time I thought about anyone here was when my mother brought them up.

"I'd be a lot better if it weren't for, you know." She motions in the general direction of the park. It hasn't even been three hours since the CSI team got here. I shouldn't be surprised, but Jesus. "She was such a sweet girl. Had a voice like an angel and always sang solos in the choir at church," she says, shaking her head. Before I can agree, she follows it up with, "What can I get you?"

"Double cap with extra foam and a copy of your surveillance video from last night," I say without skipping a beat. "Did you see her much outside of church?" I jot down a few notes as she heads toward the espresso machine.

"I've gotta call my boss to get the video for you. That'll take a bit. But about Madeline, she worked at Haven, that restaurant, on weekends, and I know she volunteered at the hospital in Rockport. I think she wanted to be a doctor or something. She got into some college already. That happened a few weeks ago—the mayor wouldn't shut up about it," she says and hands me my coffee. "Anything else?"

"Nope. How much do I owe you?" I reach for my wallet.

"On the house. Just find the bastard that did this. Come back in a couple hours, and I'll have the security footage for you."

Her eyes are focused over my shoulder instead of on me. I look back, trying to see what she's looking at. Noah strolls past the café, a laptop bag hanging from his shoulder. There's a look of recognition on her face that makes me ask, "How long has he been in town?"

She watches him for a moment before looking back at me. "He was here a few weeks ago and left. But he came back two days ago."

I nod my thanks and tuck away my notepad. I don't trust the journalist yet, and my instincts tell me to keep an eye on him. As I walk out of the café, I glance down Main Street and watch Noah slip into the hotel and disappear.

Compared to yesterday, Mayor Clark looks worn down when he answers the door, like the weight of Madeline's death is on his shoulders. Red rings his eyes, and his lips are chapped and flaky.

He offers me a pained smile and waves me into the house. "You'll have to excuse the mess," he says. There's no mess. We pass through the foyer, a pair of high-top sneakers lying near the coat closet, where they were kicked off.

"Can I get you anything?" he asks as he shows me toward a flowered couch in the middle of a very formal living room. Though the outside of the house is run down, everything inside is pressed, pristine, like it should be behind a velvet rope.

"No, thank you. I know it's very soon, so if you'd like me to come back another time, I understand. The reality is, though, the faster I jump on this, the more likely it is we'll be able to find the person who did this."

The balancing act here is difficult. Technically speaking, Mayor Clark should be considered a suspect. All parents are when a child is killed. But toeing that line is never easy.

He sneers like I said something offensive. "Person? No. It's not a person that did this; it's an animal," he growls. He wrings his hands and sits on the very edge of his seat, like he's ready to jump up at any moment. He rests his hands on his knees, digging yellowed nails into his pants. "I'll help however I can. You have to find who did this. I have another daughter, Allie. I can't bear the thought of losing her too." The last word gets caught in his throat and comes out strangled.

"We're going to do everything we can." I pull out my notebook.

"Is this related to Emma? It has to be."

Though it looks like the deaths are likely related, I can't give him that information, especially not yet. "We're still investigating. It's too early to say."

I grab my phone and pull up the picture of the necklace I found at the park. "Is this Madeline's?"

He nods. "Yes, her mom gave it to her, back before she took off a few years ago."

The necklace was found at the edge of the woods near the park. The only thing beyond those trees is the bay. This fact adds to my speculation that she was brought from the water.

"Where was she supposed to be last night?" I ask.

"Upstairs," he says as he shakes his head.

"Do you have reason to believe she left the house of her own free will? Or do you think it's possible she was taken from the house?" I'll need to check the house for signs of forced entry, though I didn't notice anything on my way in.

"We have an alarm, and it was on when I went to bed. She must have turned it off." He rubs his lips as he looks out the window behind me.

She snuck out, but he doesn't want to say that's what she did. And if she was shutting off the alarm, it wasn't the first time she'd done it. In these old houses, all the bedrooms are upstairs. Most alarms aren't connected to second story windows. But I'll need to see if she was sneaking out from the upstairs or shutting the alarm off to leave through the front door. If she was shutting it off, that would at least give me an idea of how often she was doing this.

"Did she ever get in trouble for sneaking out in the past?" If she was anything like my sister, she likely got caught at least once.

"Just once after her mom left. She hasn't done it since."

So he never caught her again, then.

"What about a boyfriend? Does Madeline have one?" I ask, forcing myself to use present tense.

He shakes his head. "No. She didn't show any interest in having one either."

The similarities make me think of Rachel. Did Madeline have a boyfriend her dad didn't know about? Or was she really not interested in dating? At least in all the interviews I've seen from Emma's friends, there was no indication she was dating.

"How about close friends I could talk to?"

He gives me the names of several girls. I'll have to interview them all this week.

"I heard that Madeline volunteers at a hospital across the bay. Is it possible that someone there might have gotten into a fight with her?" I ask while I'm still scribbling down names.

He shakes his head. "Everyone loves Madeline. If she wasn't home or volunteering, she was at the church with her choir group. She's such a good girl. She didn't deserve this."

My mom has said the same thing about Rachel a thousand times. Rachel didn't deserve it. But Rachel was anything but a good girl. She lived a secret life beneath my parents' noses. I knew they wouldn't have believed me if I'd breathed a word of it. Guilt smothers me as I think of it. Would she still be alive if I had tried to stop her from sneaking around? If I had intervened?

No parent really knows their teenager. It's not just police work that's taught me this. Whatever parents think is a well-constructed farce created by their child. They underestimate them at every turn and live in a world of their child's creation. Or maybe they just don't want to see the truth.

"What else can you tell me about Madeline?" I ask, and I try to keep my tone even, firm.

He scratches his chin and stares at the floor. He's not all here—I know that, but I need him to give me *something*. "I don't know what you want me to say," he says after a long silence.

"I'm just trying to understand who Madeline is, what she does, what her personality is like."

"I'm not sure why any of that matters."

"Everything matters right now, because even the smallest detail could help me find who did this." Sometimes it's the little things that end up being the most useful. What did she do on Tuesdays? Who was her best friend? These things could help me figure out what was different about the day she died.

There's a spark in his eyes as he looks up at me, like it finally clicks for him. It's as if I can see the fog lifting around him.

"Madeline has always been a happy child. No matter what, she finds the bright side of something. She doesn't seek happiness; I swear she made it. But something was different lately. She was *pretending* to be happy. I just don't know why."

"Was she having problems at school or with her friends? Did anyone show unusual interest in her? Notice anyone hanging around?"

"No, not that I know of," he says as he wrings his hands. "I should have pressed her more to find out what it was. Maybe I could have figured out what was going on if I'd tried harder. I just kept telling myself if it really mattered—she'd tell me. She'd come to me." His voice cracks, and his eyes flood with fresh tears.

"It's not your fault, Mr. Clark," I say, wishing there were more I could do to ease his pain.

His eyes sharpen, and for a moment his anguish is consumed by something feral. "Don't you blame yourself for Rachel?"

My chest tightens, and a heaviness hangs on my shoulders. The dark cloud that is the memory of my sister shrouds me. "Every single day." I regret it the second it's out of my mouth.

His eyes soften, my words smothering whatever was growing inside him.

"What was Madeline's schedule like? What'd she do after school?"

"She usually went to the church to help out. She used to be involved in volleyball, but she wanted to focus more on school. It was her goal to get into medical school," he explains.

"She was accepted on early admission, right? That's unusual for a sixteen-year-old. Could anyone have been jealous about that?"

"She took the SAT early and got an almost perfect score. That, combined with the letter she wrote, got her early acceptance. Her admission was contingent on her grades staying up, of course. She was going to start some classes, her general ones, next year." The tears pool in his eyes again. "Why did they have to take *her*?" He buries his face in his hands.

It's something I hear all the time. It could have been anyone else's kid, anyone else's sister—but this time, it wasn't. It's not some stranger in the news; it's a piece of you, a part of *your* life that's torn away. I know he's not wishing anyone else died instead, but I also know the desperation of loss. Bargaining to the point that you'd trade anyone and anything to get them back.

He shakes his head. "You have to find whoever did this. You have to." His eyes are wide, feral.

"I will do everything in my power to get justice for your daughter," I say, the weight of the words striking me immediately. I'm not one to make promises I can't keep. However, in this case, the reality is pretty clear—if I don't solve this, I'll be out of a job. There's enough pressure during any normal murder case, but with the daughter of the mayor a victim, the pressure is upped tenfold.

"Is there anything else you think I should know? Anything could help."

He laces his fingers together, his forearms resting on his knees. "The Warrens and the Lane family. The Warrens, they've got a boy, Ryder, sixteen or seventeen. Do you remember him? He's a bad seed. They're all bad seeds in that family, as I'm sure you remember, but he's the worst. And the Lanes, shut up in that house—they're up to no good."

I do remember Ryder, but he was a toddler the last time I saw him. He's Allen's younger brother.

The bad feeling in my stomach creeps up my throat, and though I try to swallow it, it does me no good. I've had plenty of run-ins with the Warrens. I hoped to steer clear of them this visit. Those Warren boys have been blamed for everything on this island for as long as I can remember. If the wind blows the wrong way, if a boat gets back to shore with a shitty haul, hell, if it's a long winter—somehow it's all their fault. If we were still in the 1600s, they'd be burned as witches.

"I'll look into that," I say, though there's nothing of note to look into. I need more to go on to question anyone from either of those families. As it stands, no one has given me any tangible link to the Lanes or Warrens. "There are a few items from Madeline's room that I need for the investigation. The sooner we get those, the better. But would you rather I grab them now or come back later?" As a rule, during a homicide investigation, we always start with the cell phone and computer. She didn't have her cell at the scene, so I'm hoping we find it here.

"What do you need?"

"Her devices; a journal or diary, if she has one. Did you try to track her phone?"

"I did. She always takes her phone if she leaves the house. But the app showed me the phone was off, and the last location was here at the house." He motions toward the upstairs. "She usually keeps it on her nightstand. I didn't see it this morning—that's how I knew she was gone." He looks toward the stairs. His eyes are far off, like he's waiting for Madeline to walk down.

If her phone isn't here and it's not on the body, it might lead us to the killer—that is, if it gets turned back on.

"One second, please," I say as I grab my phone and text Sergeant Michaels. We need to trace Madeline's phone. I fill him in on the details about the trace her father tried to do, but with the help of the cell phone company, we can get something far more accurate.

He texts me back almost immediately that he's putting in the request.

"I will need your permission to pull Madeline's phone records and to trace its current location," I explain to Mayor Clark. Every provider is different: some will take verbal permission, while some will require a form. Either way, I want all my bases covered so I can get it *now*.

"Of course, whatever you need."

Mayor Clark leads me upstairs. I grab Madeline's tablet and laptop. It doesn't take me long to confirm that she didn't leave her cell behind. I scan the windows and verify they don't have sensors for the alarm. If she hopped out that window, she could easily climb down the lattice along the side of the porch or down the big tree out front. Though I look for any signs of forced entry up here, there's nothing. My instincts tell me she snuck out.

"Does anything seem out of place to you?" I glance around the room. It looks like it did yesterday, the pile of clothes still on the end of the bed. I make a mental note of that.

He crosses his arms and shakes his head. "No."

"Any idea about the clothes?"

"She was going through them to get rid of the ones she said didn't fit right anymore."

Behind him in the hall, the tiny girl from the park is peering in the room. Her eyes are still ringed with red. Her long brown hair falls limp around her pale face. The way she looks at me suggests she's got something to say.

"I'd like to talk to your daughter for a minute," I say. It's not so much a request, but it isn't an outright demand. I want to be sure Mayor Clark doesn't see it as optional. It's a difficult situation, but I remember just how much sisters can know.

He glances back, seeing her for the first time. "Allie? You want to talk to Allie?"

I nod. "I do."

He heads into the hall and squeezes Allie's shoulder, and she slips into the room. She hangs back, about fifteen feet from me, close to the wall. Her arms are crossed, her eyes cast down.

"How are you doing?" I ask Allie as Mayor Clark descends the stairs.

She offers me a one-shouldered shrug but doesn't look up at me.

"I know how tough this is, believe me. There's nothing that I or anyone can say to make this better. But you will get through this." It won't help, but I wish someone had said that to me fifteen years ago. Allie isn't old enough to have been alive when Rachel died, but I'm sure she's heard the stories. Whether she's connected me to those stories isn't evident on her face.

She nods and glances at me for just a moment. "Thank you."

"Do you feel up to answering a few questions?"

"Yeah." Her arms tighten around her torso.

"Would you feel more comfortable doing this somewhere else?" I'm not sure I'd want to answer questions about Rachel in her room, especially the day I found out she'd died.

"No, it's fine."

I nod and open my notepad. "How often did Madeline sneak out?"

She chews her lip. "Almost every night. She's been doing it for a couple years, since Mom left." Tears well in her eyes as she looks down. "For a while, after she started, it scared me so bad. I thought she was going to leave me, just like Mom did."

"Why? What was she doing?"

"I don't know; meeting friends, I guess." There's an edge to her voice. She clearly wishes she had known what Madeline had been up to.

"So you never followed her?"

She shakes her head. "No. I'm afraid of heights, and Dad would have killed me if he knew."

"Was she dating anyone?"

She nods. "She had a boyfriend. I don't know who it was, though. But I heard them talking. She'd talk to someone before she snuck out."

"What made you think it was a boyfriend?"

"She'd always say she loved him before hanging up."

I note that. I'll need to talk to Madeline's friends to figure out who she was seeing. It takes me a few minutes to wrap up with Allie and get a list of Madeline's other friends for questioning. As I head out of the house and back toward downtown, I email the list of friends to Jason so he can get started on setting up interviews.

The sun flickers between the branches as I walk down Main Street, dotting the ground in front of me in dancing rays of light. My stomach growls in protest. I should have eaten breakfast, but this is going to be the kind of day with little reprieve. I'll grab a muffin, check in about the security footage, and then see if Sergeant Michaels has made any headway with the cell phone.

There are only a few people downtown, and they're staring toward the park. I shouldn't be surprised. Rumors ripple here, spreading faster than the plague. Word of Madeline's death has likely spread through the entire town already. Everyone in line at the post office turns to look at me as I pass, and I still feel the burn of their eyes as I make my second appearance of the day at the café.

"Hi, Detective Calderwood," Morgan chirps from behind the counter.

I'm not sure if the coffee is keeping her chipper or if she's always this way. Seeing how I've made myself this new friend, I may as well use it to my advantage.

"What can I get you?" she asks as she leans her hip against the counter.

"Coffee and a muffin, and I was hoping you had that security footage for me."

"Yep, I've got it in the back for you." She pours coffee into a paper cup for me. "What kind of muffin, Detective?"

"Apple. And it's Claire, please." Unless I'm formally interviewing someone, I hate feeling like I'm lording my title over them. I want her to see me as a regular person, as someone she'd normally talk to in this town—otherwise, I might not be able to get information out of her.

She passes me the coffee and a small paper bag. I lean against the counter, picking bits off the top of the muffin. For a moment, she disappears into the back, and then she reappears with several SD cards in her hand.

"Thank you. I appreciate you getting these to me so quickly," I say as she passes them across the counter.

"No problem. If you need anything else, just let me know."

"Can you get me the footage from the night Emma died as well?"

"I can." She hesitates. "I think she's got the backup of those off-site, so it might take a couple days."

"That's great. The sooner the better, but I understand that it could take time."

I grab my coffee, say my thanks to Morgan, and head out of the café.

"Hey, Claire," Noah calls. He's two shops down, walking in my direction. His worn leather jacket is open, showing a faded T-shirt beneath. His dirty-blond hair is shaggy and half in his eyes. There's a frigid wind whipping through the streets, and I feel like he must be freezing with the way he's dressed.

"Noah." I offer him a tight-lipped smile. After this morning, I have no desire to be cordial.

"Rough morning?" he asks.

Made longer by you, I want to snap, but instead I clench my jaw. "Rough, long morning," I say, sipping my coffee.

"Can I buy you a refill?" he offers with a charming smile.

"No, thanks." I take a few steps toward the station, hoping Noah will continue on his way, but he follows.

"Detective," he says, making me turn toward him again. He shoves his hands in his jacket pockets and looks down. "So can I get a comment about what happened?"

A smile born of frustration blooms on my lips, because I knew this was coming. "I can't comment on an ongoing investigation. We're following up on leads. If anyone has information, we ask that they come forward and talk to the police," I say as I start to walk again.

"Can you give me anything off the record?" he asks as he catches up to me. His arm circles mine, pulling on me to slow my pace. I wrench my arm from his and take a step back, creating a distinct space between us. My heart pounds as I glower at him.

"Noah, you know I can't make a comment on or off the record about an ongoing investigation." I'm starting to sound like a broken record. My words are harsher than they need to be, but right now I don't care.

"Maybe Mayor Clark will see the importance of this investigation now," he says in a way that makes a warning bloom in the back of my mind.

Did he have something to do with this? Did he do something so that the mayor would take the investigation into Emma's death more seriously?

"Where were *you* last night?" I ask without skipping a beat.

He furrows his brows and rocks back on his heels. "Okay, I can see how that sounded. That's not what I meant. It's not like I *wanted* her dead."

"I'm hearing a lot of things, and none of them are the answer to my question."

He maintains eye contact and says, "I was in my hotel room all night."

At least that's a good sign. That's something I can easily confirm.

"After you figure out that I'm not involved in this, do you want to grab lunch?" he asks. "No work-related questions."

"I'm all set, Noah." Thankfully when I turn this time, he doesn't follow. I huddle beneath my coat as I close the distance between me and the station.

When I walk through the doors of the station, the air is thick with the aroma of coffee. I pass through the bull pen toward Jason's desk, where he's got several folders open on top, taking up the majority of the desktop. For a couple of minutes I check in with him about the interviews, adding a few more names to his list. I know it'll take him a while to get through everyone, since Madeline was friends with nearly every kid at the high school. Then I move over to Vince to ask him to check on Noah's alibi.

I close the door to my office and pop the first SD card into the slot, and the computer chimes in response. The footage appears on the screen, and my heart races. The shot of downtown isn't great; it's a bit grainy, the contrast too high, like an old black-and-white movie. I eye the progress bar. It starts at midnight the night before I assume Madeline was killed. I fast-forward through the day. I slow down when it's just after seven p.m. The sun sets, and slowly everyone trickles out of downtown. A few cars parked on the sides of Main Street roll away. For a few hours, it's nearly abandoned. But around nine p.m., a group of fishermen head to the bar, leaving an hour later. It isn't until midnight that I see anyone again.

A woman with a slender build walks down the street, sticking to the shadows. Though I strain my eyes against the darkness on the screen, I can't make out her face. I'll need one of the guys to glance at it—maybe they'll recognize her. Not long after the woman passes the camera, she heads back in the opposite direction. Paul, the mayor's brother, passes at 12:45 a.m. and a teenage boy with long dark hair about twenty minutes after that. But neither of them ever passes by again. A dark car rolls down Main Street just as my rental car trundles past. I remember this car; at the time I thought it looked similar to my mother's. But what would my mother be doing downtown around one a.m.? I make a note to have one of the guys check who owns Jags on the island.

I peek my head out the door and call Sergeant Michaels over.

"Do you recognize this woman or this kid?" I show him the footage.

He squints at the screen. "That's Margo Lane, I'm pretty sure. And that's definitely Ryder Warren."

"They were both downtown around the time Madeline was killed, along with Paul Clark."

He furrows his brows at that. "I don't know what Margo was doing downtown. As far as I know, she never really leaves the house anymore. I'm not surprised Ryder was there, though. From time to time on patrol we pick up teens who are lingering downtown. The guys have driven him home a few times."

"Who was on patrol last night?"

"Vince. But he didn't end up spending much time downtown. There've been a couple break-ins near Calderwood Neck. He was there trying to see if he could find out who's been causing problems." He shakes his head and crosses his arms. "After Emma, I should have just had him stay near the park."

Calderwood Neck is in the northernmost part of the island, as far from downtown as you can get. My ancestors lived on that section of the island with the Carver family, or so I'm told. There's also a Calderwood Point, and many other parts of the island are named after the founding families. When we studied local geography in elementary school, I always got singled out because *two* parts of the island were named after my family—while the other founding families had one.

"Don't beat yourself up about it. You couldn't have known that was going to happen again."

"You better believe it's not happening again this time, though. Allen, Vince, and Marshall are going to be switching off staking out the park."

If this is a serial killer, which my gut tells me it might be, staking out the park isn't going to scare them off. They'll just start dropping bodies somewhere else on the island. There are plenty of secluded places a killer could choose.

Jason pops his head around the door and warns me that two of Madeline's friends are stopping by for interviews soon. That's faster than I expected. I finish up with Sergeant Michaels and meet Jenna Arey in the interrogation room. I'd just interview her in my office, but it's not set up for recording.

On my way to the interrogation room, I stop back by Vince's desk. I've already piled enough on Jason as it is.

"Claire," he says when I approach, his white mustache quirking with what I imagine is a smile underneath.

"After you check on that alibi—"

"I already called. They verified that he was there. They never saw him leave," he says.

I nod. "Thank you. Could you also check for me to see who on the island owns a Jaguar?"

"Of course. I'll have a list for you by tomorrow."

"Thank you," I say as I continue through the bull pen to find Jenna.

Jenna's face is blank. She's still got the dead-eyed stare of shock, her green irises practically drowning in white. Her long brown hair, nearly blonde toward the ends, is messy and falling half in her face. She's built small for her age, making her look a few years younger than Madeline and Emma.

"Thanks for coming in so quickly, Jenna. I'm so sorry for your loss."

She crosses her arms on top of the metal table in front of her. She doesn't say anything but just nods instead.

"How close were you to Emma and Madeline?"

"We were really close. We all went to church together. We were in the choir group. There were six of us."

"What can you tell me about them?"

"Emma had some issues, but she was super nice. She was always willing to help. She volunteered with Madeline at the hospital all the time."

"Did you ever volunteer with Madeline at the hospital?" I ask and take a sip of my coffee.

She shakes her head, and her eyes tighten. "I can't do blood. It makes me pass out. Hospitals give me the creeps." Her lips twist for a moment, and she drops her voice. "I know helping people is the right thing to do, but I just hate sick people."

"Are there any other people that you can think of that Emma and Madeline both spent time with together? Was there anywhere the two of them went together often?"

She stares at her hands for a long time before she says a word. "I mean, there were lots of people at school. Our other friends. But not, like, anyone outside of that group, that I can think of." Her teeth graze against her bottom lip, then dig into the flesh there. "I just can't believe they're dead. I keep thinking one of them is going to text me."

"I know how tough it is. It's a huge shock to lose someone. Especially when you're very close."

She looks down and sniffles. I can tell she needs a moment, so I take the opportunity to write down some notes. When it seems like she's ready again, I ask, "Was Madeline dating anyone?"

She shrugs. "No, not that I know of. Emma and I thought maybe she was going out with someone, though."

"Why did you both think that?"

"She was missing church occasionally." She bites her lip again. "We'd all sneak out sometimes, and she just kept coming up with more and more reasons that she couldn't meet with us. But it's not like she'd gotten in trouble or anything."

"So during those times that she wasn't with you while you were sneaking out, what did you and Emma think she was doing?" I can connect the dots just fine, but I need her to say it. I don't want to put words in her mouth.

"We thought she was meeting up with a guy and ditching us. She did it before when she dated Blake Smith last year. After they broke up, though, she swore she'd never be like that again."

"Did she tell you when she was dating Blake or only after they'd broken up?"

"She told us while they were dating."

"Is there anyone you can think of that she'd date but keep a secret?" There has to be a connection here. If she was secretly dating someone, her friends would have suspicions about who it could be. Everyone's favorite pastime on this island is speculating.

"We thought maybe it was Liam. They'd always been weird together. But Liam said he doesn't swing that way. The only other thing we thought is that she was dating a fisherman or something because she was at the docks *a lot,* and she always said how much she liked older guys."

I'm not sure this path is going to take me anywhere. If Madeline was at the docks a lot, though, I'll be looking into why that was. Was Madeline sending me in the wrong direction by claiming Emma was going to the docks? The docks have always had a dangerous allure for teens. There's a long tradition of fishermen providing teens with contraband. As long as it's not hard drugs, I'm not going to bust them for it. We've had a couple of mayors try to crack down on it, but it never goes anywhere. So far, it's been one of those things that the town lets slide. Their black market trade brings in money but not much of the crime you'd normally expect. "Was there anyone at school, anyone at church that Madeline or Emma had trouble with? Fights with anyone?"

She shakes her head. "Honestly, no. I don't know anyone who didn't love Madeline. Emma had a few problems with Ashley and Tara. The three of them have always hated each other, though." Based on the strength it'd take to strangle Madeline and Emma, along with the size of the handprints on their necks, it's highly unlikely a teenage girl did this. I jot down the names all the same.

"Is there anything else you think I should know?"

Her eyes well with tears unexpectedly. I nudge a box of tissues toward her. She refuses to take one. "No matter what people say about them, they didn't deserve this."

I raise a brow at that. "What people say about them? What do you mean?" All I've heard are mostly good things about Emma and Madeline, how much everyone liked them.

She shakes her head and stands suddenly. "I've got to get going. I'm sorry I couldn't help more."

Part of me thinks she might be referring to Emma's drug problems, but what about Madeline? Was she just sneaking out, or was there more to Madeline than there seems?

CHAPTER 7

When I get back to my desk, Vince pops his head in my office. His gray hair is a little rough today, falling across his forehead and sticking up in the back. Though he has the blue shirt of his uniform tucked into his pants, it has so many creases and folds that I'd guess the shirt was three sizes too big for him.

"Detective, do you have a minute?" he asks.

"Of course," I say, motioning toward the one empty chair in front of my desk. I haven't gotten around to cleaning the files off the other.

"I looked into the owners of Jaguars for you," he says, his voice much graver than I expect.

"And?"

"The only Jag on the island is registered to your mother."

That's what I was expecting, but I had to be sure. What was she doing downtown at one a.m.? "Thank you, Vince." I try to mentally prepare myself for that conversation with my mother.

"Is there anything else you need right now? I was about to grab lunch with my wife. Jason and his husband are coming with us to the Haven if you want anything."

"While you're out, after your lunch, could you please stop by the docks and see if anyone remembers Madeline and Emma being out there shortly before their deaths? I've had a few people mention it to me."

He nods. "Of course. Did you want anything to eat?" he asks.

I've been far more concerned with the case than I have been with food. "I'm all set. Thanks, Vince. Have a good time."

After Vince leaves, I turn on my computer, and there's an email waiting with the details of Madeline's phone records. Despite combing the park and surrounding beach multiple times, we haven't been able to find her phone. I glance through the files. The phone company sent the logs of incoming and outgoing calls and text messages and the location data for the GPS pings of the phone. The last place her phone pinged was on the water, halfway between the island and the coast, at 1:30 a.m. Whoever killed her could have taken her out on a boat and tossed her phone overboard.

I sigh. If the phone was tossed, or even if the murderer has it but the phone is off now, it'll be impossible to find.

Since the last location isn't going to do me any good, the next thing I need to know is who she was talking to. I match up phone numbers on the statement between the list of friends I have for Madeline. There's only one that I can't match, and it's the last number that texted her, at 12:15 a.m. I call the number, but it goes straight to a generic voice mail: no clue as to the owner. It takes me a few minutes to put in a request to find out who owns the number. It kills me that requests like this take days or weeks. The whole damn system is lacking a sense of urgency.

I look over the rest of the location tracking, trying to follow Madeline's movements. She left the house at 12:20 a.m., walked toward the school, stopped at the cemetery, and then headed downtown to the park. What the hell was she doing at the cemetery in the middle of the night? Back when I was in school, kids would skip class and hang out there because it was the only place you wouldn't be spotted—unless you wanted to hang out in the woods, that is.

On Madeline's laptop, I continue searching for connections. Though Ryder was on the surveillance footage downtown, I can't find any link between them. They're not friends on social media; no messages shared. I want to tread lightly there until I have an actual solid reason to bring Ryder in. So far, it doesn't add up, and if I can't make my case for why I need to speak to him, then it's too early to pursue.

My mind keeps slipping back to Margo Lane on the surveillance footage. I need more of a background on Margo. I don't remember much of her from when I was a kid. The guys at the station were able to give me a little info, but my mom and Margo were friends in high school—she might have details I can't get anywhere else. According to everyone I've spoken to, Margo never leaves the house, and if that's the case, what was she doing downtown?

I walk outside before I dial my mom's number. I can't dig into the hard questions over the phone, but I'm saved the trouble of asking. The moment she picks up, she insists on swinging by the station to grab me "so we can chat." Though I don't really have the time to waste, I know she'll give me more dirt in person. And right now, that's what I need to connect the dots in this case.

After fifteen minutes, my mom's jade-green Jaguar rolls to a stop in front of me. The windows are down, and she leans back against the leather seat with a silk scarf tied over her blonde hair, like a fifties movie star. The afternoon sun warms the air slightly, bringing what feels like a winter morning firmly back into fall territory, and she's clearly relishing it.

Mom comes from money. She's got enough to last our family for generations, enough to have a maid, a groundskeeper, and a chef. She could have a driver, too, but that's the one thing she's always refused. *A woman should be able to drive herself.* She loved to remind me of that when I was growing up. Something about being able to get yourself out of any situation. I'm not sure what she got herself into in the past that she couldn't get out of. I never asked.

"Come on, Claire-Bear," she says in a singsong voice. I hate the nickname because Rachel came up with it. She was obsessed with Care Bears when we were kids. She'd draw their symbols on my stomach with markers, and Mom would throw a fit. That's what Rachel told me, anyway. I was too young to remember.

I climb into the car, my slacks sliding too easily across the leather seats. "Hey, Mom," I say as I buckle myself in.

She smiles. "I'm going to take the long way home." I know it's so she can avoid having to see the park again. She must have heard about what happened, but I will not be bringing it up. It's always struck me as odd that Rachel's killer chose the small park closest to downtown. There's a much more secluded park past downtown that's normally empty since it's tucked behind the high school. It seems like a smarter place to dump a body. The significance of that isn't lost on me. The killer is saying, *Look at me; look at what I can do.* Hell, most of this island would make for a great dumping ground. Up north, we've got the quarries. I doubt anyone goes up there until the summer. There are plenty of wooded areas where a body would never be found. That's what really sticks out to me—anyone could see the locations to hide a body on this island.

"You can drive however you want. I was hoping we could talk anyway," I say.

Her hands tighten on the steering wheel, her knuckles as white as pearls. "Please, nothing about the ugliness from last night," she mutters as she accelerates. Her face is tight, the way she looks when she smells garbage or has to deal with something *unpleasant*, as she calls it. That's the face she always makes when she has to deal with me.

I shake my head. "No, nothing like that. What can you tell me about the Lanes?"

For a moment, it looks like she's chewing the inside of her cheek, something that's not a usual tic of hers. But her typical tic is booze, and it's not like she has any of that in the car. "Why on earth are you asking about *them*?" she asks as we drive through downtown and pass the high school. This route will take us past the quarries. It will take almost half an hour to reach my parents' house, but this means my mom can't dodge the question. I bet she's regretting this now. Cornering her like this is a rare gift. I'll use it to the fullest.

"A few people brought them up today, and I realized there's a lot about them I don't know. Why are they shut-ins?" I ask, tempted to pull out my notepad, but I know if I do, she'll be sealed up tighter than a brand-new hull.

She shakes her head and makes a tsk sound. "It's their own doing. That saying about making your own bed and lying in it. It's just a shame that poor girl, Jordan, was caught in the middle of it. Born in the middle of it, I should say."

"I'm going to need more to go on than that," I say.

"It was one of the biggest scandals in a long time." Her words are clipped, but there's a gleam in her eyes that tells me she's relishing this chance to gossip. She pats down the back of her scarf. It's still as tight as it can get without choking her. She clears her throat with a little *eh-em* sound, the way a teacher would to quiet down a class. "Henry and Margo were originally married to other people. Henry was married to my best friend, Violet. And Margo was married to my cousin, Richard. Violet and Henry had twin girls, such precious things. Well, around the time the girls turned two, Violet called me. It was the most upset I've ever heard her. She heard from Jane that someone had seen Henry going into the Tidewater Motel with Margo." She clears her throat again, and I swallow hard as I try to keep up. It's hard when she's talking about people I don't know and can't imagine.

"A few people had mentioned it looked like Margo was pregnant. Turns out the baby wasn't Richard's. She came clean with it shortly after finding out. She'd been having an affair with Henry. It destroyed Violet and Richard. Violet took the girls and left the island. Richard ended up leaving a few years later. But the Lanes stayed. A few months after everything went south, they got married, and Jordan was born. They kept to themselves after that. I've heard all kinds of strange rumors about why." Her lip curls like she's smelled something bad. "But it's probably just because everyone hates them for what they did." She turns to look at me, pain in her eyes. "Good people don't do that."

We've been driving for about ten minutes, and we're deep into the most wooded part of the island. Tall spindly pine trees line either side of the winding road. In a few minutes, we'll pass one of the dirt roads that lead to the quarries. I swear I spent nearly every summer swimming in those quarries.

Does anyone even still come out here? I wonder.

"There have been all kinds of strange rumors about them over the years." Her voice is so quiet I barely hear her over the wind whipping in the open windows.

"What kind of strange rumors?"

"Drugs, drinking, crazy things. For a while there was a rumor that they did something to their daughter. You remember Jordan, right? That girl was trouble. She disappeared during her senior year," she says and shakes her head. I do remember Jordan, but I don't remember her disappearing. She moved away after senior year; that's what I thought, anyway. "Disappeared?"

She shrugs. "They say she ran away, but who knows. Margo has always had a temper."

"What about the Warrens?"

She glances at me out of the side of her eye. The Warrens, from what I remember, are one of the few really large families on the island. Six kids: five boys and one girl. I went to school with four of them. The youngest two, a boy and a girl, I barely ever spoke to.

"What about them?" she asks in a voice so sharp it makes me wonder if she's got a personal grudge against them.

"Catch me up on them. I'm trying to get a feel for the families left on the island," I say, the lie coming out as smooth as a new sail.

"It'd be easier to just tell you the *few* people that moved away, or the new people that moved here over the years. Most of the founding families still have kin here. And I doubt that will ever change," she says, a bit of a barb to her words.

"Indulge me." I know if I keep pressing it, eventually she'll give in. She loves having information, and she loves even more proving she has that information.

"Matthew and Jacob moved away. Ellen and Scott, they all get by just fine. Somehow Allen made it into your police station. Ryder, their youngest, is a little hoodlum."

I almost laugh at the word *hoodlum*. I've never heard my mom use it before, and the word is thick when it rolls off her tongue, as though she's never said it aloud.

"What exactly is Ryder doing?" I ask, uncertain what exactly someone has to do in Vinalhaven to reach hoodlum status. It could mean anything from shoplifting to skipping church.

She bristles. "Skips school, shoplifts—he even stole a car once. He's always smoking." She shakes her head and glares out the window. "He's just disrespectful." It doesn't take much to be disrespectful in my mom's book, so that's not entirely definitive.

Maybe I need to talk to Ryder about that missing boat. "Whose car did he steal?"

"Father Samuel's car, but he refused to press charges. Instead he said he wanted Ryder to come to church. I don't know if he ever did." She looks at me, her lips pursed. "But I doubt it. You need to be careful around that family. They're bad news."

But I'm already very aware of that. I'm curious just how aware of that fact she is.

"I saw a car that looked very similar to yours downtown the night that Madeline died. Were you downtown?"

She bristles and makes a dismissive noise. "Of course not."

Which is what I expected her to say—my mother has always had a problem telling me the truth. She doesn't see me as a detective. I might as well be a little girl playing dress-up to her. "It's pretty clear there is a Jag on the video. No one else on the island owns one." I drop the line into the silence, the soft edges of my words not quite calling her on the lie but coaxing her to either dig her heels in deeper or give it up completely.

"Oh, that's right. I think I swung back by the church late to pick up my phone. I forgot it."

"How long were you there?"

"Probably five minutes or so. I just grabbed my phone and left," she says glibly.

"Can anyone confirm that?"

Her head snaps to the side, and her gaze narrows on me. If I were twenty years younger, that stare would be enough to level me—hell, it'd probably be enough to make a grizzly back off—but I hold my ground.

"I'm sure my phone records would confirm it. Those GPS things track everywhere you go."

I nod. That they do.

Mom curves around the winding roads with ease. Trees tower on either side of us, only parting for the occasional side street. She turns onto the street to her little neighborhood of large houses in varying shades of muted pastels. They all look exactly the same, save for the slight color variations. I swear they even have the same autumn decorations: cartoony scarecrows, hay bales, pumpkins. Each front door has a wreath made of sunflowers, mums, and tiny gourds. They're all identical, like they bought them at the same place—they probably did.

We slide out of the car, and the wind picks up, lashing against us. Thankfully, though the sky is filled with gray clouds, it doesn't seem like it'll snow today; it's warmed up too much for it. I follow Mom up the path and give my dad a little wave as he peeks out the second story window.

My mom force-feeds me cucumber sandwiches and Earl Grey tea while we catch up. She drives me home late, the sky painted in pinks and purples, and the whole time I consider what she's told me about the Lanes, the Warrens, and her presence downtown before Madeline's murder. My whole life I've felt that my mother knows more about Rachel's death than she's let on, and now with her connection to Emma and Madeline, I'll have to keep those details in mind as I investigate. After today, there's something I am sure of—my mother is hiding something.

CHAPTER 8

Over the next couple of days, I help the other officers conduct interviews of Madeline's friends, kids from school, Paul Clark, and anyone else who's come forward with information. And at the end, I'm left with nobody but the people I saw on the surveillance video from the night Madeline died. Vince also followed up on the docks for me, and he didn't learn anything of use either.

Since Ryder is the younger brother of a fellow officer, I'm hesitant to pursue him right away. Sergeant Michaels and I have decided not to mention that Ryder is in the video to Allen yet, as there's no clear link between Ryder and Madeline. So instead I follow the other leads to the Lanes.

The Lanes' house sits at the end of a street, where it's clearly out of place. Here, the other houses are kept up and decorated with the same stupid harvest decorations all over my parents' house. The house is overgrown, with paint peeling so badly it reminds me of an old sunburn.

This is a house I've never approached, never even snuck a peek inside. We'd skip over it on Halloween. As my mom put it, the Lanes are poison, and so is their candy. Rachel and I used to dare each other to knock on their door. Neither of us were ever brave enough, though.

I knock on the door after trying the doorbell three times and figuring out that it's busted. From this angle, this close, the house is in much worse shape than I thought. Grime collects in the cracking, worn wood. Rust has eaten away every bit of metal on the house. It looks like a stiff-enough wind would turn this whole place to a pile of splinters.

A husk of a woman with red-ringed eyes cracks open the door. Where her eyes should be white, they're yellow. Her waxy, sallow skin is taut over the dagger-sharp lines of her face. It's clear she hasn't been eating—not well, anyway.

"Margo?" I ask, unsure if this is the right woman. I've never seen her before.

"Depends on who's asking," she croaks.

"I'm Detective Claire Calderwood. I'm investigating the homicides of Emma Carver and Madeline Clark."

She crosses her arms. Her hands are so bony they look like bleached talons peeking from beneath her robe. Blue veins rope beneath her translucent skin. "I wouldn't know anything about that," she says and starts to close the door, but I stop it with my hand.

"Please, I have a few questions about Jordan," I say. Since there's no real consensus on what happened to her, I need to know that, at least. "We can talk here on the porch. I don't need to come in," I offer, because I have zero desire to go in this house. The air seeping from inside smells like a mixture of vinegar and old cheese. Musty and sour, it's as thick as air on a summer's day.

She glances back into the house, her face tight as she stands straighter. "We have to be quiet so we don't wake up my husband." She follows me onto the porch. "What about Jordan?" she asks as she pulls a pack of cigarettes from her robe and lights one.

"What exactly happened to her?"

She takes a long drag from her cigarette, and a ribbon of smoke seeps from her chapped lips. "She ran away after she graduated, and we haven't heard from her since." Her voice is flat, without even the smallest hint of concern. Her tone is striking. Why isn't she the least bit worried about where her daughter is?

"Are you sure she left on her own and that she wasn't taken somewhere against her will?" What I really want to ask is, *Why weren't you concerned she was taken? Why was it so easy to assume she ran away?*

"She left a note, packed her things. I doubt seriously that anyone made her do it." She takes a long drag from her cigarette and squints toward the street.

I nod and jot that down. It's still troubling that she doesn't seem the least bit concerned. I know that all families have different dynamics, that not all parents would be as worried as my mother, but it still strikes me as strange. If I left a note, skipped town, and then didn't talk to my mother in weeks, she'd send out a search party and then probably hire someone to drag me home. "Have you heard anything about Madeline?" I ask.

"Just because everyone hates us doesn't mean we hurt that girl," she says, her words barbed.

"No one said you did," I say as I make eye contact with her again. "Speaking of that, though. What were you doing downtown last night?"

She narrows her eyes, but they aren't quite focused on me. "I had to get some *things* from town. We normally have them delivered to the house, but we couldn't yesterday." Something inside the house thuds loudly, like someone falling to the floor. Her eyes go wide, and she glances toward the door. "I need to go."

Since the visit with Margo gave me nothing, I head back to town. The bell dings behind me as I head into the café. I've debated stopping to get some real lunch, but there's too much on my plate today. I've got to go over interviews and start making lists of all the other people I need to follow up with.

I grab a fresh cup of coffee and a sandwich from one of the shops on Main Street. For a few minutes, I make small talk with Mrs. Miller, but I head out quickly when I figure out she saw nothing last night. I leave with a warm coffee, a bag of food tucked under my arm, and a head full of fresh gossip. Most of it was the kind of crap my mom would blather on about over tea, but she did have some gossip about Noah. Something about him actually being a reporter for CNN trying to expose the seedy underbelly of our small fishing town. Mrs. Miller clearly believed this, so I just bit my tongue. But I know for a fact he doesn't work for CNN; he has an eclectic writing résumé, spanning everywhere from Vox to the *Washington Post*. The front door jingles behind me as she calls goodbye.

As I push through the station doors, my phone vibrates, and I glance at it, finding an email. The phone company is finally getting back to me about the request for the number that texted Madeline the night she died. John Warren is the registered owner—Ryder and Allen's dad. Which one of their phones is it? It surprises me since I haven't found any links between Ryder and Madeline. But do I really think the phone belongs to John Warren or Allen? Not likely.

An idea pops into my mind—sometimes you can link a social media account to a phone number. I navigate to Facebook and type the number in. The page loads so slowly it's as if time has skidded to a halt. After what feels like five minutes but has probably been more like five seconds, an account for Ryder Warren appears. All signs have been pointing to Madeline having a boyfriend, and this connects some dots for me. Even if they weren't dating, they were in contact the night she died. He may have answers that I can't get from anyone else.

I knock gently on the frame of Sergeant Michaels's door. He glances up and points toward the empty chair. "Sit, sit," he says as he finishes typing.

"I need to talk to you about Ryder Warren."

He pulls his hands back from the keyboard and crosses his arms. "Why?"

"His phone was the last number that texted Madeline before she died."

He bristles and thumbs the end of his nose. "That damn kid. He wants to be trouble. He wants everyone on this island to hate him."

His reaction surprises me. "Oh?" I expected him to start listing all of his crimes one by one. It sounds like he's ready to defend Ryder.

"Don't get me wrong: he's gotten into some trouble. Shoplifting, cutting class. Deep down, though, he's a good kid. He babysits for Ellen. He's even helped at the church a few times when no one was looking. He's trying to get attention in a family full of kids. It happens." He shrugs. "So you think she snuck out to see him?"

"Possibly. I need to talk to him. But I wanted your take on how to handle this with Allen." I've never had to toe the line like this and question the family member of a fellow officer.

Sergeant Michaels scratches his stubble and leans back in his chair. "I'll talk to him, give him a heads-up. You need to call his parents to arrange a time for Ryder to come to the station."

I nod. "If you've got their number, I can handle that."

"Please, just make it clear that he's not a suspect and that you think he may have just seen her downtown the night she died."

"Sure." That's not how I would normally handle the situation, but under the circumstances it'll have to work. I try not to make a habit of saying that someone is or isn't under investigation, because things can change quickly, and new evidence could come to light.

"I'll email you their number after I talk to Allen," he says as he starts typing again.

"Thanks."

I head back to my office and shut the door. Allen's always had a stick firmly planted up his ass when it comes to me. He thought I was a stuck-up bitch in high school. His favorite nickname for me was Princess Calderwood.

It takes about twenty minutes for the sergeant to get the number to me. When I call, it goes straight to voice mail. I leave a short message urging Ryder's parents to give me a call, and I hope that they'll do it quickly.

CHAPTER 9

While I wait for the Warrens to get back to me, I plan to retrace Madeline's movements. I start in my car on her street and follow the path she took toward the cemetery. Being back here, I see Rachel everywhere I go. Her ghost lingers in every shadow, the memory of her written on every street. It's as close to a haunting as my life is ever going to get. It's time for me to visit Rachel—well, her grave, anyway. I've never said goodbye to her properly. My mom didn't want a funeral, and I could never bear to come here on my own.

The cemetery is a block from the school, which is pretty poor planning, if you ask me. Instead of skipping school at the mall or wherever mainlander teenagers skip school, here they'd just walk around the cemetery and smoke, at least when I was in high school. Looking back, I cringe at how disrespectful it was.

At the end of a road lined with pine trees is the cemetery. Its bounds are ringed with a wrought iron fence, with tombstones appearing amid a field of dead grass and maple trees long since robbed of their foliage. I pull off into the spare bit of grass just inside the gates to park. The church never bothered to put a lot here. If they haven't bothered so far, chances are they never will. Things here rarely change.

I'm painfully aware of how close I am to Rachel. There's a twinge at the back of my mind, and my stomach sours with unease. My hand tightens on the steering wheel, and I glance to my right. The rows of headstones stretch all the way to the back fence.

Wind whips around me, rocking the car back and forth, as if urging me out into the graveyard. "Fine," I grumble and pop the door open.

My boots sink into the grass, and I walk slowly down the rows of graves. If it were anyone else I were visiting, I'd bring flowers, but Rachel would hate that. She hated everything Mom loved. Mom loved fresh flowers, so Rachel loathed them. Her grave is ten feet from the back fence, the headstone made of newer granite, which seems out of place surrounded by markers that look ancient.

I take off my jacket, laying it on the ground so I can sit. Even through the thick material, the earth chills my legs. I know what I need to say to her, why I came here, but my tongue may as well be tied in knots. My guts twist.

It's now or never.

"I don't know how much longer I can keep your secrets, Rachel," I whisper, my words weaker than I'd like. A shiver runs down my spine, but it's got nothing to do with the weather.

"If no one else got hurt, I would have taken them to my grave. But I can't do this anymore—not when other lives are on the line."

A tear runs down my cheek, turning icy in seconds. "God, I miss you."

Once we hit our teen years, Rachel and I fought constantly, always at each other's throats. Some days, I thought only one of us would make it out alive. Turns out I was right. I lean forward, plucking a long strand of grass from the dirt, and I slowly wrap it around my finger again and again until the tip tingles.

A shadow moves in front of me, the silhouette of a man, and I jump up. My heart pounds, and I try to catch my breath.

"Shit, I didn't mean to startle you. I didn't even know you were back here," Jason says.

He's the last person I expected to see. Hell, I didn't even know he'd left the station.

"It's okay." I grab my jacket off the ground and dust it off. "What're you doing here?"

"Today is my mom's birthday. I was stopping by to visit her," he says, brandishing a bouquet of daisies. "You all right?"

I wipe my cheeks automatically, ridding them of any evidence I've been crying. "Yeah, I'll be fine. Just here to see Rachel."

"Do you want to talk about it?"

I shake my head. "No, but thank you." I start heading back toward the fence. I've said everything I came here to say. After all, I came here to see if there were any clues to why Madeline stopped here before she was killed.

"Claire, I know it's hard. I'm here to talk if you ever need to," he calls after me.

I offer him a wave and throw a thank-you over my shoulder for good measure. I appreciate the sentiment, but I've got to figure this out on my own. Looping around the outside fence, I check for any hint that Madeline was here. At the end of the fence, toward the tree line, there's a small jacket balled up on the ground. I bag the jacket without touching it and search nearby. There's no sign that anyone has been near this jacket, not so much as a footprint on the soft earth. She wouldn't just leave this here on a cold night, but it's clear she wasn't taken here—it's not likely, anyway. I head back to the station with the evidence. I'll need to see if it belongs to Madeline and if it leads me anywhere.

CHAPTER 10

With a cup of coffee in hand, I walk to the station, leaving my rental car at home. There's no reason to use a car downtown most of the time. The house I'm renting is within spitting distance from the station, so when it's not bone-chillingly cold, I'm going to take full advantage of that. Low fluffy clouds roll across the sky above me. The air is so crisp and clear it's almost sharp. I pass the row of buildings that make up downtown, the locals waving at me as I pass. I wait across the street from the station as several cars pass by. Finally, once it's clear, I walk as quickly as I can, mindful of the steaming cup of coffee still clutched in my hands.

I throw the station door open, trading the cool air for the balmy warmth inside. Mindy waves at me as I pass through the waiting room on my way back to my office. Folders from the second round of interviews Jason did wait on my desk. One is from the witness who found Madeline's body, and the rest are from some of her other friends at school. I pore over the folders, searching for anything that might help. Madeline snuck out nearly every night, and at least one night a week, she met her friends in the park, but I'm still not sure what she did the rest of the time. If her nights with friends were anything like mine at that age, they were meeting to pass around a bottle of liquor, smoke a little pot, and bemoan their parents or teachers. But none of her friends had planned to meet her that night.

So what was Madeline doing in the park? She must have been meeting Ryder.

Though the officers asked all the right questions, there's nothing in here of substance. She didn't have a boyfriend, not that anyone knew of, anyway. She wasn't going out there to meet with any of her friends. No one has let a word slip about what she might have been doing. After the kids have had a few days to breathe, I'll ask a few more questions. Someone has to know something about this girl. I check my phone again to see if I've missed the Warrens returning my call. I haven't, so I call to leave another voice mail.

As I wait for the Warrens to call back, I flip back through the interviews and the details of the cases. There's a common thread between Emma and Madeline that has my interest piqued. They both volunteered at the Pen Bay Medical Center, the closest hospital to the island. I need to reach out to their volunteer coordinator and see what I can find out about their time at the hospital. I search online for the main number for the medical center and call.

"Pen Bay Medical Center. How can I help you?" a woman asks after two rings. Her voice is strained, like she's stressed or recovering from a cold.

I introduce myself before jumping in. "I need to ask a few questions about volunteers who have worked for the hospital in the past. It relates to a case I'm working on. Do you have a volunteer coordinator you can transfer me to?"

"Uh . . . can you hold, please?" she asks.

"Of course."

The low, chiming notes of a classical piece filter through the phone after she places me on hold. After a few minutes the line clicks, and she comes back on. "I'm going to transfer you to Aidan McConnel, the hospital director. He coordinates the volunteer program."

"Thanks," I say, but she transfers me so quickly I doubt she heard me at all.

"This is Aidan," a man says, his southern accent thick on his words.

I give him a quick explanation for my call. "I was hoping I could talk to you about Madeline Clark and Emma Carver."

"I'm not sure how I can help. They haven't volunteered in six months."

That can't be right. "Six months? I thought they'd volunteered more recently. I was told Madeline was there two weeks ago."

"No, six months ago I asked them both not to come back," he says, drawing all his words out much more slowly than I'm used to.

I quirk an eyebrow at that. Two girls who've never been in any trouble in Vinalhaven were asked not to return to a hospital they were volunteering at? "Can I inquire as to why?"

"Emma and Madeline were stealing Adderall. When we discovered the theft, we asked them not to come back."

Jesus Christ. "Was the theft reported to the authorities?"

"No, I didn't want to hurt their chances of getting into a good college over something like that. I hoped that asking them not to come back would sort of scare them straight. You know?"

"How much did they steal?" Static crackles on the line, and I pull the phone away for a second to be sure I didn't lose him.

"They stole around fifty tablets."

"Over how long of a period?" I ask. Fifty tablets is a lot for personal use. Were they selling them?

"We suspect it was within a two-week period. One of the nurses alerted me that a bottle had fewer tablets than it should have had. It appeared that they took someone else's key card to get into the prescription room. Our security guy, Craig, staked out the room and caught them in the act."

Taking a key card to steal Adderall makes me wonder if they'd done it before. Stealing fifty tablets in a two-week period seems like quite a bit for a first try. I'd bet they stole smaller amounts that went unnoticed before they were finally caught. But I file those details away in my mind.

When I'm silent for a long moment, he asks, "What is all this about?"

"I'm sorry to inform you, but Madeline and Emma were both victims of a homicide."

"They're dead?" he stammers.

"Yes. I know this must come as a shock."

"Of course it comes as a shock; they were just girls. Oh God, what happened?" His voice is pleading, every syllable of his words trembling as he speaks.

"I'm sorry, but I can't go into any of the details because it is an open investigation. While the girls volunteered there, did you ever notice anyone showing an unusual interest in them?"

He clears his throat, like suddenly he needs to sound more official. "No, not that I recall."

"Have any of your volunteers ever made any complaints about staff being inappropriate or trying to see them outside of the hospital?"

"No, there's never been anything like that. We have an incredibly clean record," he says.

"Is there anything else that you think could be of help to the investigation?" I ask.

"Not that I can recall. But I'll think about it. If you give me your details, I'll ask around and see if anyone else comes up with anything."

I give my details to Aidan and end the call. While I may not have discovered anything about the killer, he gave me some information about Emma and Madeline I never expected. If they lied about their whereabouts for six months, what else did they lie about? And if they were also selling Adderall, that could have gotten them into some trouble.

After I'm done typing up my notes on the call with Aidan, I head out of the station and walk onto Main Street. Now that I've talked to Aidan about Emma and Madeline's connection to the hospital, I need to speak with Father Samuel at the church to see if he knows anything about their time in choir together. As the cold afternoon air whips against me, my phone vibrates, and I glance at the screen as I pull it from my pocket.

"Hey, Mom," I say as soon as the call connects.

"Claire! I need you to get over here right away!" she says, her voice verging on panic.

"What's wrong?" My mom isn't the type to call and tell me to get over to her house ASAP unless there's something *really* wrong. Her words wrap around me like a vise. Is there something going on with my dad? He's had some health problems recently, chest pains, mostly, but I figured they were just a symptom of being cooped up with my mom. As she talks, I throw on my jacket and jog out of the station. My heart hammers and my breaths quicken as I fish the car keys out of my pocket and throw open the door of my rental car.

"Just get here as fast as you can," she says before ending the call, and I swear right before she hangs up I hear a strange voice in the background.

I throw open the door of the car and slide in. With my hands trembling, it's difficult to get my key in the ignition. I head west, through downtown past the station, and up the road that will lead me to my parents' house. Adrenaline burns in my bloodstream as the wood-frame houses lining the street give way to pine trees and lush landscape. I press my foot hard against the accelerator, and the car lurches forward. The drive would normally take fifteen minutes, but I make it in seven.

As I turn into the driveway, the pebbles skittering beneath the tires, my heart is thrumming away in my throat. A seed of panic was planted in me the moment my mom called, and now it's blooming in full. The house is in one piece, exactly the way it looked the last time I was here. I can't see a single thing wrong, not from out here, anyway. Crime scenes always give me a bad feeling, a sickness that grows in the pit of my stomach; here, there's nothing. But that doesn't mean there's not something wrong on the inside.

"Mom!" I call as soon as I slam the car door.

She opens the door for me, a gin and tonic clinking in her hand, a delicate slice of lime balanced on the edge. My mother has always been a drinker, not a drunk, not a lush. That being said, she likes to be seen with drinks. Presentation is everything to her, and *this* is how she wants to be presented.

"What's wrong?" I ask, looking her over, but she's as pressed and perfect as ever, as if she just walked out of a J.Crew catalog. She's got on loose beige slacks, a sharp crease down the front of each leg. Her navy-blue blouse is a bit large for her small frame, and a thin string of pearls adorns her neck. My mother isn't one for gaudy jewelry.

"I should ask you the same thing," she says as she sips her drink carefully, without smudging her coral lipstick. I raise my eyebrow, a question burning in the back of my mind, but she turns and walks toward the kitchen. She winds her way through the main hallway of the house, and I follow like a puppy. In the living room, a wall of windows overlooks the rocky shore and the bay beyond. I nearly miss Noah standing on the deck.

He sweeps his long hair away from his face and offers me a smile. I grind my teeth together as it hits me—there's nothing wrong. She called me over here because of him, but I'm not sure who to blame for this, her or him. "What is *he* doing here, Mom?" I ask, my words nearly a growl. It's not that I'm mad at him for being here. She faked an emergency, and I know it's because he's here.

"I was hoping *you* could tell me the answer to that. He showed up here and started asking all kinds of questions about your sister. And I just cannot deal with it right now."

She can't deal with it right now? Of course, all my mother can think about is herself in this situation—not that I have a murder to solve, that other girls could lose their lives while I'm here dealing with this for *her*.

For a second, I think she's going to add something else. Instead, she gives me a little push toward the sliding glass door leading to the porch.

I bite my tongue and step outside, my anger redirecting toward Noah. A swift breeze brings the smell of salt, the ocean. It feels nice now, but in a couple of hours, it will be frigid. Fall in Maine is a fickle creature, especially on an island. During the day we get a reprieve, but at night it's as cold as death.

"What are you doing here?" I ask him as I shut the door behind me, frustration edging on my words. A barrage of barbed questions slams in the back of my mind, desperate to get out. Anger still boils inside me.

He stares over the railing. "I got a strange call this afternoon." He motions toward the house. "Someone had information about Emma and Madeline. Because of the circumstances, they thought it might be related to Rachel's murder."

"And how is that, exactly?" I ask as I lean against the railing, keeping a healthy distance between us.

"I'm sure you know both Emma and Madeline were in the choir group?" He pauses, looking at me to gauge my reaction. I give none.

"Yes. That I knew. But what does that have to do with Rachel?" She might have also gone to the church, but she hadn't been in a choir group.

"Your mother leads the choir group."

My mind spins. *She leads a choir group? Since when?*

Granted, yes, her leading a group with two victims is a connection, but there's no way my mother would have killed Emma or Madeline. Then again, something nags at me. Some part of me was always frightened of what my mother was capable of. There's a darkness inside her, a shrewdness.

"Her leading a choir group with two victims is circumstantial," I say.

"The person who gave me this information had another detail." He straightens when he says this, and it's like the bottled-up knowledge has made him three inches taller.

I cross my arms as I wait. I'm not about to beg for him to tell me shit. It's obvious he'd get too much pleasure out of that.

"They saw your mother yelling at Madeline the day before she died." His eyes narrow, and he appraises me again, waiting for some explosive reaction, I'd wager.

I raise a brow. My mother? Yelling? She rarely raised her voice to me or Rachel—that's part of what made her so unnerving. She'd pinch the back of your neck, beneath your hair so no one could see, or dig her fingernails into your spine. Maybe this is why I don't like being within arm's length of her. But even with that side of her, I don't see her inflicting that on any child but her own. My mother might have a quiet cruel streak, but yelling? She's too obsessed with her image, with how everyone else on this damn island sees her. My mother might pull a lot of shit in her own home, but out in public, she's a picture of perfection. Her image is so carefully curated you'd think she had a team help her pull it all together.

"And what was she yelling about?"

"That's a detail I didn't get. They weren't sure what the disagreement was about. I was hoping you might have some info about it." He pulls a small notebook from his pocket.

"And how would I know anything about that?" I challenge. As if I would tell him even if I did know something. Noah needs to get it into his head that we're on opposite sides of this.

"Well, you don't seem surprised at all by this news, so that leads me to have some theories."

"How nice for you. Why are you here now, though?" I'm not all that surprised to find him at my mother's house. I figured it would happen eventually. But I'm not following why now.

"I came to talk to your mother to ask her side of the story. You showing up too was just a happy accident." He grins in a way that tells me that smile typically gets him out of all sorts of trouble—or maybe into it. But not with me.

"What did she tell you?" I ask. I'm not giving him *anything*.

"Absolutely nothing."

I nod and motion toward the door. "I think it's best if you leave." Though Noah tries to ask a few more questions, I refuse to entertain any of them. I'll be damned if I help him with this story.

After I walk Noah out, I find my mother staring out the back windows over the water. Her drink is half-empty, though the slack look on her face makes me wonder if she made herself another while I was talking to Noah.

"I need to talk to you," I say as I approach, careful to stay out of her reach. I feel like a fisherman carefully approaching a shark.

Her eyes flash toward me for just a moment, but she says nothing.

"I heard that you've been leading the girls' choir at the church." It seems an odd choice for her to lead the group. My mother has never shown that much interest in the church. Sure, we went while I was growing up, but she never even had Rachel or me go through confirmation. Why the interest now? She must be getting something out of it. But I know the question I really need to ask after all this.

She nods slowly. "Yes, I am. You know how important the church is to the community."

So that's why she's doing it: the perception of it. "When's the last time you saw Madeline and Emma?" I ask this question so I can gauge whether she's going to tell me the truth.

Her eyes narrow, and she takes a slow sip of her drink. "I don't remember," she says before swirling the glass, ice tinkling inside.

"Do you remember what you said to them the last time you spoke? The tone of those conversations?"

She shifts and faces me fully. "I don't recall; probably something about choir practice. It must not have been anything worth noting." A thin-lipped smile slithers across her face.

"Did you have any trouble with the girls?"

She takes another long sip. "No. What exactly is all this about?"

"I've heard rumors that you were seen arguing with Madeline before her death."

A high laugh trills out of her. "Well, that's just ridiculous."

"Is it?" I ask quickly.

"Of course. They were lovely girls. I never had problems with either of them."

I decide to shift gears, knowing if I keep going this route she'll give me nothing. "So they never lied to you?"

She raises a brow at that. "Lied to me? About what?"

I shake my head, pretending to keep my cool. "It's probably nothing. Just something a few other people said."

"I don't have any reason to think they lied to me, but if I think of something, I'll be sure to call you. You should probably get going, though—I've got errands to run," she says, motioning toward the door.

I leave my mother's house with more questions than answers. As I climb into my rental to drive back to the station, I ask myself, *What is my mother capable of?*

Back at the office, I head straight to my computer, type Noah's name into the search box, and scroll down the page. I did a general search when he showed up here, trying to figure out who he was, but now I need more details. I've really got to dig. I look over blogs and news outlets carrying his stories about the Middle East, politics, and the large earthquakes that recently hit Brazil and Mexico. For a few pages, that's all I see, article after article—until a headline catches my eye. "Maryville Teen Killed in Tragic Accident."

The small blurb tells me nothing, so I click on a link to the article.

Page cannot be found.

"You've gotta be kidding me," I growl at the screen.

What happened? How was Noah involved? I scroll back up, taking the time to look through the other articles with more care, and find a recent story published by Noah. "Another Murder Rocks Small Maine Town—Coincidence or Serial Killer?"

I click through, and anger flashes white hot inside me, burning my cheeks. Picture after picture of Grimes Park load on the screen. One of me near the body, one of Jason putting up caution tape. Several close-ups of Madeline's body. He fucking published the pictures of Madeline. I grab my coat and storm out of the police station.

As I cross the street to the hotel where Noah's staying, I gather my thoughts. Every jagged word in my mind is laced with venom. I want to drag this motherfucker out on a boat and throw him into the bay. Maybe he'll drown. Maybe I'll put some rocks in his pockets to be *sure* he does. That's what he deserves for this. Did he even think about what this would do to her family? The people on this island?

The Tidewater is a strange motel. It's not the usual truck stop type you see off every highway in America. Instead, it looks like it used to be three separate buildings that were connected probably a hundred years before I was born. Most of the motel is two stories, while the tail end is one. Along the back side, there are balconies that hang over the water. I love them, but they make most tourists turn green.

My chest is tight, pulse pounding in my ears as I throw open the door to the motel's office. Jake Stephenson, a guy from my high school, sits behind the counter tapping the screen of his cell phone furiously. Jake looks almost exactly like he did senior year, plus ten pounds, minus some hair. He glances up at me and does a double take. "I heard you were back," he says before placing his phone, screen facing down, on the counter.

"I am. Look—" I decide to cut right to the chase. I don't have the time or the patience for small talk today—or ever, really. "I need to speak to Noah Washington. Can you tell me what room he's staying in?"

"Sure," he says as he rolls up to the computer and jiggles the mouse. After a couple of seconds he says, "Room five. It's down the far-right side."

I say my thanks and rush out of the office before all the anger fizzles right out of me.

I walk up the stairs on the side leading to Noah's room. I slam my fist against the door so hard that my hand aches for a moment. But the throb is lost beneath my fury.

He opens the door, the smile on his face faltering as soon as he sees me. "Hey, Clai—" he starts. He stands in the doorway, shirtless. His brow furrows as he registers the anger on my face.

"What the fuck, Noah?" I spit the words at him as I shove into the hotel room.

"What are y—"

"Are you kidding me? Anything I say to you is off the record. Or so help me God, I will end you."

He holds his hands up in front of him like he's surrendering. He takes a step back from the door, nearly tripping over his loose flannel pajama pants. "Calm down. What's wrong?"

I laugh almost hysterically. "Don't tell me to calm down, *ever*."

He nods sharply. "Noted. So what did I do? At least tell me what I did before you shoot me."

"Shoot you? You deserve worse than that." I throw the words at him like daggers. I want to punctuate every word by poking him hard in the ribs, but for now I keep my distance.

He grins. "You're probably right."

"You published pictures of Madeline's body." I force the words out.

"The public has a right to know what's going on here. I've seen what happens firsthand when they don't. When the truth is twisted, it's soon forgotten."

"Knowing and seeing are two completely different things, and you know it. What if her dad, what if her little sister sees that? And her friends?"

He shakes his head. "It's awful. I know. But they deserve to know."

I switch gears, seeing that empathy isn't going to work with him. "You're compromising my investigation with these pictures. We specifically left the cause of death out of the media."

"I'm sorry. I didn't know you were keeping it from the media," he says, not looking at me as he speaks.

"Please take them down until this is over," I plead. My voice nearly breaks. All I can think about is how I would have reacted to pictures like that of Rachel. What if it were my family?

He looks toward his laptop, still open on the small dining table. "I can give you a few weeks, maybe a month." His voice is weaker than it usually is, like with enough prodding I could get him to relent on this. As he looks at the laptop, the screen illuminates the dark circles beneath his eyes. I didn't notice them before.

"Thank you," I breathe. The weight binding my chest recedes, if only by a little. I head to the door but stop short. "What's your connection to all this? Why do you care?" I ask as he starts typing.

He stops but doesn't look away from the screen. He pauses for a long moment, like he's not going to tell me. "My best friend's mom was killed by a serial killer while we were in middle school. The media, the police, the whole town failed her. She made some mistakes, just like anyone else, but it was the wrong place, the wrong time. The media and the police made it out to be like she was killed because she was a sex worker, but she'd never do that. It couldn't be any further from the truth."

"Damn, I'm sorry."

"She was my second mom," he says and looks at the table. After a long pause, he sucks in a sharp breath. "My mom didn't act like she even wanted us around most days, but Josh's mom, she made me feel loved. And I never even got a chance to say thank you."

"I'm sure she knew. Did they ever find her killer?"

He shakes his head. "Nope. Seven women died. And they barely investigated it. I'm sorry I've been hard on you and getting in your way.

I was afraid something like that was happening again," he says, his eyes downcast.

"I'm never letting this go. I will find out who did this, even if it kills me."

A sad smile curves his lips. "I know you will. They're damn lucky you came back. They'd never solve this without you. Look, since you're already here. I have some info that might help you with your investigation. I'd really like to help." He glances toward a stack of menus he's got on the counter in the small kitchen. "You hungry? I could order pizza."

I weigh that in my mind. He had info about my mom I didn't. I hate to admit it, but I want—no, I *need* to know what else he might know. If he has information that could help me solve this case faster, I need to take it. So far, the details I have aren't pointing me in any one direction. "Sure. Milo's delivers." After we order pizza, Noah sets his laptop on the coffee table, and I try to make myself comfortable on the god-awful floral sofa.

"So what do you have for me?" I ask as he shuffles through papers on his lap. This close to him, his woody, sweet cologne begs me to scoot closer. But I resist; I have to.

"Let me start by saying I've been looking into all of this for months. And I never planned to come to the police with it. Before you got here, I didn't think they'd have any chance of finding the killer."

I nod. He's not completely off base. I'm not sure the police here could solve a murder. They don't have the resources or experience. After all, they've never found Rachel's killer. I'm not sure how long they even bothered looking. Something about the investigation around her murder doesn't sit right with me, and I've never been in a position to solve the case myself. Once upon a time, it was just too painful, and then life got in the way.

My mom told me once, after she'd drunk too much, that the sheriff had never seemed surprised that Rachel had died—it was like he'd expected it. Maybe not that he'd expected Rachel to die, but he'd expected *someone* to die. Not long after the case went cold, that sheriff left the island. Expecting someone on this island to die never made sense to me; no one had ever been murdered before Rachel. I pressed my mom on it a few times, trying to figure out why she'd think that. But no matter when or how I asked, she never breathed another word of it. Eventually I started to wonder if it'd just been her anger or grief talking.

Noah shuffles the stack of papers in his lap and glances at his laptop. I swear he takes a deep breath before continuing. "I think you've got a serial killer on your hands," he says and looks down at the papers.

That's what my gut says too. But I can't give him that info, so I keep my mouth shut.

He purses his lips. There's a fire burning behind his eyes. "There are other victims, Jane Does, dating back almost twenty years. They've all been found up and down the shore on the mainland. They all look like they were strangled on a boat and thrown overboard. They washed up eventually, but different departments have found them, so no one has connected the dots. These killings happened before Rachel died too," he explains. "The killings have been speeding up, or maybe no one ever reported on the other murders."

"You know anything that ties them together? How many possible victims do you know of?" I understand his train of thought—proximity of the murders should be enough to link them—but I need more to go on than that.

"Six. They've all been strangled. They're all women between fourteen and twenty-one. Every one of them is blonde, same body type." By the way he says it, eyes wide, voice thick, I know that he wholeheartedly believes this theory he's concocted, that he's trying desperately to make a connection there. The reality is that most homicide victims are women. If this is serial, we'll need to draw airtight connections. But it doesn't feel right to me. Leaving the bodies in a very public space, the way Rachel, Emma, and Madeline were, is very different than dropping a body in the bay. One screams, *Look at what I'm doing; you all need to know I did this*. The other says, *No one will ever know what I did*.

While I can see that Noah is drawing parallels because of physical similarities of the victims and proximity, serial killers typically stick to the same MO. They need a good reason to deviate from established patterns.

The idea that bodies have been washing up along the mainland makes me sick. But I'm not surprised no one has really looked into this. This happens often. Town lines, jurisdictions, precincts: they do nothing but divide us all up onto our own teams. Police departments from different towns don't work together, and they sure as hell don't want to work with the FBI. Everyone's got their own fucking sandbox, and no one wants to share their toys. That's why a lot of the time it takes way too long to track down serial killers. Technology is slowly improving things, but this is a problem with roots that go down miles.

There's a knock at the door, and Noah hops up. A few minutes later, he returns with the pizzas and beer. He cracks open a beer, hands me one, and plops back on the couch.

"Where were we?" he asks as he takes a swig.

"You were trying to convince me that the other homicides must be related to the ones on the island," I say as I grab a slice of pizza. As I bite into the crispy crust, the sauce and cheese flood my mouth; I forgot how much I missed this pizza. The pizza in Detroit just never hit the spot.

"Ah yes, because it *is* the same killer." He grins and tips the mouth of his beer bottle toward me.

I shake my head. "These are two different killers, I guarantee you. People have a pattern, especially with killings. We long for a routine, even when it comes to this." A killer is going to stick with what has worked in the past. It wouldn't make sense for this killer to change now.

I studied more about serial killers in college than I care to admit. Roxie and I also had quite a few conversations about them; they fascinate me. There's something that serial killers all have in common that isn't present here—consistency. They kill in the same kind of way, over and over again. Methodical, habitual. There are very few exceptions. Bundy, Gacy, Dahmer—all the big names, they had patterns. My goal was to profile for the FBI; that's a pipe dream, though. It's way too difficult to get your foot in the door with the FBI. If I ever want to entertain the idea as a real possibility, I need at least a few more years' experience in the trenches.

"If you're wrong, you're buying the beer next."

"That's morbid, but you're on," I say as I hold out my bottle, and he clinks his against it. "And besides, until one of those bodies washes up on the shore of this island, there's nothing I can do about them. I have to worry about stopping the homicides *here*." It won't keep me from giving the other departments a heads-up, but they're not going to listen to me. They don't want me in their sandbox. Unknown dead women washing up on a shore is a problem, but I guarantee it'd be a bigger problem if the women were from their town. The death of a stranger is easier to let go of than that of someone you say hello to every morning.

He leans over and squeezes my knee. "You'll catch 'em," he says in a tone that would be more fitting for *Go get 'em, slugger*, but it still makes me smile. He glances at his laptop for a long moment before saying, "There's something I found I want to show you." He shifts his computer so it's easier for me to see the screen. "Though most of my focus was on Rachel at first, after Madeline and Emma both died, I started looking into their lives to see what I could find."

"And?" I interrupt, eager to know what he's discovered.

"They posted a lot of images on social media that they ended up deleting."

My heart pounds as I consider his words. They deleted them? Why? Is there any way to get them back?

"Luckily, when something is posted online, even if you delete it, it never really goes away completely. Based on what some of her friends said, during times they should have been volunteering at the hospital, they posted some interesting pictures." He clicks to a folder on his computer.

A picture of Madeline and Emma posed with their arms around one another appears on the screen. They take up most of the image, but in the background I can see slivers of water. Were they on the beach?

"When was this taken?"

"Two weeks before Emma died. They were supposed to be at the hospital." He scrolls to the right, showing me two more pictures from the same day. In each I see a bit more of the background, which reveals slivers of a boat behind them and water stretching toward a blurry shore.

"Whose boat is that?" I ask.

"I have no idea." His brows knit together as he scrutinizes the images, like if he stares at them hard enough, they'll reveal new details to him.

I can't tell Noah what I already know, so instead I put on my best poker face. "Can you send me these pictures and whatever you've found on the other bodies?" I've been down at the docks a few times since I came back to the island, but it's not like I spent much time looking at the boats. Even if I had, there's not much showing in these pictures to match up. But all the same, knowing that the girls were on a boat when they should have been at the hospital—that tells me that someone else took them out, that someone else knew where they were. Now I just have to find out who that was.

He nods. "I'll send you what I have."

"Thank you. Look, I've got to get going. If you think of anything else, though, call me at the station," I say.

"I will."

As soon as I head out of the hotel, I call Sergeant Michaels and catch him up on the information that Noah gave me. The other deaths in the bay may not be related or in our jurisdiction, but they're something we need to keep an eye on.

CHAPTER 11

A few days ago, I asked Sergeant Michaels for a copy of Rachel's police report. It wasn't until this afternoon that they were actually able to track down where the report was. There are a few places where old files are stored on the island since the station has very limited storage space. Dealing with this kind of shit is a whole new ball game for me. In Detroit, we had everything carefully cataloged in a database. To get Rachel's file, I've got to go to the old tailor's shop, which used to be in the center of town and has since been converted into storage, and dig through the files in the basement.

Stares follow me as I walk down Main Street and fish the keys out of my pocket. I pass the café, the post office, and a new restaurant before finally reaching the old storefront.

A hiss of stale, damp air hits me in the face when I push the door open. I imagine that the files must be pockmarked with mold. Low light filters in through the dust-caked curtains. Rolls of fabric are still piled on top of a counter that runs along the wall to my right. Sergeant Michaels warned me that the files were in the basement, so I head straight back toward the open door.

I flip on the lights, but all it does is illuminate the worn, wooden stairs in a dim, orange light. My mouth goes bone dry. I hate basements as it is, but the darkness waiting for me at the bottom of the stairs is a special brand of terror I haven't experienced in a while. For years, Rachel tormented me anytime I had to go in the basement. And I've never been able to shake the fear that there's someone waiting for me down there. I grip the banister and force myself down.

It's just a basement.

I search the wall to my left for another light switch. My hand runs across the slimy walls, slick and cold, until my fingers hit the switch. A single dim flickering bulb dangles in the middle of the room. I pull out my phone, hoping the flashlight will help. As I slide the light on, I realize I have no service in the basement.

Great. Just perfect.

The air thickens with each step I take. It smells moist, damp, like rain and rotting leaves. Somehow, it's colder down here than it is outside. Dirt and mud are tracked on the floor, crisscrossing footprints all over the cement. In the center of the room, there's an island of filing cabinets, with a few others scattered along the back, among the stacks of discarded desks.

I scan through the cabinets, looking for the number Sergeant Michaels wrote down for me. When I finally find the right cabinet, I pick through the tabs. Footsteps on the wood floor above me echo through the basement.

"I'm down here!" I call. Sergeant Michaels must have come over to make sure I found everything okay. "Don't know why he couldn't have just grabbed it for me in the first place," I grumble.

The folder isn't filed where it should be. And when I do finally find it, it's much thinner than I'd expect. I glance inside and, flipping through the pages, immediately notice that there's something missing. But the footsteps upstairs draw my attention. Liquid splashes against the floor above me. Confusion blurs my thoughts. *Did he spill his coffee?*

Every step upstairs, every splash, makes my heart pound harder. Overhead the footsteps creak against the floorboards. I head toward the door, pulling my gun from the holster as I walk, but halfway across the basement, the cold chill disappears, the thick mustiness swept away, replaced with the sharp scent of burning wood. Smoke oozes slowly through the beams above me. Someone set the upstairs on fire.

My mind races as flames lick the doorframe at the top of the stairs. I rush for the stairs anyway, knowing it's my only way out. I have no idea how I'll get past the fire, though. A cough scratches its way up my throat, and I cover my mouth with my sleeve. Smoke stings my eyes, and they water automatically, flooding my cheeks with tears. At the top of the stairs, a black outline stares down at me. The build is wide, stocky. I can feel his gaze searing my skin, but I can't make out a single detail of the man. I grab the banister to steady myself against the dizziness as smoke invades my lungs. The figure shifts, and my hand tenses around the handle of my pistol. The door at the top of the stairs slams, and the grinding metal of a bolt crushes my hopes of escape.

Who the fuck would lock me down here?

I freeze, unsure of what to do. My body moves on its own as I realize I need to find another way out. Questions rage in the back of my mind, but I ignore them for now. Smoke pours in above me, and my throat constricts as another cough rips from my lungs. Fresh tears spring from my watering eyes as the fire assaults me. I frantically search along the edges of the basement, praying for my fingers to land on anything but the cold, smooth wall. There has to be another way out of here. The haze in the basement makes it hard to see more than a few feet in front of me. I try to think back to my training—how long will it take smoke inhalation to kill me? Two minutes? Five?

Panic roars through me, and my chest tightens. I might never make it out of this place. I might die on this goddamn island. Adrenaline pours into my bloodstream, and I force myself through the wall of haze surrounding me. My heart skips a beat when I find a tiny window, painted over with black, sitting at the back of the basement. In the empty shop above me, the fire crackles, red flickering through the slats in the wooden floor. I glance back; the flames are still ten feet from me, chewing through the floorboards from upstairs, but in a matter of seconds, they could flare close enough to block my path. Smoke crawls through the air, scratching my throat, irritating my lungs.

I yank on the window, but it's screwed shut, their sorry excuse for security in this town. It wouldn't keep someone from getting in; they could just knock the glass in. It will sure as hell keep me from getting out, though. For a moment I consider shattering the glass but realize that'll just end with me bleeding out before getting the opportunity to burn to death.

As a fresh wave of smoke pours in from above, the fire roars so loudly my ears ache. The voice in the back of my mind fills me with terror: *You're going to die down here*. Every breath I take is harder as the air floods with smoke. Sweat coats my skin as the fire above turns the basement into a sauna.

Embers rain down from above, hissing when they reach the cold metal filing cabinets in the center of the room. There's no other way. I have to break the glass. I grab my gun, make sure the safety is on, and slam the handle into the window. My body is racked with coughs. Shards of glass skitter across the floor, showering around me. I gulp down a breath of fresh air before clearing the window. I thrust Rachel's file out first, onto the ground. A ribbon of smoke chokes me, and I double over, gripping my side as I try to catch my breath.

I scramble, my hands shaking, and I thrust myself out onto the damp pavement of the alley behind the row of businesses. There's a commotion on the street, the hiss of water against flames. They're trying to put out the fire.

I lie on the damp, grimy pavement as I catch my breath. The air is crisp, clean. Smoke spirals above me into the cloudy sky. When I finally pull myself from the ground, my mind screams to go back to the station, but I need to take Rachel's file home and hide it. Whoever tried to kill me didn't want me to find it. What the hell is in this file that someone was willing to murder to keep it hidden?

With the folder tucked under my arm, I jog down the alley, the smell of rotting food in the dumpsters I pass the only thing cutting through the smoke. At the end of the alley, I head toward the street and peek around the building toward the fire. Three of our firemen stand in front of the shop, one aiming a hose while the other two help him wrestle with it. Some lookie-loos have gathered behind them, watching the whole thing. I grab my cell phone, call Sergeant Michaels, and have him send everyone out to search the streets. I've got to get Rachel's file home.

Thankfully, everyone is so preoccupied with the scene that I can sneak across the street to my place. I tighten my grip on the folder and dash across the street. Just as I think I'm scot-free, one foot on the walkway, someone calls out "Hey!" behind me.

Noah stands in front of the huge Victorian that's been turned into a B and B across the street from me. His eyes go wide when I turn around.

"Holy shit, what happened? Why are you covered in ash?"

"What are you doing here?" My hackles are raised. I don't know who I can trust right now.

"I saw everyone on the street, the fire. I was trying to figure out what was going on."

I turn and march toward the house. Noah's footsteps follow along behind me. I pull my keys from my pocket, and just as I unlock the door, a tickle works its way up my throat again. A powerful cough rips from my lungs, and I double over. My hand moves to my side automatically as a sharp ache cuts through my lung.

As soon as I catch my breath, I turn on Noah. "Stop following me, Noah," I growl as I close in on the porch.

"I just want to be sure that you're okay."

I whip around, staring daggers at him. "Why, so you can report on it?"

"I'm not going to print this. I just want to make sure you're okay. I can take you to the hospital."

Rage builds inside me like a wave. But as he appraises me, it defuses my anger. This isn't his fault. He didn't do this.

"If you print a word of this—"

"I know; you'll end me," he finishes.

Reality crashes down around me all at once. I could have died. My heart seizes, and my chest tightens. It's so hard to breathe that I'd swear there were a million bricks piled on my lungs. I stand up straight, hoping it'll make it easier to get a breath in, but it doesn't. With trembling hands, I unlock the door, and Noah follows me inside.

"We should go to the hospital. How long were you in there?"

I shake my head. "I'm not going to the hospital." There's no way in hell I'm wasting my time at a hospital. I must be getting close. Someone is trying to slow me down. But I'm not going to let them.

"Claire, please," he begs as he follows me into the kitchen.

I stop and turn toward him, making sure to meet his gaze before I speak. "I'm not going to the hospital. I'm fine." My words are slow and deliberate. Too bad it sounds like I've been screaming over a concert for hours.

"Your hands are shaking," he says and takes a step closer. His proximity and the adrenaline still boiling in my blood create a mix that makes me light headed.

I take a steadying breath. "Seriously, I'm fine." The words are almost a prayer, begging them to protect me from the panic still seizing every part of me.

"You've got soot on your face," he says softly. "Are you sure you're okay?" His words are gentle, careful, as if he's afraid a harsh word will crumble my facade. Maybe right now it would.

I give him a tiny nod. "I need to go wash off these ashes," I say.

"I'm glad you didn't get hurt. If you need anything, anything at all, call me, okay?"

I nod. "I will."

I see Noah out and head upstairs. Part of me knows I need to look at Rachel's file again in more detail, but I can't yet. My stomach clenches and twists at the thought. I'll look at it later, once I've prepared myself. For now, I need to wash the ashes and the rest of this day off. After I strip off my sweat-soaked clothes, I climb into the shower. Though I desperately try to wash away the darkness of this afternoon, the stream of hot water does nothing to erase what I'm carrying around with me. After I clean myself up, I find three missed calls on my cell phone, all from the station.

I call Sergeant Michaels again, and his voice is panicked when he says, "Are you doing okay?"

"I'll be fine."

"What the hell happened?"

I go over more of the details I was too rushed to cover during the first call.

"We found a can of gas a few streets over. We think it was related. But we didn't find anyone trying to get away from the fire. Don't you worry, though—we're going to figure out who did this."

CHAPTER 12

August 2004

A warm glow seeps out from beneath Rachel's door, lighting my path in the dark hall. Behind me, snores echo, and I wonder for the three millionth time how my mother can sleep through it. I turn the handle slowly—not that Rachel would notice; she's always got her headphones on. She bobs along to a song I can't hear, her long blonde hair dancing across her back. Though it's eleven o'clock at night, she's still dressed—or, I should say, dressed again. She changed into pajamas for our parents' benefit. Now she's all gussied up to sneak out, like she does almost every night. Rachel's second life, the one she leads after they go to sleep, would give them a heart attack. This second version of Rachel, the one who only exists after she sneaks out the window and crawls down from the second floor, has a different wardrobe, different friends, and a different attitude.

They'll never know that, though, because I'm not going to tell them, and if Rachel's history is any indication, they'll never find out.

She pulls on socks, and I glimpse something on her ankle, something I've never seen before. I slip inside and shut the door behind me. Rachel jumps nearly a foot in the air, then glares at me as she clutches her heart. "Are you trying to give me a heart attack?" she asks, a sharp edge to her voice.

"What's on your ankle?" I ask, crossing my arms as I lean against the door. There's nowhere she can go to avoid the question.

"None-ya," she says as she pops her gum at me and throws her iPod on the bed.

"Don't be a bitch," I say. I'm sick of her acting like we're on separate teams. For years, we were best friends, and then suddenly, it was like I was a leper or something. Everything changed after Rachel turned twelve. Before that, Dad said we were as thick as thieves, and honestly, we were. Rachel told me everything. I knew about her friends, the rumors spreading about the middle school girls. Hell, I giggled with her when she told me about her first kiss with Scott Walker. I'd talked my dad into getting us walkie-talkies so we could keep talking even when we were in our rooms. I got them for my tenth birthday. Rachel and I used them every day, until one day she turned hers off. I kept mine on, waiting, hoping she'd start whispering midnight secrets to me again. When the batteries went dead, I gave up on the walkie-talkies—but I never gave up on the idea that Rachel might share her secrets with me again.

And eventually she did.

The first secret Rachel shared with me: she'd been shoplifting from all the stores downtown and was desperate to show me her stash. She bribed me to not tell Mom by letting me pick out anything I wanted. I chose a bracelet that I knew came from Mrs. Taylor's shop. I felt so bad about it that the next day, I went in the store and dropped it in the back. For the next few weeks, I took small things from her stash and returned them to where she'd taken them from. If she ever noticed, she never said a word to me about it.

"Don't be a narc," she says, her words almost a question.

"You know I'm not going to say anything." I try to keep my words even, though it bothers me that she doesn't trust me at all. I've kept a thousand of her secrets.

She looks away and furrows her brow, like she's trying to decide if it's a good idea or not. Finally, she tugs up her pant leg, revealing a crudely drawn cross tattoo. It's obvious it's a real tattoo, not just marker; the edges are red and crusty.

"When the hell did you get that?" I ask. I know people have tons of tattoos in New York and LA, but here, the only people who have tattoos are the fishermen. They've all got sparrows, naked ladies, anchors, you name it. Our mom made it clear, though, that tattoos aren't for those of us who belong on the island. A tattoo brands you as an outsider.

"I might have skipped class with some friends and gone to Bangor," she says with a wry grin as she brushes the hair off her shoulder.

I roll my eyes at her. "How the hell did you manage that without Mom finding out? She'd know what I was up to before I even stepped on the ferry." I plop down on the end of the bed and fold my left leg beneath me.

Rachel always has a way to get what she wants. She wants to skip class? She'll talk a teacher into giving her the hour off for some insane reason. Hell, I'm sure she could have talked our mom into taking her to get that tattoo, if she'd wanted. Of course, she didn't, though. Getting away with things Mom doesn't know about fuels her. All she's ever done is test Mom's patience. Some days, I think that's what she lives for. She's talked Mom into letting her skip class, giving her money, giving her a car on her sixteenth birthday. I don't test Mom like that because I know there's a shark lingering beneath the surface.

"We didn't take the ferry. Cameron's mom has a boat, so we took it." Her voice tells me it's not the first time they've done it, and her grin goes from wry to downright devilish.

"One day, you're going to get caught," I warn her.

"Not today, though." She slides off the bed. After brushing the curtain away from the window, she looks down into the backyard.

"Where are you going?" I ask.

"To the park, meeting up with some people from class to drink, hang out."

"So there's no one in particular you're going there to meet?" I ask pointedly. There have been rumors running rampant at school about Rachel hooking up with someone, but no one knows who. Rachel is a flaunter; she's not the type to hide a boyfriend. If she's started, that scares me.

Her face falls, like I've stumbled on something she doesn't like. Maybe she didn't expect me to figure it out. "No, there's not," she snaps after a few seconds too long. "I've got to go," she says as she slides the window open. She disappears into the night. After I count to a hundred, I follow down after her.

Though darkness shrouds me, and Rachel is nowhere to be seen, every crunch of dried leaves beneath my feet threatens to give me away or send my pounding heart straight through my chest.

A swift, cool wind cuts through the backyard and makes me wish I'd put on a heavier coat. I pull my hoodie closer, hoping it will help. I jog across the dark lawn, a moonless sky above me, and skirt the streetlights on my way to the small park where my sister usually meets her friends. This time of night, this far from downtown, her friends don't have to worry about being found. They're loud, but they haven't been caught yet.

The park is quiet and empty when I peek through the trees ringing the small playground. Next to the swing set, beneath the awning-covered park benches, I make out the shadowy figure of my sister and someone across from her. I weave between the trees, watching, staying out of view as I try to see who she's with. It isn't until they leave together, hand in hand, that I see she's with the one guy in town she shouldn't be with. If my mom saw, she'd kill them both.

—

I lie awake in bed, the memory burning in the back of my mind. It's a night that would have faded away in time, a night of little consequence. That is, if Rachel hadn't died.

I pull myself out of bed and throw on clothes for work. It's too early to go in—the sun isn't even up—but I'm too keyed up to even think about getting another minute of sleep.

I grab Rachel's file from its hiding place and tuck it into my bag. I still haven't been able to bring myself to look at it, but today I'll have to bite the bullet.

I drive the few minutes to the station. Several men in bulky jackets stroll toward the marina, getting ready to start their day on the boats. As I slide out of the car, I wave to Frank Miller, the town boat mechanic. Frank has a little shop off the marina. He hobbles a bit as he walks, though he doesn't look old enough to hobble. My mom mentioned something about Frank having cancer, and I wonder if this limp has anything to do with it. He offers me a half wave and heads on foot to the docks. I fish my keys out of my pocket and unlock the station door. Icicles hang off the edges of the roof, producing a drip, drip, drip as they melt into puddles that gather along the edges of the building. The shadow of a large oak tree dances across the side of the station like skeletal arms reaching across the facade.

The fluorescent lights buzz above my head, and I lock the door behind me. It'll be a few hours at least before anyone else gets into the station. I need to go take a look at Madeline's body, but to do that, I'll have to see which medical examiner's office we use on the mainland. It takes some digging through files, but I find the address in the paperwork. The ME is two hours away in Augusta.

My stomach churns with unease, and sweat prickles the back of my neck. There are enough similarities between Rachel's, Emma's, and Madeline's deaths that I can't ignore the connections. But talking to the ME will tell me how many there really are. After the sergeant finally gets into the office, I inform him of my plans. Sergeant Michaels tells me that he sent Jason to the burned-out store yesterday. All that was left was a smoldering shell. Though the cabinets didn't burn, all the files inside were destroyed. Jason wasn't able to find a single screw, and the windowsill was wiped clean.

With the questions about who could be responsible in the back of my mind, I pull out of the station and drive down the street to the ferry. I've got fifteen minutes to kill until the boat arrives. There's a line of six cars waiting, and I pull in behind them.

The ferry churns slowly across the bay. I know if I don't look at the file now, I won't be able to until I get to the ME's office. My stomach tightens as my fingers brush the folder. Part of me doesn't want to see inside. It's something I never wanted to face. Hell, it's something I thought I'd never have to look at. For six months after Rachel died, I honed my skills at tuning out anytime someone talked about her. I just couldn't stomach it. After that, I tried to ask my mom about it, my dad, but every time I was told that we didn't talk about *that* anymore. I wanted answers; I wanted to know what had really happened to my sister. But everyone treated me like I was too delicate, like I couldn't handle it. What I couldn't handle was pretending like she'd never existed.

I take a deep breath to settle my nerves, but it does nothing to uncoil the anxiety wound inside me. Carefully, I open the folder, as if I'm afraid jostling it too much might trigger something. A picture of Rachel's lifeless body lies on top, as though warning me about the other horrors waiting inside. It's different seeing her laid out like this, her neck purple, her lips blue. She's so pale that she's nearly the color of the fresh blanket of snow beneath her. All at once, the breath goes out of me. I knew what had happened to her, but I've never seen the pictures—I've never had the evidence scattered across my lap. My stomach bottoms out, and a bolt of pain hits my heart. I look away and catch my breath. I'm not sure this is something I can compartmentalize, but I've got to try. Her body is laid—no, posed—exactly like Madeline and Emma. The folder is as heavy as it would be if her body were laid across me.

I've seen pictures like this a thousand times, victims, cases I had to solve—but this is different. This is my sister.

I flip the pictures over and thumb through the police report. Strangled to death. In most cases like this, it'd be a ligature strangulation—a clothesline, a rope—but these girls were strangled with someone's bare hands.

There's something that sticks out about the file. There's no list of suspects, no interviews. Maybe it's because they didn't have any suspects. It's still highly unusual for a file to not have interviews. No interviews, no suspects—and the ME's report seems far too light. The full autopsy isn't here, just a few of the details. There are notes about some of the investigation details: where she was found, when, concerns about Rachel, details that were withheld from the media. There's a note toward the end of the file that the time of Rachel's death—between eleven p.m. and one a.m.—was kept as holdback information, along with the fact that flesh was removed from her ankle. A wave of nausea crawls its way up from the pit of my stomach. All I can see in my mind is someone peeling away the flesh, the tattoo from my sister's ankle, blood blooming from her pale skin as they cut the flap away. I clench my fists, waiting for the wave to pass. I can't let this get the best of me. I won't.

I can't imagine that these girls could have made someone angry enough to do this to them. Everyone loved Rachel; she rarely even got into spats at school. No one on the island hated her enough to do *this* to her.

The ferry pulls into the dock, and I take one last look at the file before tucking it away. I drive the car off as soon as I'm waved on. It takes an hour and a half through the winding roads to reach Augusta and the office of the medical examiner.

I pull in to the nearly empty parking lot and shut off my GPS. Three deep breaths later, I finally feel settled enough to get out of the car. It might be in my job description to march in there and look over the body—but that doesn't make it easy. I force myself out of the car, gripping the door a little too hard before I slam it. Turning toward the building, I take it all in. The Maine State Police crime lab is a small brick building off Hospital Street. The door is a cheery shade of blue, as if it might distract anyone from the building's grim contents. As far as these places go, the office is tiny. The ME's office in Detroit was four times the size of this one.

The lobby looks like it could double as a dentist's office. Uncomfortable-looking plastic chairs line the walls, and a receptionist sits behind a waxy wooden desk. After showing her my badge and signing in, I wait for the medical examiner to collect me. The air is sharp with chemicals, but it still manages to smell vaguely stale, bottled.

A tall woman in a white lab coat strolls through the double doors and glowers over her glasses at me. She looks frazzled, like she doesn't even have time to breathe. The thick lines on her wide face make it look like she hasn't smiled in a long time—not that I blame her. I'm not sure how often I'd smile if I had to cut up murder victims all day. She's got dim green eyes, the kind of eyes that have no life left behind in them, no spark. I guess everyone here is dead.

"Detective Calderwood?" she asks, as if she's skeptical I'm actually a detective. I take no offense to it, though. It's not the first time it's happened. My first sergeant told me I looked like I should be teaching preschool. There's nothing about me that screams *intimidating* like most of the others I encounter on the force. I've considered dyeing my hair brown a thousand times so people will take me seriously, but I know it won't do me much good. I'd need to grow a dick for the guys on the force to see me as a *real* cop.

I hold my hand out to shake hers. She has a firm grip and papery, delicate skin. Her hands are covered in powder, the result of wearing latex gloves all day. I expect her hands to be cold, a symptom of working in a morgue, but they're surprisingly warm.

"Dr. Sabrina White," she says as she nods at me.

"Dr. White, I'm here to see the body of Madeline Clark and pick up her autopsy report," I say as she leads me down a long hallway lined with doors. We pass labs filled with technicians and head down to the morgue.

"You're not new to bodies, are you?" she asks as she peers at me over her shoulder. With the way she looks at me, she must think I'm sixteen.

"No, ma'am. I'm originally from Detroit PD," I explain.

She chuckles. "Ah, so you've seen more bodies than I have."

"Probably not that many." I've seen quite a few, but I doubt it compares to what any ME has seen.

Three metal tables stand empty in the middle of the morgue. The mixture of antiseptic and alcohol in the air prickles in the back of my throat. One of the guys I made friends with at the Detroit ME's office told me they do that on purpose to stifle the stench of some of the riper corpses. Though I've got a jacket and a long-sleeved shirt on, the cold creeps beneath my clothes and settles under my skin.

Dr. White walks along a wall filled with small metal doors and slides the body out. "Do you need her on a table?" she asks.

"Sliding her out is enough." I step closer once she walks across the room to grab a clipboard.

She flips through the pages, then reads, "Five foot two, ninety-five pounds, COD manual strangulation," she rattles off.

"Any thoughts on time of death?"

"Most likely between ten p.m. and two a.m.," she says as she flips to the first page.

All the similarities are enough to make the back of my neck prickle. I brush my hand along it, trying to smother the feeling. It does me no good. What if the person I'm after is Rachel's killer? I never thought I'd have the opportunity to hunt down her murderer. The thought overwhelms me, tightening my throat. I've always hoped that somehow they'd track down Rachel's killer. But bringing him in myself? I'm not sure I could arrest him and not seize the opportunity to snuff out the bastard myself. I want justice for her and justice for me. My entire life has been defined by my sister—or the absence of her. Maybe with this I can finally be set free.

"Anything else?"

"There was a four-inch-square incision made on her back, removing a strip of flesh there entirely," she explains, flipping through the pages. "There are pictures, if you want to see."

I know immediately what it was; Madeline told me about the tattoo she shared with Emma. The idea of the killer cutting flesh from these girls makes me queasy. "Was the flesh cut off pre- or postmortem?" For Rachel's sake, I hope it was post.

"Post," she says.

Deep down my instinct says the killer is keeping the flesh as a trophy—sick bastard. "Was she sexually assaulted?" I ask, though at the scene it didn't look like she had been.

"No. There are no signs of assault. She was around fourteen weeks pregnant, though."

My heart nearly stops. Madeline was pregnant? Is this serial killer hunting teenage mothers?

"Was Emma Carver pregnant?"

She shakes her head. "No. There were no signs of pregnancy."

"Is there anything else that sticks out to you?"

She flips through the paperwork again. "Like Emma, we found fibers in her lungs, indicating her face was likely covered while she was strangled."

I swallow hard. The physical similarities between these girls are alarming. This serial killer, if that's what we have, preys on teenage girls who are small, popular, blonde. But more than the physical similarities, the details of the murders—flesh cut from the body, strangled, face covered while being strangled—stick out to me as if a neon light is flashing *serial killer* in front of my eyes.

"Did she have any drugs in her system?"

She shakes her head. "No drugs or alcohol in her hair follicles or urine. Seems like she was a pretty good girl, and she wasn't drugged into submission. I can't tell you how many girls this age we get in here filled with oxy, heroin, you name it. We had a thirteen-year-old OD two weeks ago," she says and hangs her head for a moment. Even when you see death every day, that's not something you ever want to see. "Fentanyl," she adds, pursing her lips. Even by Detroit standards, thirteen is really young. It wasn't that often I heard about something like that.

I never expected that Maine would be a hotbed of teenage overdoses, but then again, when there's nothing else to do, that's a common path for teenagers to take.

"You're sure there was no Adderall in her system?" I ask. If Madeline was making her own trips to the docks, I have a feeling she had a vice of her own. Since she and Emma were stealing Adderall, my assumption is she liked it as well.

"I didn't look for Adderall. I can check, but it'll take several weeks to get back."

I leave with few answers, two heavy folders, and a bad feeling I just can't shake. Questions boil in the back of my mind. Madeline and Emma both had the tattoos cut from their backs, and Rachel had flesh cut from her ankle, where she also had a tattoo. It can't be possible that this is really Rachel's killer, can it? As I drive, I go over the evidence again and again in my mind. There are too many similarities for it to be a coincidence, but maybe I just don't *want* to believe it could be Rachel's killer, because that would raise the stakes way too high for me. If my emotions get too tangled in this investigation, it could cloud my judgment.

After driving back to the port, I roll onto the ferry, most of the day already burned away. Halfway through my return ferry trip, I get a call from Ryder's parents letting me know he'll stop by tomorrow at four to answer my questions. I add it to my calendar and start mentally preparing what I want to ask him. When the ferry docks in the marina, I drive off and back toward Main Street.

My wheels crunch as I maneuver into the station parking lot. When I exit the car, I see Mayor Clark across the street from me outside the café. I raise my hand to wave at him, but he just glowers. I shrug it off and head inside. As I walk toward my office, it catches my eye that the sergeant's door is closed. It's *never* closed. Inside there's a droning of voices. I can make out the sergeant's voice just fine; the other, not so much. It sounds familiar—I'd almost swear it was Noah.

I leave my office door open and try to focus on reviewing interviews while I wait for their meeting to end. Just as I slide from my seat to grab a cup of coffee, the door pops open, and Noah strolls out. I expect him to head out of the station, so I'm surprised when they both cross the hall into my office. I plop back in my chair.

"Claire, I wanted to let you know that I've decided to bring on Noah in an unofficial capacity to help with your investigation into Rachel's murder." The sergeant's rough smile tells me I'm supposed to be pleased about this information.

I open my mouth to protest, to say how unprofessional and just plain stupid it is, but he holds his hand up as if he knows exactly what I'm going to say.

"He has a degree in criminal justice, Claire, and he's done investigations like this before. Let's give him a chance. After all, I want you to be able to focus on Madeline and Emma." There's a gleam in his eye, something that tells me this may not have been his idea.

I hate when he frames things like that, in a way I can't argue with. There's nothing I can do other than bite my tongue, since Noah is still here.

"He's also agreed that while he's working with us on this, not a word of it will make it into print. And neither will any pictures."

My eyes widen. Did Sergeant Michaels bring him in here for that? Was he hoping to keep all this out of print until the investigations are wrapped up? Maybe my complaints about Noah being halfway up my ass actually did some good.

"Thank you," I say to Sergeant Michaels as he heads back to his office.

Once he's out of earshot, Noah says, "I'm really glad he asked me to come in. I think this will work out really well for everyone. I've got a lot to show you."

"This better not be some ploy, Noah."

"I'm going to prove to you that I'm in this to help, even if it kills me."

It might kill us both.

I knock gently on the doorframe of Sergeant Michaels's office as soon as Noah leaves. I need to catch him up on what happened at the ME's office. "You got a minute?" I ask when he looks up at me.

He offers a slow nod and motions for me to take a seat.

"Why are you really doing this?"

He leans back and crosses his arms. "If we don't do this, he's going to publish the crime scene photos. He's going to publish articles saying we're not taking this investigation seriously, and after what you already told me he's found, I think he can help with Rachel's case so that you can focus on Madeline and Emma."

Anger flares inside me, and I clench my jaw against it. This is a prime example of why I hate journalists.

When I say nothing, he continues, "We'll work with him, we'll close this case, and we'll move on knowing we did everything we could. We're not doing anything wrong. How was Dr. White?" he asks, his voice thick.

"She seems fine," I say, not sure what information he's after. No part of me wants to drop the issue with Noah, but I have a case to focus on.

"She and I go way back," he says with a grin. "If I had played my cards right . . ." He shakes his head. The ME has to be a good ten years older than the sergeant. I'm not sure when or how they met the first time, but honestly, I don't give a shit.

I offer him a tight smile and hand him a folder. "I brought you a copy of the initial autopsy."

He hesitates and rubs his eyes. This is wearing him down. It might be too much for him. The second I start to take the folder back, he finally snatches it from me.

"What'd she have to say?" he asks as he stacks the folder on the pile nearest to him.

I go over everything the ME said, which isn't much. "I think we have a serial killer."

He shakes his head and pinches the bridge of his nose. "I don't want you to be right about that. But I think you may be." He slams his fist on the desk, and everything rattles. "We've got to find who's doing this."

I understand his frustration, but the truth of it is there aren't any places this kind of thing doesn't happen. This is the world we live in. Monsters kill girls; the rest of us suffer and wonder why. No matter how many answers we get, it will never be enough. "We'll find them. I know we will." We just don't have much to go on yet. It could be *anyone*.

"We'll keep digging," I say, not sure who I'm trying to convince. Rachel's murder has been unsolved for fifteen years. Who am I to say we're going to do any better with these other deaths? But if we don't, so many lives hang in the balance. We can't let more girls die. And we can't afford for this guy to slip away again for another fifteen years.

He nods. "You doing all right with all this?" he asks. He narrows his eyes at me, like he's inspecting me for battle damage.

I offer a curt nod in response and push up from the chair. Though I appreciate his concern, I don't talk about my problems to coworkers.

CHAPTER 13

Sergeant Michaels knocks on my door the next day and hovers just outside. The creases around his mouth look deeper today, like he hasn't smiled in a while. Though he's normally got his shirt starched and ironed to perfection, the wrinkles are starting to show today. I've been here less than a month, but I swear he's aged already.

"Do you have a minute?" he asks in his low, rocky baritone.

"Of course," I say.

"I want you to meet with Noah today to go over everything we know about Rachel so far. Don't clue him in to anything about the current investigations—I don't trust him with that—but he needs to be caught up if he's going to help."

There's still a lot I don't have, but if he wants me to talk to Noah, I will. As long as it keeps this out of the news. I nod. "I'll call him a little later."

"Thank you. I sent his contact information to your email."

After Sergeant Michaels returns to his office, I open the email and dial. He answers on the third ring, a little breathless, like he ran for the phone. "This is Noah," he says.

"Noah, it's Detective Calderwood."

"Oh, hi," he says, his voice high. Obviously my call has caught him off guard.

"I was hoping you could come by the station today so we could discuss Rachel's case," I explain. Having this discussion with him makes me uneasy. I've never worked with someone outside law enforcement like this on a cold case. More importantly, I wouldn't make the choice to involve a reporter. But if Sergeant Michaels wants me to do this, I really don't have much choice.

"Yeah. I'm just finishing something up. I could be there in an hour?"

"That's fine," I say.

We end the call, and I gather my notes, readying myself as best I can for the unpleasant conversation I know is coming. Around an hour later, Mindy calls for my permission to send Noah back. He opens the door tentatively, like he's afraid I've changed my mind about him being here, but I wave him in with whatever smile I can manage given the circumstances. Though Noah said he had something to finish up, instead it looks to me like he spent an hour getting ready. His button-up shirt is freshly ironed; I can practically see the steam still rising from it. The ice-blue shirt is tucked into khakis that hang a little loosely on him. Noah perpetually dresses like someone who has never endured a real winter. He never has on a thick jacket, gloves, anything.

"Is it okay if I sit?" he asks as he motions toward the chair.

I nod and can't help but wonder if I've gotten a different Noah to show up to this meeting than the one I've encountered before. He's not the same brash, in-your-face asshole as he was the first time he came in here. Though it still makes me fume that he showed up at my crime scene with a camera, this version of Noah I can stand. For now, anyway.

For a moment we sit in silence, and then I open Rachel's folder in front of me with the notes I've written on a legal pad on the right side. Though I've practically memorized what I want to say—and with any other case I'd be fine—with Rachel, I can't be sure of myself.

I want to remain stoic and unfeeling as I look over the details of the case again, but it's like a vise is tightening around my heart.

"Are you okay?" Noah asks, leaning toward my desk.

"Fine," I say and clear my throat. *Stick to the details, just like any other case.* I swallow hard, but my saliva may as well be made of nails. "The autopsy in the file is incomplete, leading me to believe pages were taken. I haven't been able to chase down the state records to find their copy with everything going on here. What we do know about her homicide is the following: she was strangled and dropped in Grimes Park, and flesh was cut from her body where a tattoo had been."

"I'll see if I can find any details of the autopsy on my own. And what was the tattoo of?" he asks as he takes notes on the details. His brows are furrowed, shadowing his blue eyes.

"A cross."

"Was flesh removed from the other victims?" he asks with a raised brow. The detail clearly doesn't shock him, but he still looks uneasy.

"I can't tell you that, Noah," I say, my voice firm. I want it to be clear that I will not waver on this.

He looks at me, his brows furrowed like he's going to argue, but after a beat he thinks better of it.

The next detail swims in my mind and forms a lump in my throat as sharp as a shard of glass. "Rachel was also pregnant."

"Do you know who the father was?"

"I do." I'm not about to volunteer the information.

"Would you share that with me?" he asks gently.

All I can think about is what a betrayal that would be. Rachel would never have wanted me to tell anyone. And I know Jacob didn't do this to her. Well, that's what I want to believe.

"You don't have to tell me. I just want as much of the picture as possible," he says when I say nothing.

"I need some time to think about it. I want your help. I want you to have the information, but it feels like I'm betraying her."

He nods. "It's fine, really. Do you mind if I ask you some other questions about her?"

My stomach flip-flops. "Questions like . . . ?"

"Just things about Rachel, so I can get a better understanding of her. I think it helps to know more about the person I'm investigating, helps me think like them."

"As long as I can tell you that I'm not comfortable answering certain questions, and you won't pressure me to answer them," I say, hoping my words make it clear that my demands are nonnegotiable.

For a moment he pauses, then says, "Deal," somewhat reluctantly. He flips the page of his notebook over and readies his pen. "How old were you when Rachel died?"

"It was a couple days before my sixteenth birthday," I say. Two days exactly. That's part of the reason I hate birthdays. The other part—somehow all my birthdays ended up being about *her*. Every bad thing in my life centers on birthdays now. They're cursed.

"And she was . . ." he starts.

"Seventeen." She hadn't even graduated high school.

I expected better questions out of this guy, but I recognize the line of questioning. It's the same way I'd start out if I were trying to get a read on someone in an interview. It's surprising, the things you can learn from a person's answers to very basic questions.

"Was there anyone at the time she didn't get along with? Anyone you could imagine doing this to her?"

I look down at my desk and cover the pictures of Rachel's strangled body with my notes. My thoughts bottle up inside me, begging to come out. "Noah, there's no one on this island that I could imagine doing *that* to my sister. She was popular. Everyone liked—no—loved her," I say, and there's an edge to my voice. No matter how hard I try to shake it, it only gets sharper. In that way, she was so like the other victims.

"When did you find out that Rachel was dead?"

"It was first thing in the morning. There was a lot of talking, commotion, in the living room. It was directly beneath my bedroom. It woke me up. When I went downstairs, I saw the cops, my parents crying. That's the moment I knew," I explain, staring at the paper in front of me. But I'm not seeing it; I'm reliving that moment and the detached numbness that settled over me. They didn't have to say a word to me. No one ever officially told me she died. They shuffled me through grief counseling, to church every week to pray for her. But the moment Rachel died, so did my faith. I couldn't believe in a God that took her from us. My parents became hollow shells afterward; they were just decoration. They sat around me; they were always there—but no one was ever home.

"What can you tell me about her that most people didn't know?" he asks, and the lump creeps back into my throat.

"What do you mean?" Rachel had so many secrets that if he's not specific, I won't even know where to start.

"I don't know, general stuff. What did she want to be when she grew up? Where did she want to go to school?"

"You can get this info from *anyone else* on this island." I expected he'd ask me stuff with a little more substance. Is he trying to take it easy on me?

"I can get some of the answers from the other people on this island; you're right about that. But I want to know what she told you, what you saw. The versions of ourselves that our siblings see are much different than the versions the people on the street see."

I guess I can see his point. "She wanted to go to a college in Maine. She loved it here. She changed her mind a lot, though. Senior year, she wavered between computer engineer and programmer," I say. It was weird: senior year I joked that she had become a supernerd. Before that, she'd wanted to be a chef, and before that, a fashion designer.

"Really?"

"Yep, she loved computers. She wanted to be the next Bill Gates." It's too bad she couldn't see how far they've come. Rachel would have lost her shit over an iPhone.

"What was the last thing you two said to one another?"

His question is like a punch to the gut. I grab a pen from my desk and dig my nails into it, just for something to do with my hands. I have to catch my breath. That's not something I ever want to have to remember. But the words are still there, burning in the back of my mind. A tear rolls down my cheek. I don't realize until it turns ice cold.

"Shit, I'm sorry," Noah says as he closes his notebook.

I shake my head. "No, I'm sorry. It's just harder than I thought it would be," I say as I wipe the tears on my sleeve. "I haven't talked about it to anyone since it happened. The last people I really talked to about Rachel were the police." Even with my shrinks during grief counseling, I barely talked, and I definitely didn't give them all the details.

His eyes go wide, and he leans toward my desk. "Anyone?"

I shake my head.

"I'm such an asshole," he breathes. "I figured you've been asked all these questions a thousand times."

"I've been asked a lot of things about her a million times, but I don't answer. That's part of the reason I moved away from here." I lower my voice and prop my elbows on the desk. "Living here, I felt like there was never any chance I'd get out of her shadow. Half of my life was buried in that grave with her. Out in the world, though, I wasn't the sad girl with the dead sister anymore." I want to tell him more, but I snap my mouth shut. If I don't stop myself, all my secrets are going to pour out, and he is the last person I should be saying all this to. I'm not sure if it's him or if maybe I just really need to get all of this out; it's all been bottled up inside me for so long, and returning home hasn't helped.

He nods. "I'm really sorry. I think we should call it here. You can catch me up on other details later." He shoves his notebook into his laptop bag, slings it over his shoulder, and stands up.

"Noah, before you leave," I say before he can disappear through the door, "could you look up what you can on Jacob Warren for me?"

He raises a brow at that. "Are there any details you want to give me for that?"

I shake my head. "Just see what you can find."

He stands up without another question, grabs his things, and leaves my office. I know he's giving up on his questioning so easily to grant me a reprieve from the memories, and though I won't admit it aloud, I appreciate it. I've always seen journalists as soulless, smarmy weasels, but maybe this journalist has a soul after all.

CHAPTER 14

September 2004

I lean back in bed, computer propped on my lap as I scroll, my eyes nearly glazed over. The door creeps open, and I try to peek at who it is. It's too late for my parents to be up, and Rachel should have snuck out an hour ago. Her blonde hair comes into view first, followed by her sweatpants and a baggy T-shirt. Rachel never dresses like this.

"Can we talk for a minute?" she asks as she shuts my door. Her eyes are red, like she's been crying. That's also very unlike her. Concern grips me.

"What's up?" I snap my laptop closed. Something feels wrong here—Rachel never comes to talk to me like this anymore. Is she messing with me?

She walks over slowly and sits at the end of my bed. For a few moments, she twists a loose string from my comforter around her finger before pulling her legs to her chest.

"What's the deal, Ally McBeal?" I ask. It's something she always asked me when I was feeling down.

"I've gotta tell you something, but you have to swear you won't tell Mom." Her voice is deadly serious.

"Okay, fine," I say as I cross my heart.

She chews her lip and tightens her grip around her legs. Her hair falls in her face, but she doesn't bother moving it.

"Just say it. You'll feel better," I urge her. The way she's acting is giving me anxiety. This isn't my big sister.

She straightens up, like she's gathering her strength. "Saying it out loud makes it seem more real, you know?"

I nod. I know exactly how that feels.

"Claire-Bear, I think I'm pregnant." Her voice shakes.

My jaw doesn't just drop to the ground; it falls straight through the whole planet. My heart races. What is my mom going to do to her?

"Jacob and I started dating a few months ago." My mind spins. I can't believe she's actually admitting it. Though I saw the two of them together, she has no idea that I was there. Jacob Warren is a senior and someone pretty much every girl on this island is forbidden to date. The Warrens are off limits, especially for us. I never knew Rachel had even the slightest interest in him. "We were going to keep it a secret until we left for college." She laughs, but there's no humor to it. "We figured once we left, no one could stop us from being together."

"Are you sure, Rach? Are you positive you're pregnant?"

"Pretty sure. I haven't taken a test yet, but I haven't had my period in three months."

"Why haven't you taken a test?" I ask, but as soon as it's out, I already know the answer. If she bought a test, everyone on this island would know.

"I can't get one."

"We need to figure out a way to get you one," I say.

"If I am, Jacob says we can leave together. We're planning to leave in a couple weeks."

"Do you really think that's a good idea? I really think you should tell Dad." Dad will know what to do.

"You have to swear you won't tell anyone."

The next morning, Rachel hovers beside me on Main Street. I'm so nervous that I shove my sweaty hands in my pockets to keep them from shaking. I've never stolen anything, never had any desire to. But here I am, planning to go in the drugstore to steal for her.

"Why can't you do this yourself?" I ask as I swallow hard. I've probably asked fifty times. I'm just stalling at this point.

"I can't steal it myself. If someone sees me, if that gets back to Mom—" She looks down at her shoes. "She'll kill me."

"Like she won't kill me?"

"You're not pregnant," she snaps, like that'll do me much good.

"You might not be," I say, because I desperately hope that she isn't. That would change everything. If she is, I'm going to lose my sister. She'll leave. No more Rachel. She'll leave me here with *them*. Without Rachel to keep her attention, Mom is going to make my life a living hell.

She shakes her head and bites her lip. Tears gather in her eyes. My heart seizes. Rachel never cries, ever. Seeing her upset forces me into action. I can't just stand here with my sister crying on the sidewalk.

"How do I do this again?" I'm putting it off to try and rally every ounce of courage I've got. Hearing Rachel explain it calms me. Maybe with her voice in my head, I'll be able to get through this.

"Let your sleeves hang loose. Pick it up, slide it up your sleeve, and wander the store a bit. Then leave. You can do this, Claire-Bear. No one is going to think that you're stealing," she says, then squeezes my shoulder.

I take a deep breath, trying to steady my pounding heart. But it does no good. If anything, it makes it beat faster, like I'm standing at the edge of a cliff with seconds until I jump off. Rachel gives me a little push toward the door and offers me a thumbs-up. With the way my heart is racing, I don't know how no one else can hear it. The door dings above me as I push inside. Mrs. Miller is tucked behind the counter, where she usually is. She waves when she sees me. "Hey, Claire!"

"Hi, Mrs. Miller," I say as I dart down the first aisle. Most of the time, after saying hello, she'll just leave me be. But I'm nervous this time might be different. What if she comes over to talk to me?

Though Rachel wants me to just take the test and get out, I can't do that. I've got two bucks in my pocket so that I can buy some candy. I walk down the aisle searching for the tests, grab the first one I see, stick it up my sleeve, and dart to the candy aisle.

I plop the candy bars on the counter, careful not to reveal the box hidden away in my hoodie.

"Just the candy?" she asks as she presses the buttons on the register.

"Mm-hmm," I say as I pretend to be interested in the magazines behind the counter. Really I'm just trying to keep my heart from pounding straight through my chest. And I'm afraid if I look her in the eyes, she'll know.

"Dollar and sixty-eight cents," she says, and I hand my money over.

"Thank you," I say as I grab the candy with my left hand and shove it in my pocket.

"Claire," she calls to me as I dart toward the door.

I'm ten feet from getting out, from getting away with this. Rachel stands outside, wide eyed, waving for me to come on.

"Yeah?" I look back over my shoulder.

"Be sure to take that test first thing in the morning."

I swallow hard. "What?" My stomach jumps into my throat. That can't be what she really said. I must have misheard her.

"The test. Be sure you take it first thing in the morning."

My eyes well with tears, and my mouth drops open. So many apologies try to swarm from me at once that they all bottle up in my throat. She shakes her head. "It's fine. Go," she says as she shoos me out.

I round the corner when I don't find Rachel waiting outside. I find her parked a street away and climb into the car. The moment I shut my door, she slides the keys into the ignition.

"What the hell happened?" she snaps at me as she shifts the car into drive.

"She must have seen me take it. She told me to be sure I used the test in the morning."

"Shit," she breathes.

I sink lower in the seat. "Shit? I'm dead, Rachel. Mom is going to kill me."

CHAPTER 15

When I moved from Detroit, I hired movers to haul my crap across the country and unpack it for me. This morning I received a notification that my stuff finally arrived in Maine. I left the key under the mat, texted them its location, and headed into the office. But since it's been a few hours since they started, and I'm heading in the direction of my rental anyway, I decide to pop in to check on the progress. The moving truck is still parked along the side of the house, but the movers must all be inside. It looks like they've cleared out half the truck. I'm happy to see that my car arrived safely and is parked in front of the house. I grab my keys from the workers and climb into my Mustang, relishing the feel and the smell of it. I've had my rental for too long; I've missed this car. Since I'm satisfied that things are going well with the movers, I move on to the interviews I need to chase down today.

I've meant to talk to Father Samuel at the church, hoping he could give me some insight into the girls, but so far things have kept popping up, sidetracking me. Before something else can get in the way, I have to pounce on the opportunity. If Madeline and Emma were both involved in the church, they must have seen him often.

I head to the large Catholic church that I swear the rest of the town was built around. It's the most ornate building downtown. With its old stone and stained glass windows, it looks like something that dropped straight out of another century. The air inside is thick with sandalwood and something floral, maybe roses. Nothing has changed since the last time I was here when I was a kid. Wood pews stained a dark chocolate brown stand on either side of the room, creating a clear path down the middle to the altar. Father Samuel stands near the altar, a surprised smile on his face as he looks back to see me.

Father Samuel hasn't really aged in the last fifteen years. He's a bit over six feet tall, lanky, with a potbelly that's out of place on his frame. On either side of his head, his dark hair is dusted with gray, the only real hint that he's gotten older.

"Claire?" he asks, his voice high, boisterous.

"Father Samuel, it's good to see you," I say as he meets me in the middle of the room and ushers me toward the front pew.

"I didn't know you were back. It's so good to see you." He clearly doesn't get out enough to hear gossip if he didn't know I was back. "What are you doing here?" he asks.

"I took a position at the police department. I'm working as the detective now."

He glances down at the rosary gripped in his right hand. "Investigating the murders?" he asks, and his eyes darken.

I nod. "Unfortunately."

He leans closer and grips my shoulder, making small circles with his thumb for a moment. "They were both so much like Rachel. It breaks my heart when children are taken from us. Especially girls like them," he says as he leans his arm along the back of the pew. "The only comfort is knowing they're with God now."

I take a deep breath as the questions swim in the back of my mind. Technically, I know he's not supposed to answer the question I want to ask him, but I have to try.

"I was hoping I could ask you a few questions about Rachel, Emma, and Madeline. They spent a lot of time at the church. You might have information about them that no one else does."

"I'll help however I can," he says, and his grip tightens on the rosary.

"I've heard that my mother heads up the choir group all the girls are in. Did you ever hear of issues between my mother and the girls?"

"Your mother can have a bit of a temper. The girls did make a few comments. I spoke with your mother, and she has been working on it," he assures me. He doesn't seem the least bit concerned about it.

"Do you know why she was angry with them?"

He shakes his head. "No. That I don't know. I've heard from other girls that sometimes they could be disruptive during practice—talking, laughing, that sort of thing. But that's all I've heard of."

My mother has always been so careful about the face she shows others. If she was willing to yell at teenage girls in public, they had to have been much more than disruptive.

"Could you give me a list of girls in the group?"

"Of course. I'll email them to you when we're done here."

With all the questions about my mother out of the way, I move on. "Father, did Emma or Madeline confide in you that there was anything going on? Anyone that was giving them trouble?"

He shakes his head. "Heavens, no. If the girls had said anything about someone giving them trouble or threatening them, I would have already gone to the school or the police."

"Is there anything that either of them might have said that you think I should know?"

He looks away, his eyes far off. "There was a boy I overheard them talking about who was aggressively pursuing them."

"Did you catch the name of this person?"

"Unfortunately, no. They didn't mention it." His voice falls as he says it.

"Is there anything they said or did recently that alarmed you?" I ask, because there has to be something, some hint here.

He looks toward the altar, lost in thought. "About two or three months ago, Madeline stopped coming so often. She seemed distant, withdrawn, even. It wasn't like her. She asked some questions about whether God's forgiveness covered *everything*. But when I pressed her about what she meant, she wouldn't say."

Was she asking about the pregnancy or something else?

"And she never gave you any indication as to why she stopped coming more often?"

"She told me that she was volunteering more at the hospital, that she couldn't find time for both. I don't want to say that I didn't believe her," he says as he crosses his legs.

"But you didn't believe her."

He nods.

"Did you have any idea that Emma or Madeline was sneaking out of the house at night?"

He shakes his head. "If I'd had any idea that they were up to something like that, I would have warned their fathers. It's not safe for them to be downtown at night with all those fishermen."

"What about Ryder Warren?"

He raises a brow at that. "What about him?"

"I heard he got into some trouble a few months back, that he might have helped you in the church after that."

"He did." His voice is low as he looks toward the stained glass windows. "Ryder's a good kid. He wanted to help around here, helped me with some chores around the church. But he made sure that he was here at off hours. It seemed to me that he didn't want anyone to know he was here."

"So he never interacted with Madeline and Emma, then?"

For a moment he looks at me but doesn't respond. "I'm sure there were a few times they talked. But the girls never mentioned any problems with him." His face grows more serious. "I don't think he would have done anything to them. He's gotten into trouble—harmless kid stuff—but he'd never hurt anyone." Insistence is thick on his words.

It doesn't mean much that the girls might have talked to Ryder a few times. They all went to school together. It's not like they were strangers. I was hoping he'd have more for me. "Well, thank you for your time. If you think of anything else, please give me a call at the station."

"Claire, should I warn the other girls who are part of the congregation that whoever did this is a danger to them too?" he asks, his brows drawn, his features tight.

"Father, between the two of us, there's a pattern. And that pattern very distinctly touches girls who go to this church. I'd advise that if there's anything you can say to keep these girls from sneaking out at night, you say it." My voice has more of an edge than I mean for it to, but I hope it gets across how serious this is. I can't say for certain yet that the church really has anything to do with these murders. Saying something to him might keep these girls safe. Maybe they'll listen to him.

He opens his mouth, but words fail him. He just nods instead.

I glance at my watch and realize I've got to get back to the station soon to prep for my next interview. Ryder will be by in an hour for his interview. Father Samuel and I say our goodbyes, and I head back to my car. The afternoon sun is shrouded by a thin veil of gray clouds. Cold, sharp air bites at my cheeks. As my hand brushes the handle of my car, a familiar scent catches me off guard.

Gasoline.

I circle my car, stooping to look beneath it. Near the rear tire, there's a growing pool of liquid. When did my car start leaking gas? Was it damaged when they shipped it here? I grab my phone and call Carl, the local mechanic, and in twenty minutes he's got my car towed to his shop. As he looks it over, I hang back, giving him space to work.

"Where'd you drive this morning?" he asks as he glances over his shoulder at me.

"From my place to the church. That's it. I just got it back from the movers. Why?"

He waves me over and points up at my car. It's hovering a few feet above us on the lift. "You see that?" he asks as he takes a step forward, urging me to follow.

I squint as I try to make out what exactly he's pointing out to me. As I scan the undercarriage of the car, finally I see what's out of place: a blue handle sticking out of a rounded metal tank.

"What is that?"

"Someone stuck a screwdriver in your gas tank."

I ask him to clarify, because I must have heard him wrong. Once he's explained it to me three times, I ask, "Is it possible I drove over something and it bounced up there?"

He shakes his head. "I doubt it. I think someone stuck that in your tank."

"How long would it take after piercing it for all the gas to drain out?"

"It'd be immediate."

It must have happened while I was in the church. "How long will it take you to fix?" I ask, thankful that I haven't had a chance to return my rental car yet.

"A few hours. Worst case, tomorrow."

I grab a plastic bag from behind the counter, wrap it carefully around the screwdriver so I won't mess up any fingerprints, and yank it out.

CHAPTER 16

As soon as I get to the station, I head to Sergeant Michaels's office. I pop my head in his office and catch him midswig from his coffee cup, his eyes intently focused on his computer.

"Afternoon," I say when he finally looks up at me.

"Afternoon." He eyes the bag in my hand.

"Someone stuck a screwdriver in my gas tank. I'm going to send it off for prints."

"What the hell is going on in this town?" he growls as he leans back in his chair. Red is creeping up from his collar. "Between you and me—and technically Jason—I've launched an unofficial investigation into the fire. Give him that screwdriver. These things might be related."

I nod. "Did he find something in the basement?"

"There was a partial print on the window. But we haven't been able to match it to anything in the database." He furrows his brow and looks down at his desk. "The whole basement was filled with fireproof filing cabinets, yet all the files inside were burned. Like someone set fires inside each one."

"Are you saying they went back and set the fires? Because they couldn't have done that while I was there."

He nods. "The fire marshal found evidence someone had come back there."

Someone wanted those files destroyed real bad if they returned to the scene. Maybe the fire wasn't just to kill me after all.

"Jason also questioned Danny at the Gas-N-Go. No one that he saw had filled up gas containers the day of the fire. Nothing was seen on surveillance either."

Who would have the motive to burn all the files down there? Someone who didn't want us to find out about something.

"Thank you for opening the investigation."

He nods. "Of course. I find it deeply disturbing that someone would put one of the officers on this island at risk like that. And I will find out who is responsible," he says.

We chat for another few minutes, catching up on my progress, and then I hand over the screwdriver to Jason. When I get into my office, I've got an email from Father Samuel with names of all the girls from the choir group. I forward the email to Allen and ask him to handle interviews. It'll probably take a few days to get them all to come in, so I want to get started as soon as possible.

I've watched the clock tick down to four p.m. And then slowly past. I've called Ryder's mom twice, and so far there's no answer—he's still a no-show. I can't just sit around here and wait. I *need* to talk to Ryder. I grab my bag and keys and tell Sergeant Michaels where I'm headed. Just as I reach my car, someone calls my name from across the street. Noah jogs over. Seeing him lifts some of the weight from my shoulders, and I stand straighter. My heart starts to race, but I try to play it cool.

"Hey," he says.

"How's it going?"

"Pretty good; just got a new story to write on some of the political turmoil," he says with a grin. Clearly it's the kind of story he enjoys writing.

"Sounds thrilling," I say with a laugh.

"How's the case coming?"

"You know I can—" I start.

"Can't comment on an ongoing investigation, I know. I'm more checking on how you're holding up. It's so similar to Rachel. I'm not asking for details. I'm asking about *you*."

"I'm fine," I say, clipped, almost defensive. "Thank you."

He nods and shoves his hands in his pockets. "A few of the teenagers I've talked to said the Warren kid has info about Madeline," he says in a tone that's almost hushed.

I raise an eyebrow at that. There's no way I'm telling him that's where I'm headed, but he's piqued my curiosity all the same. "Oh?"

He shrugs. "No one would give me details. That's all I've got for you."

"So you haven't talked to him?"

"Oh, I've tried. He won't talk to me."

"Look, I've got to get going. Thanks for the tip," I say before walking to my car to drive to the Warrens'.

The Warrens have one of the newer houses on the island. The kind of sleek, contemporary house that belongs in the Hollywood Hills, not here. While most of the other houses in Vinalhaven are three-story classic Victorians, this one is three stories of sharp lines, large panel windows, and concrete. It looks like something a modern-day Le Corbusier would have designed.

I step onto the porch, the boards whining and groaning beneath my feet. A cool breeze sweeps past me, blowing my ponytail against the back of my neck. The front door creaks in the wind, catching my eye. The door swings in, opening about six inches.

"Hello?" I call into the quiet house. The silence inside is thick, palpable, and though I listen for a response, the rush of blood in my ears is deafening.

I push the door in, my hand hovering over my gun. I try to keep my mind busy, flooding my brain, cataloging everything I see. After all, if my brain is busy with that, there won't be any room for fear to sneak in. Through the first floor, I creep slowly. It's eerily empty, decorated in the sleek, modern style you'd expect for a house like this. Minimal, austere. As I weave my way through the house, I pass a sleek kitchen. The whole thing is gray, from the flat, unadorned cabinets to the glittering granite. I touch my knuckle to the coffeepot and find the carafe still warm. Someone was here recently, at least.

Glancing up the cement stairs, I try to discern if there's anyone in the house. Something clinks upstairs, like someone dropped a coin on tile. I climb the stairs, straining to hear any other indications of where they are over the pounding of my heart. Droplets glistening on the white marble landing catch my eye. The small red beads form a trail between doorways.

Blood.

It's not enough blood to be a mortal wound—it's more the kind of trail you'd leave after nicking yourself while cutting an onion—but my heart hammers as I throw open the door in front of me. The room is dim, the curtains closed. Stretching my fingers out against the rough wall, I feel for the light switch. Turning on the light doesn't help much. It illuminates the dirty laundry piled next to the bed. But there's no blood in this room. The trail leads me to another door, but when I try the handle, it's locked.

"Leave me alone," someone says from inside. The voice is low but not deep enough to be a man. *Ryder.*

"Ryder, open the door," I say, forcing my voice to be steady, calm, as my training takes over. It doesn't stop the nag of panic at the back of my mind. This situation grates on my nerves—the blood, the locked door.

Something rustles on the other side, and the shadows of his feet shift beneath the door. "Who's there?"

"I'm Detective Claire Calderwood. We were supposed to talk today. Are you okay in there?"

It isn't until I hear the water running inside the locked room that I realize Ryder is in the bathroom. His feet scuff against the floor. I listen, trying to figure out what he's doing.

"Just go away. Leave me alone," he growls.

I try the handle again, jiggling it as I twist, but the knob won't budge. Behind the door, he coughs, and something rustles again. My heart beats frantically as I try to figure out how to get the door open. Ryder starts to talk again, but something slaps hard against the tile floor. I drop to my knees automatically to peek beneath the door. Through the three-inch gap at the bottom, I see Ryder's body collapsed on the plush pink bath mat, a growing pool of blood next to him.

I push off the wooden floor and kick the door over and over, landing my heel close to the doorknob. Finally, with a crack of splintering wood, the door flies open and rattles on its hinges. Ryder is limp on the floor, his face pale. His long black hair covers most of his face. Deep gashes cut across his pale wrists, oozing red on the floor. The sink is flooded with red water spilling over the brim and trickling onto the floor. He must have submerged his wounds so that he'd bleed out faster.

He needs to get to a hospital soon, but the closest one is across the bay. There's no way I can wait for a boat to get him. We'll have to take him to urgent care to stabilize him. I grab my phone and call Jason. I need his help to get Ryder to urgent care, and I may need him to perform CPR while I'm driving if things get much worse. I put the phone on speaker and search the drawers for something to wrap up his wrists. The best thing I can find is Ace bandages and toilet paper.

"Jason, I need you at the Warrens', now." My words are rushed, but I catch him up on the situation. Luckily Jason's out on patrol today. I don't have to worry about him alerting Allen. He can't know until Ryder is stable. Otherwise, he'll just get in the way.

After five of the longest minutes of my life, Ryder's arms are bandaged, and Jason calls my name from downstairs. "Claire?"

"Up here!"

Jason's feet pound against the stairs, and he freezes behind me.

"We've got to get him to urgent care. You can do CPR, right?"

"Uh, yeah," he says with zero conviction to his words.

"Help me carry him downstairs."

Jason grabs Ryder beneath the armpits, and I take his feet. Ryder is tall and lanky but heavier than he looks. After we slide him into the back of Jason's patrol car, we drive to urgent care in two minutes. I wish there were some way to get him out of here without anyone in town seeing, but that's not an option.

My heart pounds as we carry him through the doors. Ryder is so pale I'm not sure if we're too late. There's no telling how much blood he lost when he plunged his arms into the hot water.

"How's he doing?" I ask as Jason helps me carry him out of the back seat.

"He's still got a pulse. It's weak, though."

The nurse looks at me wide eyed from behind the desk as we come through the doors. "What the hell happened?"

"Suicide attempt," I say.

"We can bandage him, but he's going to have to be transported to the hospital. There's not much we can do for him here."

I knew she'd say that. But we've got to get the bleeding under control. Otherwise there won't be any chance that we can get him to the hospital. The makeshift bandages I gave him are barely doing any good. While Ryder is back with the doctors, I call Sergeant Michaels to give him a rundown of what happened. And though I offer to go to the hospital, he informs me that he's going to take Allen ahead and wait there. I want to head to the hospital in hopes I can question Ryder once he's stable, but Sergeant Michaels orders me to stay behind on the island. Anger flickers through me. Ryder may have answers I can't get anywhere else. But I know better than to argue with a sergeant.

Jason heads back to the station, and as much as I want to jump right back into the case, I need to go home and clean off the blood. I walk down Main Street, my hands still trembling with adrenaline. Thankfully the movers are gone when I get back to my house. After I've showered, changed, and grabbed some water, my nerves are still on edge. And though I try to push today's events from my mind, I know I need to talk to someone to unburden my mind. But my options are limited. Noah's the first person who pops into my mind. I need to see what he's looking into anyway. I'm sure he wouldn't mind going out for a drink.

I head downstairs and glance at Noah's contact info on my phone. There's a war raging in my mind as my finger hovers over the call button. Maybe I shouldn't bother him with this. Maybe I should just keep these issues to myself. My finger ventures closer. Finally, on the third attempt, I give in.

"Hey, Claire," he answers.

"Hey. I know this will probably be weird, but would you want to grab a drink?"

He clears his throat and says something muffled that I can't quite make out. Maybe I shouldn't have called him. "When and where?" he asks.

"Now, at the Sand Bar."

"Oh," he says, and his voice falls.

"Too short notice?"

"Never. I'll be there in ten. With bells on."

I head to the bar and wait outside for Noah. The doors are propped open with rusty anchors, letting the cigarette smoke and the dull roar of gossip spill into the street. In a couple of minutes Noah walks up the sidewalk toward me, picking up speed when our eyes meet.

"Never thought you'd ask me to get a drink," he says with a sheepish grin. Noah's got on a tight faded AC/DC T-shirt with a leather coat open over it. He's wearing distressed jeans that hang on him in just the right way.

"Don't make me regret it," I warn in a way that makes it clear I *might* not be serious. Somehow, just seeing him unwinds the anxiety that's been wound around my chest all day.

The large oak bar is already full, but that's no surprise. It's full every night. This place is always packed as I drive home from the station. Several women are teetering on their barstools precariously. It looks like they're a heartbeat from smacking their heads on the grimy floor. I lead us toward a table in the corner, as far from the others as we can manage. I'm not worried about any of them spreading rumors about seeing me here. I don't want to be bothered with stories about my childhood—or worse, Rachel.

Noah and I take a seat in the dim corner, and a few seconds later, a waitress who doesn't look old enough to drink drops by our table. We both order beer, and I watch the other patrons gather like a school of fish in a group by the bar.

"So what did you want to talk about?" Noah asks as he slides out of his jacket.

I glance toward our waitress, who's still lingering behind the bar. I give him a rundown of what happened without giving him any details about *who* hurt themselves.

"Holy shit," he says as he leans back. "Are you okay?"

I nod. "Yeah, I'll be fine. Just processing all of it."

"You sure you're all right?" he asks. The question is more serious than what I'd expect out of him.

I nod and press my lips together. "Yeah. I'm glad it wasn't worse. But I'd really rather talk about *anything* else." I need to get my mind off the case. "What have you found? Catch me up."

"Well, I looked into Jacob Warren like you asked. Since I wasn't sure what you wanted on him, I'll give you a rundown of what I found. Jacob lived in Vinalhaven and went to school with Rachel. Like the other Warrens, it seems most people did not care for Jacob. After 2005, I couldn't find anything on Jacob, but then I discovered that he killed himself."

I shake my head. My mom told me he'd moved off the island. There's no way she doesn't know that he killed himself if that's what happened. Why would she hide that from me?

"They were dating, weren't they?" he asks, his brow furrowed. His eyes tell me he already knows the answers.

"Is this on or off the record?" When I first met Noah, making a distinction was easy—but now, with the lines so blurred, I don't know what to think. My worst fear is letting my guard down and finding all of this in print. I can't be too careful. There are a million other things I'd let him write before *this* ended up all over the internet. This was Rachel's big secret, the one she didn't want anyone to know. Hell, she didn't even want me to know. She only told me because she thought she was pregnant.

"Unless you tell me otherwise, it's all off the record. What would it matter if it weren't, though?"

I shake my head. It makes me feel like I'm speaking ill of the dead. "It was a secret Rachel and I had," I say as I try to get comfortable on the plastic booth cover. "I really don't want to get into it, though."

Though he doesn't look pleased, he says, "I also spoke to some of Rachel's old teachers, but they didn't have anything for me other than a few memories that Rachel seemed distant and was skipping some classes leading up to her death."

Our waitress drops off our beers and lingers at the table a bit longer than I'd like. "You guys know anything yet? Do you know who killed Madeline and Emma?" she asks in a hushed voice.

"We're working on it, but I can't comment any further on an ongoing investigation," I answer. She narrows her eyes, deflates, and stalks away.

"I can't believe Rachel was skipping her classes," I say, but what I mean is that I can't believe Rachel was skipping her classes and didn't tell me about it. Even after all this time, it feels like a betrayal. I wish I knew why she stopped trusting me, why she started building a wall around herself out of secrets.

"That's all I've been able to find so far. I'll keep digging, though," he says, pulling me from my teenage misery.

Since Noah doesn't have anything else about Rachel, I say, "So tell me more about you." I hope that if he talks about himself, maybe it'll distract me from all this. There's already an unfair balance here: Noah knows way too much about me, and I know next to nothing about him.

"I have no idea where to start," he says with a nervous laugh.

"Tell me the weirdest thing about your childhood."

"I made replicas of all the furniture in my bedroom out of cardboard," he says without skipping a beat.

A laugh slips from me. "You what?" I ask, because I couldn't have heard him right.

He sighs and leans into the table. "My mom had an obsession with QVC. She could never sleep, which I blame on a penchant for diet pills, so she'd stay up late ordering shit from infomercials. We got so many boxes every month that I told my mom there were enough to build a whole other house out of them." He pauses to take a sip of his beer.

"So let me guess: you started with your room."

He laughs. "Nah. I started in the backyard and built the living room first. Just as I finished my room, as luck would have it, a rainstorm came through, destroying all my cardboard. I was so upset. I just wanted to prove to her that I could do it."

A laugh bubbles out of me and keeps coming until I can't breathe. "That's the most adorable and saddest thing I've ever heard. How old were you?"

"Eight or nine, I guess." He shakes his head and takes a swig from his bottle. "Your turn," he says with a grin.

"Ugh, no way am I telling you an embarrassing story." I bite my lip and shake my head. I wish I had a less embarrassing story, but only one comes to mind.

"Oh, come on," he urges me after I've been silent for too long.

"When I was in ninth grade, I had this *huge* crush on a senior. One of the few guys who didn't grow up here. I loved the idea that he was a mainlander. It seemed so boring to me that people would date someone who already knew everything about them, their whole history. Part of the fun is supposed to be exploring one another, getting to know one another."

He nods. "I can see that." He takes a swig of his beer, and I spend way too long staring at his lips.

"Dating when you live in a small town seems like you're just hooking up with someone from your extended family, you know? Your families share a history. Everyone on the island is entangled with everyone else." I laugh. "Incestuous small towns. Anyway," I say as I sip my beer, "I was in love with him pretty much immediately. Not like normal teenage love. I was obsessed. I memorized every fact about him like I was going to be tested on it."

"Everyone has a crush like that," he says, and I'm sure it's to make me feel better.

"It wouldn't have been so bad if Rachel hadn't found out. Once she figured it out, she decided to do me a *favor* and tell him during lunch. In front of the whole school." My cheeks burn.

"That's awful. Why would she do that?"

I shrug. That's a question I asked myself a lot. *Why would Rachel do that?* I'm not sure she even knew most of the time. Dad said it was because Rachel had a weird way of protecting me. I think it's because Rachel needed to control me. She may have hated Mom and wanted to be nothing like her, but when it came to controlling me, they were one and the same. "Who knows. That wasn't the worst of it, though. I've always had a nervous stomach. All those eyes on me—I tried to run out of the cafeteria before I was sick, but I ended up puking in front of everyone. And that's how I ended up with the nickname Chunks Calderwood." I take a big swig of my beer, hoping it'll calm the burning in my cheeks, but it does nothing.

"That's awful," he says again.

"I can't believe I told you that." God, I should have just made up a story.

Noah reaches across the table and takes my hand. "It's fine, really." He looks down, and his cheeks redden. "My brothers used to call me Nonie Pony Macaroni."

I laugh so hard I start to cough. "Why on earth did they call you that?"

"Two of my brothers were too young to pronounce Noah properly when I was born, so they called me Nonie. Then once I got a little older, I was obsessed with this pony toy my mom and dad got me. I have no idea where macaroni came from, though; I think my brothers just added it because it rhymed."

I shake my head as I try not to laugh. "That's rough."

He shrugs. "It was when they'd call me that at school; then everyone would start chanting it. But it doesn't matter now."

My own embarrassment fades.

"What happened to you after Rachel died?" he asks and takes a sip of beer. I narrow my eyes. He holds his hand up in mock surrender. "Not for the article—just for me."

"I can't believe you have the nerve to ask anyone about their past when you'll barely talk about yours. All you've given me is cute anecdotes. Give me some meat."

"You tell me something about your past, and I'll tell you something about mine," he says with a smirk.

I look down at the table and play with one of the coasters. That's not a game I'd normally indulge. But I want to know more about him. "I lost it after Rachel died. Kinda went off the deep end and got into some trouble." That's as specific as I feel like being. "Your turn."

"I dropped out of high school in my sophomore year. A lot of shit happened while I was in middle school. When I started high school, it really didn't get any better. I couldn't handle it and school. Something had to give, and that something was school. When my parents found out I'd dropped out, they kicked me out of the house, and I ended up staying with my uncle."

"Shit." The word escapes me with a trapped breath.

"I didn't actually talk to my parents again until I was in my midtwenties. After my brother, Cameron, urged them to talk to me again." He takes a long swig of his beer.

"How'd you end up going to college?"

"Got my GED when I was nineteen. Then did night classes while I worked as a lifeguard."

"And your parents, how'd they feel about that?"

"Every job I've ever had is *beneath me*. That's the nice way of putting it. I believe their exact quote is *I'm wasting my fucking time*."

I roll my eyes at that. It's exactly what my mom thinks of my job. My dad would be thrilled with me doing anything as long as I was happy, but my mom—I swear, anything short of bringing in a seven-figure salary isn't what she wants for her daughter. Her expectations sting more than they should, because she didn't have any until Rachel died. It's as if all of her expectations for both of us ended up falling on me, and now no matter what I do, it'll never be good enough—because I can't become her.

"So why'd you get arrested?" he asks with a quirked eyebrow.

"Jesus Christ, you really did some digging. Hardly anyone knows about that." I shake my head. It never went on my record, and after my mother finished yelling, I never talked to anyone about it again. That was one of the worst times in my life.

"I'm good at digging," he says with a grin.

I don't want to share. But he did, and I want to know more about him. To get that, I've got to give a little. "After Rachel died, as I said before, I fell apart. I made some *really* bad choices. I did some awful things and hurt people in the process. It was two or three weeks after Rachel died, and I needed someone to talk to *so bad*. And my parents wouldn't say a word about it. I swear it's like they enjoy pretending she never existed. Every day, the silence killed me a little more. I couldn't stand it anymore. I had to get out. I wanted to go somewhere where no one had even heard of my family. I stole a boat."

Noah's eyes go wide. "*You* stole a boat?"

"It's not like I was born a cop. I got into trouble."

He laughs at that, like he can't imagine any of it.

"Anyway, I stole Mr. Barton's boat, went across the bay, and ended up in Rockland. I had a backpack full of stupid stuff that would have done me no good in the real world. And I had no plan to speak of. I spent a very long night in the park. In the morning the police found me, arrested me, and dragged me back to the island. Mr. Barton wouldn't press charges after everything I'd already been through and insisted that he'd just forgotten that I borrowed his boat." I pause to sip my beer. "It was all just one big misunderstanding, he said."

"Holy shit, you got lucky," he says, then winces when he realizes what he said. "Sorry, you know what I mean."

"Yeah, guess I discovered the perks of having a dead sister that day."

After I've spent a couple of hours drinking and talking with Noah, it's like all the weight has lifted from my shoulders. He listens so intently when I talk, as opposed to just waiting for his turn to speak. It's a nice change of pace. God knows he's the first guy to see me as more than a cop in a long time. His touch and the beer work together, making my skin hot and tingly. The alcohol takes down some of the walls I've built. I can't help myself. I imagine those warm, strong hands venturing to other parts of my body. It takes too long for me to dislodge the thoughts. It's like after weeks around Noah, I'm seeing him for the first time. That's when I realize I need to get out of here. I need to get away from Noah before I'm in over my head.

I glance at the time on my phone. "It's getting late. I'm going to head back to the station for a little bit."

He raises an eyebrow at that but nods. "I'll walk you."

We weave through a crowd of fishermen that's just filtered in the door and start down Main Street toward the station. The full moon illuminates the streets, and the sidewalks are powdery white, as if they've been dusted in sugar. I bundle my coat a little tighter around my chest as the cold slips in, and Noah wraps his arm around me as we walk, pulling me closer to him. His warmth bleeds into me. His proximity and the beer mix inside me, heating my core and blurring my thoughts. I'm so lost in my own mind that it takes me a moment to realize we've made it to the station.

"Thanks for walking me," I say as I step toward the door, but Noah grabs my hand before I can get inside.

I turn around, facing him. There's an intensity in his eyes, a desire that I swear mirrors my own. He reaches for me and brushes his hand along my cheek. I close my eyes automatically, relishing his touch. All I want is for him to close the gap between us, for him to kiss me. I don't care who sees. There's only a breath of space between us. My heart pounds as his chest brushes against mine.

"I'll see you later, Claire," he says, and when I open my eyes again, he's gone.

I stand for a long moment, frozen, before finally heading into the station. Once I sit down at my desk, I'm finally able to shake the thoughts of Noah and get my mind back on the case. The facts of the girls' murders keep going around and around in my mind. In Detroit, eventually the evidence led us in a direction, but right now it seems everything I've got could apply to most of the people on this island. I grab my phone and scroll through my contacts. I want to bounce my ideas off the most qualified person I know, and someone in particular comes to mind.

I hold the phone against my ear with my shoulder and flip open my notes.

"Hey, stranger," Roxie says as soon as the call connects.

With the case taking up every single second I've had to spare, I haven't had time to miss her, but hearing her voice makes my chest ache. I'd never been really close to anyone at the station until Roxie joined. We clicked immediately and worked most of the murder cases side by side. She'd been a profiler for the FBI but wanted to move back to Michigan to be closer to family.

"Hey, Rox."

"How's Maine treating you?"

I cut right to the chase, because that's how Roxie and I have always been with each other. "I think I've got a serial killer on my hands. And I was hoping to bounce some ideas off you."

While Roxie passed along some of her profiling knowledge to me, I've never exactly had to put it to the test. I never worked a serial case in Detroit.

"Really?" she asks, a bit more excited about it than I'm feeling.

I give her the details of all three of the murders and go over any of the elements I think might be important: where the bodies have been found, the method of killing, and how alike all the victims have been. Then I add in what the strongest fact is for me: that they all had tattoos cut from their bodies. Though I've never gone into great detail about what happened to Rachel with anyone else, Roxie knows a bit about the history—but thank God she doesn't grill me for the rest of the details now.

"Based on the proximity to the water, my guess is they're killed on a boat, then dropped in the park," I add. I don't know that for a fact; so far that just lines up with Emma's murder. But seeing how Madeline was also killed somewhere else and dropped in the park, my guess is the killer takes them onto the water for the privacy.

"They all had flesh removed?" she asks after a long pause.

"Yes, a religious tattoo was cut from each of the girls."

"Pre- or postmortem?"

"Post."

"Any signs of sexual trauma?" she asks. I knew that'd be her next question.

"None on any of the victims."

"It seems like your killer either is single or has a wife who works nights, since he's able to capture these girls and kill them in the middle of the night," she says as she clears her throat. "The cutting off of religious symbols makes me think the killer suffered a trauma from a member of the clergy."

As far as I know, the church scandals have never touched Vinalhaven. So could it have been a trauma that happened off the island?

"The long cooling-off period between Rachel and Emma makes me wonder if the killer was off the island for an extended period of time, or if the new killing was an anniversary of sorts," I say.

"Or there was no one who really fit the profile the killer needed, or maybe your killer was locked up for a while."

"The real thing I want to be sure about is covering the faces of the victims. Is it because he can't stand for the victims to see him, or is it because he's imagining someone else as he's killing them?" I ask.

She pauses for a moment. "It could be either, really. Since all these victims are likely people that he knew very well, he may not be able to stand looking them in the eye when it's time to kill them."

"I'm worried I'm not going to be able to find him before he kills again."

"With fifteen years between the first and second kill but such a quick turnaround for the third victim, I have to wonder if there were other victims elsewhere. Maybe in other towns? Other places. The MO would be similar."

"There have been a few other bodies found in the water. The women were strangled, but none had flesh cut from the bodies as far as I know."

"Does your gut tell you that they're unrelated or related?" she asks.

I lean back in my chair and tap my pen against the desk. "I don't think they're related." Though I've gone over it in my mind many times, I just can't see how they're connected—why don't the victims in the water have flesh removed? Why would the killer drop some on the island and others in the water? If I can't find a solid answer to these questions, I have to assume there are two killers.

"I've got a friend who still works at the FBI. She's got access to a tool that allows us to cross-reference MOs to see if the killers were actually active anywhere else in the US. If you want, I can see if they've got any hits on this."

"Thank you. I appreciate any help I can get."

"It doesn't sound like you need much help. You're on the right track."

Roxie and I catch up on what I've missed in Detroit. And once she's got to go, I realize how much I miss working with her.

CHAPTER 17

After my drink with Noah and call with Roxie, I continue working on the case, going through the interviews Allen has done with the girls in the choir. Finally, I've looked at my screen for so long my eyes have gone from blurry to lost cause. They burn, and no matter how many times I rub them, it does me no good. It's time to pack it in. The sun set hours ago, and the clock is ticking dangerously close to ten p.m.

I grab my bag, tuck away the files I know I'll want to look at again tonight, and shut down my computer. As I flip off the light and head out to the main room, I realize I'm not alone. Allen turns around slowly, his long dark hair falling in his face. Though I've been working here nearly a week, he hasn't said a single word to me.

This close to him, alone, a bad feeling imprints on me so deeply I'm sure its fingerprints are on my soul. He drags the back of his hand slowly across his lips. Something lingers behind his eyes, and I swear they sharpen. When Allen stands, he's got a foot on me; it doesn't help that he's also at least a hundred pounds heavier. Though I've got a gun at my hip, it does nothing to calm my nerves. After all, he's got his own.

I swallow hard and walk toward the door, pretending that he doesn't exist. When I'm ten feet from being free, my heart pounding, Allen steps in front of me, blocking my only path out.

"You shouldn't be here." The words practically come out as a hiss.

"Well, I'm heading home now," I say, swallowing back the snide comment I want to hurl at him. I always feel like I've got to be careful as a woman in this world. Men can get away with anything in criminal justice. Women, though? We have to fight tooth and nail to get where we are. When we lose ground, it's not just an inch—it's a mile.

"No, you shouldn't be on this island. You should have never come back here." He spits the words, looking down at me like I'm shit stuck to his shoe.

"And why is that, exactly?"

"You know why. Ryder tried to kill himself because of you," he growls. But it isn't anger lingering behind his eyes; I swear it's pain. If he's so worried about Ryder, why is he here and not at the hospital? Did he come back just to confront me?

"Because of me? I hadn't questioned him. He wasn't a suspect."

"He knew you were asking about him. It was only a matter of time until you tried to pin this on him, because that's what everyone else on this island does." He clenches his fists at his sides.

Frustration piles inside me, brick by brick. "If I hadn't shown up, Ryder would be dead. I'm not out for him. I'm not out for your family—as much as you seem to want me to be."

Allen has always been a loner, always clung to his family and protected them viciously, even back in school. That's the one thing about him that I admire. He's never liked me, but then again, I don't know if he's ever liked anyone on the island. He's never been downright hostile, though.

I consider cutting him some slack until he adds, "Just go back to wherever you came from. We're better off without you."

"I don't know what your problem is." I launch the words at him, hoping they'll put him in his place, but he doesn't bat an eye.

"Your whole family is my problem. Boo-hoo, your poor sister. That's all anyone talks about. What about what her death did to my family? To me?"

I cross my arms and sigh. Rachel's interest in Jacob was something I had hoped would stay secret, something I would have taken to my grave if I could have. I'm not sure how he found out or who else knows. Secrets don't stay buried here.

"To you? What the hell are you talking about?"

He snorts a laugh, and his eyes narrow. "Did someone erase your memories when you left the island? Don't act like you don't remember spray-painting my car and spreading rumors about me."

My mind spins. I never spread rumors about him, and I sure as hell didn't spray-paint his car. "What are you talking about?"

He pinches the bridge of his nose. "You seriously don't remember?"

"Allen, I had nothing to do with any of that. I hadn't even heard about it."

"Is everything all right?" Noah asks as he pops his head around the doorframe. His brows are furrowed, and he's holding two foam cups I suspect are filled with coffee.

He steps around Allen and stands beside me, so close his arm brushes mine. All the tension rushes out of me at once. If he hadn't shown up, I'm not sure how this would have ended.

"Everything is fine. I was just leaving." I take the chance to skirt past Allen and make my way to the door. As I pass Allen, he grinds his teeth together so loudly it makes my teeth ache.

We exit the station together and turn right toward the parking lot. Night shrouds the island. The moon huddles behind a thick blanket of clouds. Streetlights cast long shadows across the sidewalk. The night is so cold it burrows beneath my clothes. It's not until I'm in the parking lot with Noah at my side that I'm finally able to take a deep breath. In a few seconds, the uneven beat of my heart steadies, and I look up at the inky sky above us.

"Thank you," I say to Noah as I walk to my car. He follows closely and hands me one of the cups he's holding. The warmth bleeds into me, and for the first time, I realize I'm shivering; I'm unsure if it's from the cold or the adrenaline still buzzing in my blood.

"No thanks necessary; I thought you could use some coffee." He glances toward the door. "Turns out you needed something else."

"The way my heart is racing, I don't think I'll ever need coffee again." I chuckle weakly.

"What was going on back there?" He motions toward the station.

"Get in. I'll tell you about it," I say as I unlock the car doors. The cold of the seats seeps through my pant legs, making goose bumps prickle along my flesh.

He slides into the car, and I sip my coffee, hoping it will warm me up. I drive the few minutes to my house while I go over what happened with Allen. There's not much to tell, but I give him a rundown all the same.

"The last thing I expected was for Allen to jump down my throat," I say as I pull in to the driveway. I know he's angry that Ryder tried to kill himself, but I didn't expect him to take it out on me. The house is dark. With the moonlight spilling across the sharp lines of the old house, it looks haunted. "I think he's got some pent-up issues from high school. I know part of it was because Rachel was seeing Jacob." I drink from my coffee cup, then ask, "Why did you head back to the station?"

A look of recognition flashes in his eyes, as if it just occurred to him that he came back to the station for a reason. "Oh, right. I found another death I wanted to talk to you about."

I get the sense it's going to be a long story, and I want all the information he's got—among other things. "You want to come in?" I ask.

He smiles and nods.

We head into the house. My black couch and end tables are shoved against the back wall, the small coffee table in front of the couch. A vase of tulips sits in the middle of the coffee table. A lacy tablecloth I've never seen before covers the table in the dining room, and a vase filled with lilies sits atop it. That's not a touch I expected the movers to add; I'm not much of a flower person.

"Nice place," he says like he's somewhat surprised.

"Thanks. You want anything?" I ask as I go to the kitchen to grab myself a bottle of water.

"No, I'm fine," he says after a long pause.

"So what have you found?" I ask as I sit on the couch and sip my water.

Noah takes a seat at the other end of the couch and turns toward me. I wish he were closer, but I push the thought from my mind. *Stop it, Claire.*

"While researching Vinalhaven to look for other clues and to see if there were any other deaths linked to Rachel's, I found something else that sparked my attention, if you don't want to count the six that were found in the bay. A girl who drowned in the midseventies."

"Drowned?" I ask. I hadn't heard of anyone drowning on the island in the seventies. Even if a death like that was accidental, I'm sure I would have heard of it growing up at some point.

He makes a face that tells me he doesn't think a drowning is the full story.

"Aha, so you think the drowning is covering for something else."

"They could have also just mistaken a murder for an accidental drowning. Things were different back then. Their ability to investigate homicides was so limited. They could have easily assumed it was a tragic accident when it was a homicide, especially if nothing like that had ever happened on the island before."

Could that really be the case? If the first murder happened in the midseventies, that would mean that murders have been occurring on the island for over forty years. The idea that someone could have been hunting down victims and hiding murders for that long terrifies and sickens me.

"Who was the victim?" I ask after silence has grown between us for a long time.

"That I don't know yet. Everything I've found—which is very little—has just mentioned a Jane Doe."

"Do we know what she looked like?" I ask.

He nods. "Blonde, between the ages of eighteen and twenty-five."

Too similar. Could this Jane Doe have been our first victim?

"I'll keep looking to see if I can track down her identity or any clues as to who she was."

"Thank you," I say. "Have you found anything else?"

He shakes his head. "I've been asking a lot of questions, but instead of getting answers, I'm mainly getting gossip and more information than I'd ever want in my life about this island."

I can't help but laugh at that. "That seems about right."

"I'm so glad I didn't grow up in a small town like this. I can't even imagine what people would have said about me."

"A bad boy, were you?" I ask as I laugh. It's hard to imagine Noah trying to be a bad boy.

"I got into my fair share of trouble." He chuckles. After a few moments of silence, his brows furrow, and he looks toward my front door. "I was hoping I could ask you about Jacob and your sister," he says, and I nearly flinch.

"What about them?"

"How long had she been seeing Jacob?"

I shrug. "She didn't tell me when it started. I was the annoying little sister. Eventually Rachel told me she was planning to run away with Jacob because of the baby." Spilling this information to him feels like a betrayal, even all these years later. I sip my coffee, trying to distract myself from the thoughts. My attention shifts back to Noah.

He runs his hand through his long hair, and all I can imagine is what it would feel like against my fingers. I wish the thought away as soon as it crosses my mind, but it won't budge. Being around Noah, I feel like something is slowly building inside me, and if I don't distance myself, whatever it is will explode. But I don't want distance, not even a little.

My phone vibrates, and I slip it out of my pocket. A text from my mom is waiting on the screen, but I don't look at it. All I see is the time—it's almost eleven.

"Shit, it's getting late," I say as I stand up and stretch my legs. I have to get some sleep—the rational part of me knows that. The part of me that wants to drag Noah upstairs, however, is fighting a very loud battle in the back of my mind. Noah would take my mind off of everything in the best and worst ways possible. His shirt is tight over his chest as he gets off the couch, and I can imagine easily how muscular he must be without it. The leather jacket he always wears hangs open and begs for me to lace my arms around his back beneath the material. But I force the thought from my mind.

"Yeah, I should probably head back to the hotel," he says, but his voice lacks conviction.

I walk him to the door, and with every step, I swear I feel the heat building between us, like electricity gathering in the air before lightning strikes. My skin hums at our proximity, and heat rushes to my cheeks. If this is how I feel with a foot between us, I'm not sure I could handle him being any closer. I chew the inside of my cheek at the thought.

"Thank you again for the coffee, and for being there," I say, but it doesn't feel like enough thanks. I owe him—*really* owe him.

"No thanks necessary. I may have to make it a habit." He brushes a stray strand of hair that's fallen out of my ponytail away from my eyes. His fingers brush my cheek for just a moment, but it's enough to kick up the embers already swirling inside me. He leans closer, and my heart gallops as my chest tightens. His lips are so close to mine that the heat of his breath warms them. All I want is for his lips to meet mine. Fuck the consequences. The craving for him runs so deep it vibrates in my bones.

A car horn outside makes us both jump, and he pulls back, the moment shattered. I curse whoever interrupted us. But despite the persistent pulse of desire in my core, maybe it's for the best. He sighs, and I open the door. He starts to walk past me but stops and presses a feather-light kiss against my cheek. His lips are warm and soft. A bolt of panic and excitement shoots through me at his touch.

"Good night," he whispers, and the moment the heat of his breath hits my ear, the tickle of a shiver plays down my spine.

I close the door and lean against it, trying to get my heart to slow down. I have no idea how much longer I can resist him. For the first time since I got here, this place feels empty, and I wish I weren't going to bed alone.

CHAPTER 18

I didn't remember to set my alarm, but I'm still up before dawn. From the moment I wake up, thoughts of Noah pool in the back of my mind, but I shove them aside. There are other things I have to focus on.

The roads are empty as I pull the rental car out of my driveway. As I drive slowly through downtown with the window down, cold morning air hisses against my cheeks. Close to the marina, thick fog oozes off the bay and seeps through the streets. I love seeing the city like this, with the empty streets.

When I pull in to the parking lot of the police station, Noah is leaning against the building, waiting for me. He's holding coffee and a bag from the café. Seeing him here, here for *me*, makes butterflies bloom in the pit of my stomach.

I hop out of the car, a grin spreading from ear to ear. "I'm starting to think I'll never have to buy coffee again."

"After yesterday, it seems like you're going to need coffee deliveries more often," he says, his drawl more pronounced than usual.

We walk together into the station, and I breathe a sigh of relief that Allen isn't in. I'll have to face him eventually, I know, but the longer I can put it off, the better. Maybe once Ryder is discharged from the hospital, Allen will loosen up. He can't stay pissed at me forever.

Noah hands me a coffee and a muffin. "I was hoping we could do something in a bit," he says.

I rip a piece of my muffin off and pop it in my mouth. "Oh?"

"I've been taking walks along the beach since I got here. Will you come with me later?"

"You like long walks on the beach?" I ask, and I can't help smiling. "I thought writers were supposed to hate clichés."

"I would have never known if I hadn't come here. There weren't any beaches where I grew up." He leans back in the chair as he chuckles. "There are beaches in South Carolina, but they're packed, so I've avoided them."

"You've never spent time at the beach?" I ask, shocked. Growing up on the coast, I've spent most of my life within minutes of the beach. Hell, I could see the rocky beach from my bedroom window.

He shakes his head. "My mom likes skiing on vacation. She hated the water, so she never took us to the beach."

"That's a shame. Of course I'll go for a walk with you. I need to check the beach near the park anyway." The guys did a sweep a few days ago, but I always feel better if I do another just to check.

We finish our breakfast and steer toward the beach on foot. Eyes follow us as we walk through downtown toward the park.

"It feels like I'm under a microscope here," he says as we near the beach.

The rocky shore crunches beneath my feet as I steer us toward the beach closest to the park. Luckily, it's usually abandoned. It's not the nice kind of place where you lay out your towel and work on your tan. There isn't a smooth part of this beach. There's no white sand. What sand there is, littered with pebbles and tiny shells, is as gray as the sky. It's impossible to go fifty feet without tripping over driftwood.

"Yeah, imagine growing up here," I say sarcastically.

It's low tide, so we've got much more shore to walk than usual. Foamy waves slip up and down the shore, swallowing our footsteps as we walk. The hiss of the water is soothing, the slow inhale and exhale of the sea. Our feet crunch across the tiny shells scattered on the rocky shore. Being out here puts me at ease, like maybe the waves will wash away all my problems.

"I can see why you come out here. This is what I missed the most about this place."

"Miss the most? What else did you miss?"

Rachel.

I consider that for a moment, but I really can't think of anything else. "I guess this is it, actually." The thought weighs on me. I shouldn't have come back.

"What's your favorite memory of living here?" he asks.

I don't even have to think about it. It's one of my favorite memories of Rachel. "My first month of high school was *bad.* Looking back, the problems were stupid. But they all just kinda piled up at once. My boyfriend broke up with me. I failed three tests. Someone was spreading rumors about me—basically I would have rather drowned myself in the bay than spend another minute on the island. Rachel had just gotten her license. She talked Mom into letting us skip school and take the ferry so we could go to the mall in Bangor. There'd been a wall between us since Rachel turned twelve, but that day, it came down, and she was my sister again." The knife that's been in my heart since she died twists at the memory. What would she be like today? Would we be close? Maybe she'd be married, and I'd be an aunt.

"She sounds like she was great," he says as he squeezes my hand.

"When she wanted to be. Those years were really tough on both of us." My survivor's guilt is uniquely defined by the number of times I wished my sister were dead when I was fifteen. It's normal. That's what the shrink told me. *Everyone wishes someone were dead when they're a teen.* The difference is most of them don't wake up with a dead sister.

"It's still tough with my brothers, but I can't imagine losing one of them," he says, squeezing my hand gently. The warmth of him bleeds into me, comforting me.

"Tell me about your brothers?"

He looks out over the water, and his brows knit together. "There's not much to say."

Why doesn't he want to talk about them? Something about it doesn't sit right with me. "Why not?"

He looks out over the rolling waves. "I'm just not close to my family anymore. I don't fit into the family, and they don't want me to. I try not to think about them." There's an edge to his voice, but it's clear it's not directed at me.

"How many do you have?" I ask. I won't ask details about them if he doesn't want to discuss it, but I'd like to know more about him.

"Three," he says.

As we walk along the beach, something pale, almost bluish, catches my eye, the flicker of fabric caught in the pull of the waves. My mind screams to a halt. *Is that a body?*

I drop Noah's hand and run toward it. But as I get closer, my pounding heart steadies. It's just sun-bleached driftwood with a ripped pillowcase caught in the branches.

"Jesus," I breathe. "I thought it was a body," I explain as Noah jogs up beside me.

"It's the color of one," he says. "Is that a shirt?"

"I think it's a pillowcase. I'm going to have it bagged just in case." The killer is using something to cover the victim's faces. Though we found a pillowcase at the scene with Madeline's body, to my knowledge none was ever found for Emma's murder. Could this be it?

My phone vibrates in my pocket, and I nearly jump. I grab the phone and unlock it. "Detective Calderwood."

"This is Tim Armstrong with the coast guard. Sergeant Michaels gave me your cell."

"How can I help you?" I ask as goose bumps prickle the back of my neck.

"We found a boat, and your sergeant said to call you about it," he explains. The man's words are clipped, like he's rushed.

"What boat?"

"The name on the hull is *School Marmalade*." That's Paul's boat. There's a long pause that makes my stomach churn. Something rustles on the other end of the line. "I think you need to get out here with a CSI team, though. We can't tow this back to Vinalhaven."

A CSI team? My heart pounds, and my mind swims with all the horrible possibilities. Is there another girl on the boat? "Why? What happened?" Deep down, I know why. But I need to hear him say it.

"There appears to be blood all over the inside of it and down the side of the hull."

"Is there a body?"

"Not that we saw, no, ma'am."

Just because they didn't see it doesn't mean it's not there, unfortunately. He gives me the coordinates. I'm going to have to use the station boat to head over there.

My heart pounds, and my mouth goes dry. Thoughts swarm in my mind, clotting together. Is it the same killer? Was it someone from our island on that boat? Whose blood is it? No one else has been reported missing. Bile floods my mouth. I clench my fist, cutting half moons into my palm.

The second I hang up the phone, Noah takes a step closer. "Is everything all right?" His brows are furrowed, and concern swims in his eyes.

I shake my head. "The coast guard found a boat we're looking for off the coast." A shiver creeps up my spine. Though the coast guard didn't find one, I have to wonder if there's a body in or near that boat. All the murders I dealt with in Detroit were revenge, gang violence, or crimes of passion. Honestly, those are easier to deal with. They're cut and dried. A serial killer is a whole new ball game. I want to bag this motherfucker, but a thought nags at the back of my mind. Am I even capable of finding this guy? Sure, most serials get sloppy, and that's how they get caught. But for that to happen, more girls have to die. That idea is enough to turn my stomach.

"Are you okay?" he asks as he cups my cheek. "You're really pale." His thumb brushes against my cheekbone, the gentle caress grounding me.

"I'm floundering. I should have something by now—a hunch, a thread—something should point me in the right direction. There isn't a single lead that's taking us anywhere right now." With every word, I expel some of the weight piling up around me. I'm so used to bottling things up that I forget how good it can be to purge some of the toxic thoughts I have swimming in my head.

"You're being way too hard on yourself. Do you have any idea how many murders go unsolved every year?"

"One-third." I remember the figure from a test in college. I don't give a shit what the averages are. What's *good enough* for other precincts isn't good enough for me. Having cases go unsolved for years would eat away at me. Maybe that's why I focused on working homicides where things were pretty clear cut—or maybe before now I've gotten lucky.

"Correct," he says with a smile. "I believe in you. I know you can do this. I don't think you're ever going to see yourself as part of that one-third, but if you don't give yourself a little bit of a break here, you're going to drive yourself insane before you get a chance to solve this."

"Thank you. I needed that," I say as I sigh.

This is a side of Noah I didn't expect. Not that I mind.

Noah heads back to the hotel as I call the CSI team and coordinate for them to meet me at the cove. Though I don't know what we'll find out there, we need to process this as a crime scene.

Low gray clouds roll across the sky, warning that rain or snow might be closing in. I need to get to the cove where they found the boat fast, before any evidence washes away. Back at the station, I grab

Jason, a tarp, and the keys to the boat. While Jason drives the boat over the choppy waters, I keep an eye out for other boats, scanning the sprawl before us intently. We cross the open water, Vinalhaven shrinking behind us before being swallowed entirely by the gray mist filling the bay. It takes fifteen minutes to start closing in on the cove, and the whole time, my nerves gnaw at me. The moment the cove appears in the distance, my heart starts to gallop, and a few fat drops of freezing rain land on my arms, warning me we've only got minutes to preserve evidence.

These aren't ideal conditions for a crime scene. The evidence has already been exposed to the elements. Some of it could have washed away. But my plan is to set up the tarp over the boat to at least protect what we can until the CSI team gets here. Jason and I pull the boat up and tie it to the small dock on the cove. During the summer, some of the tourists who journey to Vinalhaven for small-town charm and to get away from it all end up at this cove. It's a great beach when the weather is warm. In the off-season some of the high schoolers come out here to party. The beer bottles that lie half-swallowed by the sand are evidence that's still true.

My feet sink in the wet sand as I walk toward the large fishing boat with *School Marmalade* painted on the side. Jason and I work quickly to put the tarp over it. When the coast guard mentioned blood, I wasn't sure what to expect. There's brown smeared all over the floor in a few spots, and there are smeared handprints, too large to be from Madeline or Emma. I lean in for a closer look, trying to discern if we could get fingerprints from this evidence, but they're too smudged. We won't be able to get anything from these. Is this where the killer was cutting flesh from the victims?

After we've got the tarp set up, we take some photos of the scene. And I notice something odd. Near the steering wheel, there's a floral backpack shoved under the controls. The pattern looks familiar, but it takes me a minute to place it. It looks similar to the pattern that

Madeline had on her shoes. I won't be able to check the bag until after CSI gets here to take in all the evidence. Jason and I take photos as the rain pelts the tarp. About thirty minutes after we arrive, the CSI team pulls up in their boat.

We hang back as they catalog the scene, take swabs and photos, and gather all the evidence they can. They unzip the backpack and sift through the things inside. I flip through a notebook once CSI is done with it, sift through some papers, and it becomes clear the backpack belonged to Emma Carver.

After the CSI team is done, I head back to the station with Jason. As we pass through the doors, he says, "Allen sent me the interviews for the rest of the choir girls you requested. If you don't need me here for the boat, I'll finish the rest of those."

It annoys me that Allen blew off his assignment, but I'll let it go for now; I have something more pressing. I need to talk to Sergeant Michaels about Paul's boat. No matter what Paul might say, finding his boat covered in blood doesn't look good.

I rap my knuckles lightly on Sergeant Michaels's door and offer him a pained smile as I peek my head in. Over the stacks of folders, it's clear he had an accident with a cup of coffee this morning but hasn't bothered to change his shirt. A trail of brown circles in varying sizes leads down the front of his yellow button-up. I give him a rundown of what we found at the cove.

"There's not enough here to arrest him. But I could go to his place to ask him a few questions," I offer.

He steeples his fingers on top of the desk. "It's going to be a week at least until we have the forensics back on the boat. Even then, it's not going to be enough to pin it on him, since he reported it missing," he explains, like I didn't know all that. "We have to be careful how we handle this since it's Mayor Clark's brother. I think it's best if you talk to him at his house; that way it's not going to come off like he's a suspect. We can't afford to raise any red flags for him if he knows what happened."

"Are there any other reasons he might be looked at that I don't know about?" I ask.

He points toward the door. "Shut that." Once I've shut the door, he continues. "Three girls have made allegations against him, but they all ended up recanting. Without evidence or a confession, there isn't much we can do."

"Allegations of what, exactly?" My stomach shifts, and I swear I know what's coming.

He clears his throat and leans closer to the desk. "Sexual assault. The girls said he raped them. But they changed their stories."

"They recanted?"

He nods. "And afterward they all left the island," he explains.

Did they really leave? Or did they end up dead? The Jane Does Noah told me about linger in the back of my mind.

"Who were they? Do you have files on them?"

He shakes his head. "That outage about six months ago. Wiped out everything we didn't have paper copies of. And apparently our backups weren't working properly."

"Perfect," I mutter to myself. Is this really bad police work, or is this something else? "Do you have their names at least so I can look them up?" Heat flares under my skin, and my pulse pounds in my ears. I clench my fists against the thoughts raging in my mind.

"I'll look through my files to see if I have them written somewhere."

Everyone knows everyone here. How could he not know their names? All of this is adding up to spell something really bad.

"I'll stop by today to ask Paul some questions."

His eyes narrow. I hold up my hand, because I know what he's thinking. "I know. I'll be careful about what I ask," I say before he gets a chance to warn me.

Clouds blanket the sky when I leave the station. I timed it so Paul should be out of school and back home. The air is crisp, the way it always is before it snows. The only snow so far this year was the night Madeline died. I hop in my car and snake my way up the long winding roads of the island. My phone vibrates in my pocket as I pull in front of Paul's house. I sit in my car and finish my coffee, letting my nerves settle before I head to the door. I grab my keys from the ignition, throw open the door, and walk up the path to Paul's house. I have to keep knocking for a while, and by the time he answers, I've almost given up.

Paul eyes me up and down, making my skin crawl. He tightens his robe around himself, plaid pajama pants sticking out from the bottom. "Sorry, you've caught me relaxing after a long day. It's good to see you, Claire," he says without an ounce of sincerity to his words. "What do you need?"

"I'm very sorry to hear about your niece. How are you holding up?" I ask. I've never been great with my bedside manner, so to speak, but I want to be as compassionate here as I can—before I have to ask him about the boat, anyway.

He gives me a smile that looks forced. "As well as can be expected, I suppose. My brother and I aren't incredibly close, but the loss has been very hard on him. We'll all miss Madeline. But I'm sure you didn't come over here just to talk about that."

"I was hoping I could talk to you for a few minutes about your boat," I explain and take a step toward the door. I'm not going to give him a chance to say no.

"Of course." He waves me inside, and we take a seat in his living room. "Did you find it?"

"Yes, we did. That's what I'm here to talk to you about." I look down, taking a moment to gather my thoughts. "We found your boat in Arey Cove. We've had to take it in as evidence," I explain.

"Evidence? Why?" he asks, and I have to give it to him—he does seem genuinely baffled. But I still don't buy it. Being in the same room with him makes my skin crawl. I've always felt something off about Paul, and now I know what it is. Beneath that calm demeanor lurks a predator. If he's been assaulting girls on this island and silencing them, I have to ask myself, What else is he capable of?

"It's clear a crime was committed on the boat," I say. And that's all the information I'm willing to give him. I need to know if he's involved in this or if someone really stole it. "Can you tell me again about the last time you used your boat?" I ask without skipping a beat.

His eyes narrow, and he looks away, staring off into the distance. For a long time, he says nothing, and then he scratches his cheek when he looks back at me. "I can't remember. It's been a while. I think the last person who used it was Madeline; sometimes she and Emma would borrow it, go out on the water."

"Weren't they a little young to be out on the water alone in a boat?" I ask as I quirk my eyebrow. Though I saw it plenty when I was growing up, you've got to be sixteen years old now to operate a boat, and you have to complete a course to get a card to drive one. Even with that, most people don't want to turn their boats over to sixteen-year-olds.

He shrugs. "They had sea legs just like everyone else on this island."

"What did they use it for?"

"Just relaxing with friends on the water." He clears his throat as soon as he's done speaking and crosses his legs.

So was that the boat in the background of the pictures that Noah showed me?

"Do you think they would take your boat without permission?" I ask.

He shakes his head. "I don't see why. I've always let them use it whenever they wanted."

"Did either of the girls ever leave anything on the boat while they were using it?"

He crosses his arms and furrows his brow. "Yeah, now and then."

"How well did you know Emma Carver?"

He looks toward the windows and picks at his left knuckle. "She took driver's ed with me a few months ago." Just as I finish making a note of that, he adds, "I've taught driver's ed to nearly every kid on this island."

"Is there anything else that you think could help?"

He shakes his head. "If I can think of anything, I'll be sure to let you know," he says as he stands up, signaling our conversation is over. Paul rushes me out. I get the impression he's got no interest in helping. If my boat had disappeared and the police were investigating a murder, I'd have a million questions. I'd be doing everything I could to help the cops.

After talking to Paul, I spend most of my day downtown, checking in with the shop owners and combing the park again. Being in the park, standing in the spot where Rachel, Emma, and Madeline were found, makes a bad feeling slither beneath my skin. Even though this isn't where they're buried, it's their final resting place. I can still feel them here. Before I sweep back through Main Street toward the station, I pop back into the café to see if Morgan has the security footage from the night of Emma's murder. As soon as I ask, she grabs the SD cards for me and hands them over.

I shove them into my coat pocket and head back out onto Main Street. Downtown is nearly empty as I cross the street back to the station. Mindy smiles at me as I throw the front door open and walk back toward my office. When I pop the first SD card into the computer, it chimes in response. It takes a few moments for the files to appear, broken up into one-hour increments. It's likely that Emma died between eleven p.m. and three a.m. based on what we know.

The first icon I click on is for ten to eleven that night. As before, the angle faces down Main Street toward my rental. The hotel and the police station sit behind the camera, out of view. Most of the cars are already gone from the sides of the darkened streets of downtown. At around ten thirty Morgan locks the café and walks to her car. But nothing else. I click to the next video, from eleven to midnight. A few fishermen stroll down the street toward the Sand Bar; one diverges, crossing the street to see if one of the other restaurants is open, before returning to his group. I move to the next video. At 12:13 a.m. Emma strolls down the street, her hands shoved in the pockets of her dark coat. She stops about ten feet from the camera and glances back over her shoulder, like someone might be following her. But from this angle, I can't see anything. She continues walking a moment later, passing out of view, and a figure emerges at the end of the street, cloaked in shadows. The figure is wide, tall, definitely a man. My heart pounds as I move to the next video, but he's gone. He never walked past the camera.

I may not know who he is—it's impossible to tell—but my gut tells me that's him. That's Emma's killer.

CHAPTER 19

The next morning, I walk into the station with a box of muffins and a coffee for each of the guys. When I get in, Jason's already at his desk, typing away. In all the years that I've worked in law enforcement, he's one of the few people I've encountered who actually make it to the office before I do. Hell, from what I know about the guy so far, I'm not sure he ever actually sleeps.

"Morning," I say as I hand him a coffee.

"Donuts?" he asks as he glances at the box.

"Muffins." I set the box down and take a sip of my coffee.

"Thank God. With all the donuts around here, I feel like I'm sweating frosting."

I dig in my bag and pull out a printout of the man from the surveillance video last night. It's a blurred mess. The chances we can get anything out of this are pretty slim, but we have to try.

"I know it's a long shot, but could you take a look at this, maybe ask some of the fishermen if they saw this guy the night of Emma's murder around midnight?" I ask.

He takes the paper from me and scrutinizes it. "I'll try, but I wouldn't hold your breath."

"Thanks," I say as I start to turn toward my office.

"Oh, Claire," he says, and I turn to face him again. "I conducted some of the interviews with the girls from the choir, and two heard the argument between your mother and Emma. Both think Madeline may have been there as well."

"And?"

"Jenna Arey said that your mother was mad at Emma because she had told Father Samuel that your mother treated them poorly. But your mother also yelled at Madeline and Emma because she thought they'd stolen money from her purse."

Stealing from her purse? I could see how that would get a rise out of my mother. She will not abide being *disrespected.* My mind reels as I try to figure out what role—if any—she could have played in this. "Thank you, Jason. I'm going to give her a call. Please let me know if you find anything else." I head back to my office. There's a voice mail waiting for me, a doctor from the hospital notifying me that it'll be at least a week before I can talk to Ryder. Though I'm frustrated about the holdup, there's nothing I can do about it.

I call my mother while debating if I should just show up at her house—I really don't have time for that today, though. She picks up on the third ring.

"Hello, Claire," she says in a distant tone, like she could just be speaking to a gardener or a stray cat.

I don't have time to draw this out, so I cut right to the chase. If I surprise her, she's much less likely to lie to me. "What do you think Emma and Madeline stole from you?"

She's silent for a beat. When she does speak, her voice is high, unusually so. "I have no idea—"

"Cut the shit, Mom," I say, my tone as hard as her granite countertops.

"That seems a little extreme." A high, humorless laugh filters out of her. "Fine. They stole money from my purse."

"And how do you know they stole it?" I counter. I ask this because my mother *loves* holding grudges. If there were a sport for holding grudges, my mother would have a medal—actually, she'd have a roomful. The worst part of her little games is that if she can't find the appropriate reason to hate someone, she'll invent one. When I was in third grade, she decided she hated my English teacher, Mrs. Blake. She tried to get this woman fired, spread rumors about her, made her life a living hell, all because she invented a sordid glance in my father's direction.

"Because there's no one else it could have been." Her voice goes up in pitch, like she's losing the battle of keeping herself calm.

"So other than your purse being in proximity to Madeline and Emma, your purse was either on you or in your direct line of sight the rest of the day?"

"Well, no—" she stammers.

"Okay, if it wasn't in your sight the entire day, how can you be sure it was them?"

Silence falls over the line. "They were disrespectful little liars who hated me and took every opportunity to show it," she seethes.

This is turning out worse than I thought it would.

"Emma and Madeline were spoiled brats who were never told no in their lives. The second I said a single word to them, they'd run off to Father Samuel about how *mean* I was to them." Her words are laced with venom.

And now we've reached a point where I have to ask, "Where were you the night of October thirteenth, Mom?"

She laughs. "You're being ridiculous."

"If I have to ask you again, it'll be in an interrogation room."

She clears her throat but doesn't speak, and I think I'm actually going to have to drive out there. She finally says, "The night Emma died I was home until I realized I'd forgotten my phone at the church. I went back to get it. I was there for probably ten minutes. The night Madeline died I never left the house."

"Would you be able to verify your story?"

She scoffs.

"Mom, I'm serious." The man I saw downtown definitely didn't fit my mother's description, but if I'm going to rule her out for anything, I need solid reasons for doing so. I won't make it look like familial ties have any bearing on decisions I make.

"Yes," she says finally.

We finish up the call with my mother being so standoffish to me that I'm hopeful she may not talk to me again for *weeks.*

Noah hasn't been able to find anything in his search for records of Rachel's autopsy or the items missing from her file. There are details about the autopsy that I need to make connections in the case, and there's only one other option I can think of—reaching out to the medical examiner who worked on Rachel's case.

It takes me three hours of searching to find the medical examiner who worked in Augusta when Rachel died. As luck would have it, when she retired, she stayed in Maine in a small city right off the bay. Now that I've got the info on the old ME, I need to head there and ask her some questions about Rachel's file. I pop my head into Sergeant Michaels's office. He's hunched over his keyboard, anxiously hunting keys.

"Sarge, I'm heading up to see Barbara Valloy."

"You should see if Noah is available and take him."

"I'm sure he's busy," I say, because I really don't want him tagging along.

His face grows serious. "He's helping with Rachel's investigation—that's where this falls. Let him help, Claire. He's got a good perspective on things like this."

I nod to Sergeant Michaels, grab my coat, and dial Noah's number on my way out of the station.

"You up for a road trip?" I ask as soon as the call connects.

"Always."

"Meet me at the ferry in fifteen."

"Deal," he says, and I swear I can hear his smile.

I pull my car up to the ferry and drum my fingers against the steering wheel as I wait for Noah. Across the bay, the boat is churning toward us, but at the speed it's going, it'll take at least another ten minutes to get here. My door pops open, and Noah slides into my passenger seat.

"So where are we headed?" he asks as he hands me a cup of coffee.

"We're going to see Barbara Valloy, the ME who worked on Rachel."

The ferry finally docks, and we're able to drive on. With the car locked in place at the front, we climb the stairs to the top to take in the sights. Evergreen trees crowd the bay, some of them still dusted with the snow that fell last night. In the few weeks since I came here, the autumn leaves have succumbed to winter and coated the ground in a blanket of brown.

"Where is this place?"

"It's right off the coast, about a twenty-minute drive after we get off the ferry," I explain and take a long sip of my coffee.

"Do you like snow?" Noah asks, catching me off guard.

I laugh. "Sometimes. Why?"

"People who grew up with snow all the time have a very different opinion of it than people who didn't," he explains. "In Tennessee, it hardly ever snows, unless you live in the mountains. Where I grew up we got it maybe once a year. So it's magical, not annoying. People from up north hate it, because they're stuck with it for half the year."

"I liked the snow better when I lived here. It didn't seem to ever get in the way. It was part of life. In Detroit, snow was a constant pain. It slowed things down, made life more difficult," I explain. "I like snow on Christmas, though. It makes the holiday feel special."

He nods. "It doesn't feel like Christmas without it."

"Does it snow in South Carolina?"

He shakes his head. "Not that I've ever seen. I've only lived there a few years, though."

The ferry horn lets out a long, low, billowing sound. It's a sound that sets my teeth on edge, loud enough to make your ears ache. It's the kind of sound you feel in your bones.

"Where do you want to live?" he asks after a long silence.

"What do you mean?"

"It's clear you don't like the island. You're here because you have to be, not because you want to be. So where would you rather live?"

I let out a little chuckle. "Virginia," I say automatically.

"Why Virginia?" he asks, his eyes wide, like that was the last place he expected me to say. I guess most people would say New York, California—someplace big, someplace that's alluring for most. But that's not for me. I'm never going to be a big-city, downtown kind of girl. Detroit was as close as I'll get, and it never fit me quite right.

"My dream has always been to work for the FBI," I explain. "So it's not so much about the place; it's about the job."

"So why don't you apply?"

I laugh again, louder this time. "I barely have any experience. There's no way I'd get a job with the FBI." It takes some people twenty years to do it—unless they've got connections, that is.

"You don't know if you don't try. After you solve this case, you should try. Otherwise you might end up stuck here." He offers me a smile.

He has a point. I don't want to spend the rest of my life here, the lead detective of a small town. It's not for me. And I'll never have a chance of getting out unless I try. If I worked for the FBI, I could do what I love every day. I could hunt down the guys who do this. Some detectives, they want space from this; they want to be able to take a step back, have some breathing room. I want to be in this up to my eyeballs. I need the opposite of space.

Deep down, I know it's because I'm compensating. I had a chance to save Rachel, but I didn't take it. If I had talked to someone then, if I hadn't listened to her, she might be alive right now. And the day after she died, I had a chance to help them find her killer, and instead I kept my mouth shut. That's the kind of power Rachel had over me. Even in death her grip on me didn't waver. All I ever wanted was for her to love me.

"Looks like we're getting close," Noah says, pulling me from my train of thought.

The dock is still a good half mile from us, but being able to see it clearly makes Noah feel better. A few miles out, just as I could make out the blurry dock in the distance, the tension in his shoulders started to fall. It'll still take us at least ten minutes before we can drive off the ferry.

"How's your search coming?" I ask, knowing we've still got a little time to talk it through before we need to get back to my car.

"A lot of information about Rachel seems to be *missing*. I tried tracking down the sheriff who worked on her case, but he died. It feels like dead end after dead end."

"At least we found the ME who performed the autopsy."

He nods. "Yeah, at least there's that. There was one other thing I found," he says, his voice a little unsteady. "Her friend Angela, from high school, found out about my research and reached out to me."

I rack my brain for a memory of Angela. I'm not sure that I would have called her and Rachel friends. Instead, my guess is that Angela got wind of Noah's research—and how cute he is—and wanted to squeeze into the spotlight.

"And what did she say?" I ask, trying to keep the skepticism from my voice.

"She said that Rachel was planning to leave the island. She suspects your mom found out about it and got angry—there might have been a fight between them." He eyes me, obviously waiting for some kind of reaction.

I knew Rachel was planning to leave; that doesn't surprise me. It does surprise me that she might have told Angela. I just don't buy it. And if my mom had found out that Rachel was going to leave, she probably would have locked her in her room, and I'm sure I would have heard the fallout from it.

"Did Rachel say anything to you about leaving?" he asks when I say nothing.

"Well, yes. But I don't think she told Angela that, and I sure as hell don't think my mother hurt Rachel. She wouldn't kill her." My mind flashes to that night, and I clench my eyes closed just long enough to burn the image from my mind. "It wasn't her."

"How can you be sure?"

"I just am," I snap.

As the ferry bounces against the docks, we climb back in my car and drive toward Rockland, Noah silent as a stone since I snapped at him. I don't mind the silence; I'll take it over a barrage of questions any day. It takes us twenty minutes to get to the house of the old medical examiner. We're an hour early, but I'm bad at two things—waiting and killing time. So I decide I'm fine with being the kind of asshole that shows up an hour early.

The house is a tiny cottage with bright-green shutters and daisy-yellow siding. White details line the house—edging, roofline, and ornate porch. It's as cute as an overdecorated cupcake or a Victorian gingerbread house. The former medical examiner, Barbara Valloy, is hunchbacked and frail. Her face is bloated, taking away some of the lines that should be there. A spiderweb of blue veins peeks from beneath her translucent, milky skin. Barbara is the kind of old that disturbs me. I can see in her dim eyes that she's going to die soon. I can't imagine her ever being young; her features are too far gone for that. Saying she's got one foot in the grave would be a kindness; it's more like she's clinging to life with her splintered fingernails. I introduce myself and offer her a thin smile.

"Detective Calderwood? Are you early? Or did I take an extra pill this morning?" she asks, and it isn't until she laughs that I realize she's joking.

"I'm sorry we're early."

"Oh, pishposh, I'm an old lady. What the hell else do I have to do?" She cackles in an unnerving way as she ushers us into the house.

Her house is well kept, pristine, the kind of house that doesn't see grandchildren often. There are no toys, no candy dishes out; there isn't a single stain on her carpet. The furniture in her living room looks like it belongs in a dollhouse: dainty, floral, carved into unnatural curves and loops. The wall closest to the door is covered in pictures of the family that doesn't visit her. A smiling family, arms looped around each other as they hover together at the beach.

"That's a beautiful family you have." I nod toward the pictures.

"You didn't say you were bringing your partner," Barbara says as she smiles at Noah and sweeps her long white hair behind her ear.

I almost correct her, but Noah reaches out and introduces himself as he shakes her hand.

"It's lovely to meet you," she says, smiling at him and leading him to the living room. I follow behind them, forgotten.

Noah and I take a seat side by side on the couch, and Barbara sits across from us on a plush pink chair. Between us on the coffee table, there's a half-finished crossword puzzle. We might be side by side, but Noah is clearly all she can see.

"Barbara, like I said on the phone, I was hoping I could ask you a few questions about your time at the medical examiner's office in Augusta." There's already a lot I know about her. She retired a few months after Rachel died. Rachel would have been one of the last bodies that Barbara saw, so I'm hoping that makes her stick out in her mind.

She nods. "Ask away."

"Do you remember seeing the body of a girl who was murdered in Vinalhaven in 2004?" I ask as I flip open my notebook.

"That's the sister you mentioned on the phone, right? Rachel?"

I nod. "Yes, that's her."

"I do remember her. It's not often with all these small towns that we get something that . . ." She pauses and purses her lips. "Gruesome. There are things I've seen a lot. Stabbings, gunshot wounds, poisonings. Things that are ritualistic like Rachel, though—that's not something that I came across often."

"It's happened again," I say before I can stop myself. She needs to know what's at stake here, that other girls could die if I don't stop this. "Two girls in Vinalhaven were killed in the same way."

She shakes her head and rubs her cracked lips. "It's a damn shame they never caught the bastard that did it."

"That's why I'm here. Information from Rachel's autopsy and police reports is missing," I explain.

She leans back, crossing her legs and draping an arm over her knee. "I wish I could say that surprises me, but it doesn't. Not in the least."

"It doesn't surprise you?" I ask, my eyebrow raised.

"Things got lost a lot back then. The security isn't anything like it is now."

"Just for my own peace of mind, who would have access to the ME's files?" I ask.

"Only someone who worked for the medical examiner's office or for the police station. Technically no one from the station should have been left alone with our files, but not everyone was on top of following those rules, us all being on the same team and whatnot." An undercurrent of annoyance taints her words. It must have happened often. More often than it should have, anyway. "If you don't mind me asking, what in particular was missing from each report?"

"From the ME's report, time of death and details about the body—they were all gone. From the police report, suspects and interviews were all missing. Images of the crime scene, toxicology, notes about the case, details that weren't released to the media—they were all there."

She shakes her head. "That goes deeper than it should. Her official cause of death was strangulation. Also, based on the evidence I saw, it appears she was strangled with cloth over her face. There were fibers in her mouth. The police also found a pillowcase near the body. One thing I really remember was discovering grease on her body and traces of fuel, like she'd been on a boat. Her feet were grimy, bare. Dirt was caked between her toes. Not to mention the flesh that was cut from her ankle; that was just bizarre." After she says this, she purses her lips, as if the words themselves are sour.

The other girls weren't found with grease, dirt, or fuel on their bodies. Did Rachel try to escape? She had shoes on the last time I saw her, and winter clothing—there's no reason she would have had dirt on her feet.

Barbara sighs and crosses her arms. "I'm not sure if it's in your police report or not, or in the copy of the report you have, but I made a few notes about her death and the hours thereafter," she explains. "It was clear the body had been moved. Since there was no blood on the scene, the flesh must have been cut from the body outside of the park. There was also sand on her pants, like she'd been on the beach."

While our beaches are mostly pebbles, if you kick those up, you can find sand underneath. Considering my previous thought that the killer was bringing the bodies from the water and into the park, that'd make sense. But she would have had to dig her heels in to get some kicked up. Or was there sand wherever the killer took her? "Do you remember seeing any deaths that reminded you of Rachel's?" The question is a little more open ended than I'd like. She likely saw way more murder victims in the thirty or so years she worked for the ME's office than I ever have. For a long moment, she furrows her brows and sips her tea.

"There were two that I can remember before Rachel died. The bodies of two women were found in the bay, about nine or ten years apart.

They got caught in the nets. Both had been strangled and had a patch of flesh removed. They were Jane Does, though."

"Did anyone from Vinalhaven ever come to identify the bodies?" Typically, if a Doe is called in from the ME's office, all local stations will check their records and try to match the Doe to any missing persons in the city.

"We notified all the departments about the similarities of the homicides. The sheriff from back then who worked with me on those, Sheriff Dyer, came to see both. He said they weren't from Vinalhaven. He didn't seem concerned about it at all." She takes a long sip of her tea. "Back then, no one had ever been killed in Vinalhaven, though."

"Would the ME's office still have records on them?"

She nods. "We did last I was there. All the unidentified files are kept there, in the computer now."

That's how it was done in the Detroit ME's office. We'd have to get dental records or DNA to match to the Doe we thought matched a missing person. But the question is, Who were these victims?

"Do you remember when these bodies were brought in?"

"One woman in '89, the other in '98," she says and crosses her legs. Rachel died in 2004.

"Were you able to tell how long they'd been in the water?"

"It's hard to get an accurate read on that, especially when the water is cold. The one in '98 didn't seem like she'd been in the water long. The one in '89 seemed like it'd been a while, at least a few months. It'd been eaten quite a bit by the crabs." She purses her lips and stares off into nothing for a long time. "Sheriff Dyer passed away. For a long time he was at the memory hospital, though. It was terrible—dementia." She shakes her head.

The hospital that Margo Lane worked at. I'll have to talk to her and see if she remembers the sheriff ever saying anything about it.

"Do you remember ever seeing the body of a girl who drowned in the midseventies that washed up on the shores of Vinalhaven?" I ask, remembering the Jane Doe that Noah told me about.

She purses her lips in concentration, and then there's a flicker in her eyes. "Ah, yes. That was another Jane Doe. She did not have any flesh removed from her body."

"Are you sure she drowned and wasn't strangled?"

"It was very hard to tell. When the body was found, there had been quite a bit of decomposition. But I did find water in the lungs, so it appeared likely—back in those days—that she had drowned."

I jot down a note about that. "And did Sheriff Dyer come to see that Jane Doe?"

She nods, and her eyes bulge a little. "Yes, and something really stuck out to me about that. He claimed that he did not know the girl, but he was clearly shaken. It struck me as very strange. I felt like he knew her but didn't want to say so."

"Thank you so much for your time, Barbara," I say as I stand. A puff of perfumed air follows me out of the couch cushions.

She nods. "Of course. Don't be a stranger if you've got more questions." She shuffles along after me to the door.

After we're out of Barbara's house, I feel like I can breathe again. The weight of all the questions I had piled inside my mind lifts. It's not that I feel better; I don't. But the more I can piece together about Rachel's death, the easier it is to cope with—like if I know exactly what happened to her, it'll finally fill the hole inside me that her death left. In a way, I'm relieved.

The drive and ferry back to the island seem to take twice as long as they did the first time around. As I chew my lip on the drive back, Noah reaches over and squeezes my hand gently. The subtle reassurance brings a smile to my face and a warmth to my core.

The air between us thickens as I pull in to the hotel parking lot. Noah turns toward me, and I hold his gaze. I want to lean closer, to close the distance between us, but I can't because we shouldn't be doing this at all. It doesn't stop the heat from creeping up my neck. Noah takes the lead, leans closer, and tucks a stray piece of hair behind my ear. My breath hitches in response. I want his hands on me. What I wouldn't give to be anyone else so I could close the distance between us. My mind clots with all the reasons I can't kiss him. *Coworker, journalist, the enemy.*

"Is this all right?" he asks as his hand moves to the side of my neck. The gentle brush of his fingers against my flesh is enough to make my stomach jump and goose bumps creep up my spine. He's close enough that the mint on his breath mingles between us. His proximity isn't enough to make me back off or say no. I nod slowly. Anticipation builds inside me. I want to lean in, want to feel his lips against mine. The heat blazing beneath my skin is almost enough to turn every reservation I have to ashes. My core pulses like a beacon, calling to Noah, begging him to come closer.

But I can't do this. I can't let him in. If the situation weren't complicated enough with us working together, I'm terrified of letting someone else in. Because I know if I let my walls down, I'm opening myself up to just get hurt again. I don't know if I could make it through losing someone else like I lost Rachel.

I tear myself from him and turn away; it makes my head spin. "You should go," I say and motion toward the car door.

Noah's shoulders sag, and he opens his mouth as if to argue but comes up short. There's a cloud of disappointment surrounding us, and I'm not sure if it's his or mine. Brick by brick, I build the wall back up around myself. My fingers wrap around the steering wheel, and I force myself not to look at him. If I do, it'll shatter my resolve. "See you later, Noah," I call while he climbs out of the car. By the time I reach my rental, I hate myself.

It's for the best, I tell myself over and over. Maybe one day I'll believe it.

For twenty minutes, I've lain in bed regretting not kissing Noah. I should have. I should have balled his shirt in my fists and kissed him until my lips ached. I should have dragged him inside and fucked him until my legs turned to Jell-O. I could drown in all my should-haves.

I toss and turn for nearly an hour. Unable to purge Noah from my mind, I crawl out of bed. My heart races as my body commits to a decision my brain hasn't agreed to yet. I throw on jeans and a T-shirt, pulling my coat on before I reach the door.

I climb into my car, the cool cloth shifting beneath me. I drive without thinking to the hotel, nearly chewing a hole in my lip the whole way. My brain keeps giving me reasons I should turn the car around, but I'm done listening to it. It's time that I do something for myself. For a long moment, I sit in the parking lot. The cold night seeps in through the windows. If I don't do this now, I may never be brave enough.

I throw open the car door and run up the side stairs to Noah's room. I let out a heavy breath when I see his door.

You shouldn't do this, one side of me screams.

You should have done this an hour ago, the other side shouts back.

My mind is at war, but it's too late. The desire is flooding through my body, and there's no way I can fight it. I knock quietly at first, then louder. The part of me that's been fighting for this, that's wanted this for weeks, has won the war.

Noah's hair is tousled when he answers the door. His groggy blue eyes gleam, even in the low light. A pair of plaid boxers hangs loose from his sharp hip bones. I spend more time than I'll ever admit memorizing the muscular lines of his chest and the curve of his bicep as he holds open the door. The sight of him lights a fire inside me. The heat builds until a primal need for him is so strong it's all I can do to not launch myself at him.

"Claire?" he asks, leaning against the door.

Self-doubt threatens to consume me. What if I'm reading into things? What if he doesn't want this? Have I just made a fool of myself?

He smiles and shakes off the remnants of sleep like he'd thought this was a dream. Every single thought in my head vanishes except one. *Kiss him. Fuck everything else.*

I step forward, and he opens the door wider, letting me pass. He shuts the door and asks, "Is everything all right?"

Gathering all my strength, I close the distance between us, and my lips meet his. The kiss is stiff at first, but then Noah relaxes and wraps his arms around me. A warmth radiates from the kiss and reverberates through my body, heightening the growing throb between my legs. I grasp his shoulders and pull myself against him, the firm lines of his body pressing against me. His soft, warm lips fold against mine, and I sigh against him. I know nothing but that this is *exactly* where I'm supposed to be. We kiss furiously, our movements rushed. His tongue brushes against mine, and my pulse quickens. My mind spins and swarms all at once—I swear I'm drunk on lust. His hands shift, and I pull away to rip off my shirt. In seconds my bra is shed too. His thumbs graze my nipples, and I throb in response. There's hesitation in his movements, and I know what he's thinking, because his eyes mirror my thoughts—*Are we really doing this?*

To destroy any lingering doubts, I go in again for another kiss, pressing my body against him, skin against skin. He moans against my mouth as I start to undo my pants. I only get the top button undone before his warm hands are on mine, wanting to take over as his tongue slides down my neck. His hands tighten around me, and I swear if it weren't for his firm grip around the small of my back, I might just sink to the floor. Everywhere his hands touch, my skin blazes in response.

"You're gorgeous," he says into my ear before his mouth travels back down my neck toward my breasts as he slides my pants and underwear off.

Not wanting to be the only one naked, I push down his boxers, needing to feel his body against mine. His cock throbs between us, and I slowly stroke him. A low moan rolls from his lips. With his head tossed back, I run my tongue slowly across his neck.

"Oh fuck," he groans, his grip on me tightening.

I drop to my knees and tease the head of his cock. Noah inhales sharply, and his eyes intensify with pleasure. The control over him, the ability to coax a reaction out of him, excites me. I open my mouth, taking him in over and over again.

He moans so low it's almost a purr. I'm so tempted to finish him, but my body aches for him.

His fingers lace through my hair as he guides me. He pulls me up to face him and seals his lips desperately over mine. There's a frenzy to his movements, like he's afraid I'll change my mind. I curve my hand around the length of him again, coaxing and teasing. Noah scoops me up before tossing me playfully on the bed.

I lean back into the pillows as he crawls over me, his eyes wild with desire. I've never wanted anything so badly. I spread my legs, not sure how much longer I can wait.

His eyes flare as his head dips so his mouth can close around my breast, sucking on my nipple, sending a wave of pleasure through me. A sharp moan slips from my lips as my core aches for him. His finger rubs against my clit, and my back arches in response. I'm not sure how much longer I can take it. Tongue lashing against my nipple, his fingers slide into my wet slit, matching the rhythm of my rocking hips until I beg him to fuck me. My body moves on its own, responding automatically to his touch.

Noah traces kisses lower, across the sensitive skin of my stomach and further still until his tongue slides against me. His fingers push me toward the edge. I moan and bite my bottom lip as my hips buck into his hand. He intensifies the pressure as his tongue rolls again and again. Pleasure builds inside me. His lips brush against me one last time, finally throwing me over the edge. I cry out as I clutch the sheets, arching my back.

The tremors ease, and I pant as I recover from the orgasm. No guy I've been with has had skills like this. Now that I've had a taste of what Noah can do, I might be hooked. Noah sits between my spread legs and brushes his cock along my swollen lips. The way he teases me excites and infuriates me at the same time. Though I'm spent, my need for him jumps back to life. I don't just want him inside me; I *need* him inside me. He rolls the head across my slit again, and a wave of pleasure shoots through me like lightning. He pushes and enters me slowly. My body stretches to accommodate him, sending a delicious ache through me. A moan slips from my lips as he fills me to the hilt.

He thrusts inside. "Are you all right?"

"Was the moaning not enough confirmation that I'm all right?" I ask with a smirk.

The weight of Noah's body against mine fills me with warmth. My arms lace around his shoulders, pulling his muscular chest against mine. Though we're this close, somehow, I still want to be closer. Noah's rhythm is slow and building. Each time his breathing quickens, he slows, taking time to coax me closer to the edge again.

"We should have done this sooner," he murmurs into my ear. And he's right; we should have. Having Noah inside me fills a void I didn't even know I had. He pulls back, his thumb rubbing me as his rhythm increases. With Noah moving in me, his low moans drive me over the edge again. I push against Noah's chest as I pant, urging him onto his back. The waves crash over me again and again, filling my head with static.

Climbing on top, I slowly guide myself down onto him and ride him. His eyes flicker closed as I grind against him. Noah's hands wrap around my hips, and as he groans I know he's close. I quicken my strokes, bringing myself onto him over and over, until finally he moans my name. The pressure builds inside me as his hands grip my hips tight. His cock throbs inside me as he finds his own release, his eyes squeezed tight. His groans of pleasure throw me over the edge again. I smile with the knowledge that I've satisfied him as much as he's satisfied me.

I ease myself off him, knowing I'll feel it tomorrow. A delicious ache is already setting in, but I don't care. I collapse next to him, and we lie together, panting, the room thick with sex. He slides an arm around me, and I rest my head against his shoulder, waiting for my heart to slow.

"So was that on or off the record?" he asks with a wicked grin.

I smack his chest playfully.

"Mmm, harder," he teases.

"Don't tempt me," I say as I smile back at him, and I pinch his nipple.

"I'm not sure I can help myself, knowing you've got the cuffs and all."

I laugh. "I'll have to keep that in mind for next time."

He looks at his wrist, where a watch would be if he had one. "So in ten minutes, then?"

"Good luck with that." I chuckle. "I'll need at least a couple of hours of sleep before work."

"Are you going to sleep here?" he asks self-consciously, as though this could have been a wham-bam-thank-you fuck.

"Do you want me to?" It's been a long time since I've spent the night at a guy's place. But I remember well enough that there are plenty of them who don't want you to stick around.

"Of course I do," he says as he kisses me on the top of the head.

I offer him a sleepy smile, and I fall asleep in Noah's arms, feeling for the first time in a while like I'm home.

CHAPTER 20

Noah's fast asleep, and the steady rhythm of his breathing beside me almost coaxes me into staying. Waking up in his arms was surprisingly natural, like it's exactly where I should be. I force myself up and write Noah a quick note. I've got to get to the station, but I don't want him to think I freaked out about last night and took off.

As mind blowing as the sex with Noah was, there's a knot in my stomach. Something prickles at the back of my mind. It's not quite regret, but I need to think about last night.

I might be taking off before Noah wakes up because I've been second-guessing myself from the moment I opened my eyes. He feels right—this feels right—and that scares me shitless.

Just as I make it into my office, my phone rings. I've got folders and a cup of coffee in my hands, and it takes a minute to get it all on the desk.

"Calderwood."

"It's Matt, from the Augusta CSI office. I just got back the DNA of the blood that was found on your boat," he says, and papers rustle in the background.

My heart pounds. If it's from a new victim, it'll kill me.

"There was blood from Madeline Clark on the boat." He clears his throat. "However, we also found trace amounts of other blood that had been poorly cleaned."

The fact that the killer tried to clean up the blood tells me a lot about their mental state. It means they probably won't be able to plead insanity for this. Cleaning up after a murder shows the suspect was of sound enough mind to know what they were doing was wrong and to try to cover it up. The blood, though, that's what has me excited. Was it the blood of our perp? Did we actually get his DNA? My heart races as I consider it. If we have the perp's blood, if we can match it, this could be case closed.

"The blood was Emma Carver's."

My heart sinks. I'd hoped that we'd get something from the perp, too, something that would help me connect the dots.

"Thank you. Did you find anything else?"

"Actually, yes. We put all the DNA that we find into the database, just in case it ever matches any other evidence that's found, or for familial DNA matches. Whenever we add new DNA, it automatically runs against the Doe database. The body of a woman found in the bay in 2000 matched Emma Carver's DNA. It's not a sister, but based on what I see, I'd say they're cousins."

My jaw nearly drops, and anger floods through me. No one informed me that another girl was missing. In all the questioning I've done on the island, how did no one bring that up? Was she a runaway?

"Thank you," I say and rush him off the phone. I've got to talk to Sergeant Michaels about this.

I grab my coffee and cross the hall. He's standing up, typing, with a muffin clutched in his jaws. When he sees me, he grabs it and sets it on the desk. "Morning."

"Are there currently any open missing persons investigations at this station?"

He raises a brow at that. "No. If there was, the mayor would be so far up my ass about it that he could see out of my eyes."

"One of the guys from the CSI office just informed me that a Jane Doe in their database matched Emma's DNA. They think she's a cousin. The Doe was found in 2000."

He shakes his head. "If a Carver girl had gone missing back then, we'd have known about it. *Everyone* would have known about it."

"Did anyone move away around then?" I ask. It seems like a stretch. Wouldn't the family have noticed by now that they hadn't moved and were just missing?

"Chloe did, and so did Samantha. They were sisters. The daughters of Butch Carver. He had six girls and one boy."

Though I was too young to really know either of them well—they were about ten years older than me—I remember Chloe being trouble.

"Butch still lives on the island, right?"

He nods. "You gonna talk to him?"

"I sure as hell am," I say as I grab my keys.

Butch lives in Calderwood Neck, on the northernmost part of the island. He owns a blue farmhouse I've passed a thousand times but never been in. In second grade, I befriended one of the Carver girls, Georgia. But my mom put an end to that. The Lanes, the Warrens, and the Carvers were off limits to us, though she never told me why.

I approach the front door, and Butch pops his head around the side of the house. He's got a hammer in one hand and a piece of wood in the other. Butch Carver is a small guy, not built wide and tall like many of the other men on the island. His name doesn't suit him. He raises an eyebrow when he sees me. "Claire?"

I nod. "Good to see you, Butch."

"Here to talk to me about my niece?"

I shake my head as I approach. "No, sir. I was hoping I could talk to you about Chloe and Samantha."

He nods and walks over, waving for me to take a seat on one of the benches pushed up against the porch railing. "Why are you here about them?"

"When's the last time you spoke to both of them?"

"Samantha, about a week." He scratches his stubbled chin and stares off toward the tree line. "Chloe, though—it's been eighteen, almost nineteen years." His voice is as far off as his eyes.

"Why is that?"

"We had a big falling-out, and she decided she wanted to move to California. She went to stay with one of her friends, and she never spoke to me or her mother again after that."

"Weren't you concerned that something might have happened to her?"

"We were for a while. We spoke to Sheriff Dyer about it a couple of weeks after she left. We wanted to make sure she got there okay. She wouldn't return our calls, and she shut her cell off. He said since she was over eighteen, there was nothing we could do about it. But he reached out to the Los Angeles Police Department. They confirmed that she was fine but that she didn't want to talk to us anymore."

"What was the falling-out over, if you don't mind me asking?"

He shakes his head and looks down. "A boy."

"Who?"

"Zach Miller," he says. Zach is Mrs. Miller's son. He's a few years older than me; Rachel had a crush on him when she was in middle school and he was in high school.

"And she's never contacted you since?" I ask. Eighteen years is a long time to hold a grudge.

He shakes his head. "No." He furrows his brow and crosses his arms. "Why are you asking about Chloe?"

My heart is heavy as I consider how to continue. With everything I've learned, it's possible that the Jane Doe is Chloe. But I'll need his DNA to be sure. There's no way to ask for his DNA without alerting him. "I'm sorry to have to tell you this. There's a Jane Doe who was found in 2000." I give him a rundown of how they found the match and what it means to him.

For a long moment, he's stoic, silent. "If I give DNA, could they test it to see if it matches?"

I nod. "You or Chloe's mother. I can have someone from the CSI team reach out to get the test run for you."

He looks down and crosses his arms. "If she's been dead this whole time and we didn't know—no one knew—" Red rings his eyes. He's seconds from crying.

"There's nothing you could have done. My hope is that it's not Chloe, that she's safe in California like you were told." Because if she's not—what could that mean? Did Sheriff Dyer lie and never make the call? Could he have known what was really happening to these girls? Or worse—was he involved?

I head back to the station and call to arrange the DNA match for Butch. A few minutes later, right as I'm digging into an autopsy report about a Jane Doe, Noah knocks on my door.

"You know you don't have to knock," I say as I smile at him.

"Oh, come on, it's part of that southern charm you love so much," he says as he winks at me, handing over a cup of coffee.

"Thank you." I take the coffee. I have to admit I'm loving this daily ritual we have. "Can you shut the door?"

He nods and shuts it before sitting across from me. "What's up?"

"I'm going over the autopsy and the info that we gathered in Rockland about the Jane Doe that might be Chloe. It all seems pretty familiar: age estimated sixteen to nineteen, blonde, strangled, and"—I lower my voice—"a piece of flesh removed from her lower back."

Barbara mentioned the MOs being similar, but seeing it laid out like this, there's no denying that this fits the pattern perfectly.

"Jesus," he says and blows out a hot burst of air from his nose like a bull. He passes me a muffin.

I nod. Noah may have really been onto something about these bodies dropped in the bay.

"I found something for you." Noah slides a folded piece of paper across the desk to me.

"Oh, you shouldn't have," I joke as I grab it. As soon as I've got it in my hands, I open it up. Inside I find a rough, streaked photocopy of an article.

> Rash of Runaways Rocks Vinalhaven
> March 13, 1981
>
> The small town of Vinalhaven, Maine, has been suffering from an alarming pattern. In the past six months alone, four girls have run away, leaving their friends and families heartbroken.
>
> I've reached out to Sheriff Dyer for comment . . .

I look up at Noah, my eyebrows raised. "Where did you find this? How?"

"Well, it goes on to say the sheriff confirmed all the girls were fine. They're over eighteen and wanted to move. There's nothing anyone could do about it. You can't drag an adult back to the island. There were just so many that ran away or moved away during that time: Camille Norton, Bessie Smith, Delilah . . ." He trails off.

I scan the article again, looking for names. The Carvers, Thayers, Smiths, and Nortons all had girls leave. One of the names catches my eye, though: Dovey Thayer. She's one of my grandmother's nieces—I guess that'd make her my cousin, but I never knew her. My grandma never mentioned to me before that she'd moved or run away.

There's a missing piece, a connection I'm starting to feel. "I'm going to talk to my grandma. Maybe she can tell me something." Were some of these girls victims and not runaways?

He leans over the desk and gives me a feather-soft kiss on the cheek. "Text me if you need anything."

"Thank you. I will." The butterflies in my stomach when he's this close to me make me feel like I'm thirteen. He floods my senses. His woody smell, the brush of his stubble against my cheek, the heat of his breath—it all works together to make my head swim. "I'll try to be at the hotel by five."

He offers me a smile and grabs his coffee. "You better be, or I'll come get you," he says with a playful laugh.

When Noah leaves, I expect to hear the door shut, but instead a dark figure looms over me, and I find Mayor Clark glowering at me. Dark circles hang beneath his bloodshot eyes. His cheeks are sunken, his skin sallow and waxy. He looks like—well, he looks like his daughter died less than two weeks ago. It's clear from his greasy hair and thick stubble that he hasn't been taking care of himself, not that I blame him. I wouldn't be in any better of a state.

"How can I help you, Mayor Clark?"

He swings the door shut, and red creeps from his collar. On the left side of his neck one of his veins throbs insistently, making it difficult for me to maintain eye contact.

"You're supposed to be solving Madeline's murder, not schlepping around town with your mainlander boyfriend," he seethes, his fist clenching at his side.

It takes far too long for the words to register, because I'm convinced I didn't hear him properly. By the time I finally come to my senses with a reply, my heart is pounding, anger stabbing the back of my mind. My thoughts circle dangerously, like sharks. It's so tempting to hurl an insult before I think it through.

"Excuse me? What did you say?"

"You heard me," he snaps. "You've been all over town with that backwater reporter while you should be tracking down Madeline's killer."

I push all of the air trapped in my lungs out at once. Though anger builds inside me like a toxic cloud, I won't let it out. I know he's angry. He's hurting. It's not the first time a family member of a victim has yelled at me. I know better than to lash out. It will only make this worse.

"We're doing everything we can to find Madeline's killer. I've been here every day, sometimes twelve hours a day, trying to solve this. The other officers are working on it as well." I'd tell him about the other girls, that this might be a serial killer, that I was nearly killed in a fire, but we've all agreed to keep it under wraps. It will only cause panic, and that's the last thing we need.

He crosses his arms and sighs. "Do you have any suspects yet?"

"We have some people we're looking at," I say, because if I go as far as to say suspects, he's going to want the list. He's going to go after someone. I know what it's like to need answers. I know what it's like to want to fix it yourself, to do *something* because you're so helpless.

"Like who?"

"I'm sorry, but I'm not at liberty to say."

"Of course you're not," he growls and heads to the door. As he reaches for the knob, he turns back. "Solve this, or I will end you."

I know he means my career. He's closer to the truth than he realizes, though. If I don't solve this, it will likely kill me.

I trace a path up the long winding roads north, past my mom's house, past the quarries. The further north I drive, the more civilization disappears as nature claims the island. Finally, the trees thin as I reach the coast and cross the small, narrow bridge to Calderwood Neck. My grandmother's house, of course, is on Calderwood Point. She loves living out here. It's her badge of honor, even though she married into the Calderwood name.

Her grand Victorian overlooks the ocean. It's from her side of the family, the Thayers. Thayer Manor, she's called it jokingly. The original Calderwood home is about a block away, a twelve-room Victorian dressed in maroon and light blue. My grandma's changed the color since I last saw her house; the siding is the color of a faded daisy, with teal accents around the windows and a wraparound porch. Even after all these years, it's pristine.

I ring the doorbell and have to keep myself from pacing the porch. It's been over fifteen years since I saw her last. I didn't even think to tell her I was back in town. She and my mother had a falling-out after Rachel died. I don't know all the details, but I assume it had something to do with Rachel's death. After that, Grandma wasn't at Christmas or birthdays. I wasn't even able to talk about her; there was no more Grandma and no more Rachel. In one fell swoop I lost them both. I've never felt so alone in my life as I did then. My parents didn't seem to consider that I had lost Rachel and Grandma too. It wasn't my loss, just theirs.

She opens the door, and the sight of her takes my breath away. I expected her to be ancient, to be a brittle, frail old woman. But it doesn't look like she's aged a day. Her long blonde hair falls across her shoulders with a braided strand mixed into it. It's hard to see her big blue eyes behind her thick turquoise glasses, but I know they're there. The only thing different about her is that she's started penciling in her nonexistent eyebrows since the last time I saw her. They're darker and higher than they should be, making her look surprised. Or maybe she actually is surprised.

"Claire?" she breathes as she grabs me and pulls me into a hug. Her paisley dress billows around me, enveloping me. My grandmother, Bea, has always looked like she'd fit right in at Woodstock. She's too ethereal. She doesn't belong on an island like this. A free spirit tethered to this island is a tragedy. After my grandpa died, I figured she'd travel, explore, but she never did.

"Hey, Grandma," I mumble as she squeezes me. She's surrounded in a floral, powdery smell, a scent that brings me back to my childhood, back when I still had her and Rachel. My eyes tear up. God, I missed her. But I bite back the tears. I refuse to cry.

"What are you doing here? Your mother is going to kill you," she warns as she takes a step back, appraising me carefully.

I roll my eyes. "There's nothing she can do about it. I'm working here as the detective."

She waves me through the door. "Well, come on in. It's cold enough to catch your death out there." Once I'm inside, she offers me a warm smile and holds me by the shoulders. "I always knew you were going to do great things."

The air is thick with patchouli and something else, maybe vanilla. She's always had the house decorated with rich colors. She told me it was Moroccan while I was growing up. I sit on the gold crushed-velvet sofa in her living room. Mismatched gauzy curtains hang on every window, dyeing the light spilling in orange and blue.

"You want some tea or anything?" she offers.

"No, thank you. I was hoping I could talk to you about something, actually," I say, and my voice sounds much weaker than I mean for it to. This is one of those topics I never imagined I'd talk to my grandma about.

She perches on a burgundy chair across from me. "Oh?"

"What I'm going to say needs to stay between us," I say, and I wait for her to nod before I continue. "I'm sure you heard about the murder of the mayor's daughter and Emma Carver."

She nods and purses her lips. "Poor girls."

"Because of their deaths falling so close to the anniversary, we think it might be connected to Rachel. But there are pages missing from

Rachel's autopsy, and the police report is spotty at best." I swallow hard and try to gather my thoughts. "I can't ask my parents about this. They won't tell me the truth. So I was hoping you remembered something."

She shakes her head, and sadness paints her features. "You know, I think you might be the first Calderwood to try to help a Carver."

"Why is that?" I know my mom hates the Carvers, but she's never told me why. There are so many pieces of Vinalhaven history that are a mystery to me.

"It's a long story."

"A story I think I need to hear," I urge.

She nods. "I suppose you're right. Not long after the island was founded, your great-great-great-great-aunt married Abner Warren. They had a very contentious marriage. The families had been happy about the marriage, though, because it helped their two fishing companies merge, and they no longer had to compete. Abner started spending less and less time at home and more time on a boat. Your aunt got fed up with it and started seeing William Carver. She got pregnant while Abner was away, and shortly after he returned, she was found dead—drowned at the bottom of one of the Calderwood quarries. A week later, they found William in the same place."

"Jesus." This town has more secrets than I expected.

"After they both died, the families all split. The Warrens, the Carvers, and the Calderwoods were never on good terms again after that. There was a lot of finger-pointing."

"Mom's not a Calderwood, though. Why would she care about the history of it?"

"She and the other Millers always sided with the Calderwoods. So they've always had the same enemies." She sighs and leans back in her chair. "Usually an awful thing like this will bring a community together. But no one wanted to bury the hatchet. Maybe with you on it, though, you can fix this. You can set some of these awful things right."

"I wish I could help more," I say.

"None of these girls deserved what happened to them. I couldn't get any information from the sheriff when Rachel died. Maybe your mom and dad had an easier time. But they wouldn't tell me anything." Her face grows pale, and she looks at the floor. "I had a good friend who worked for the medical examiner's office. When your mom found out I was looking into Rachel's death, she disowned me, and your father went right along with it." Pain swims in her eyes. My mom robbed her of her family, and for what? "She wanted nothing to do with me anymore. I was just trying to find out who did this. Your mom wanted me to leave it alone. It's partly my fault. When we got into a fight about it, I asked her if she even wanted this to be solved."

Why would my mom not want this solved? How could she really disown my grandmother over trying to solve Rachel's death? All she wanted were answers.

There are other questions I have to ask, questions about her niece. "Whatever happened to Dovey?"

Her eyes go wide, like that's the very last thing she expected me to ask about. "Why?"

"I saw an article today mentioning that she was a runaway."

She nods and looks toward the windows. "Dovey never liked the island. She hated it, even. When she was little, sometimes it felt like as soon as she started talking, she was saying that she wanted to leave. At sixteen, she told me and your grandfather that she was gay. It was a shock, to say the least. But I accepted it. Some of the other family members, though . . ." She shakes her head. "Some didn't understand. Every time I turned around, someone was giving her hell about it. As soon as she was eighteen, she took off."

I can't believe she never told me about any of this. "When's the last time you spoke with her?"

"About two weeks ago."

"She's not missing, then?"

"Missing? Of course not. She just doesn't want anything to do with this island. That's why you've never met her. And it doesn't help that your mother froze her out as soon as she left." She reaches over and squeezes my hand. "You know as well as anyone how complicated families can be."

With the Jane Does we've seen so far, this is shaping up into a pattern that spans decades, generations. I need to find out which girls really did make it off this island and which ones didn't. If it wasn't Dovey, it could have been someone else. "The station doesn't have any of the records of runaways from the eighties or nineties. Is there anything you remember from back then, a murder, anything?"

She shakes her head. "I don't know of a murder ever on the island before Rachel. In the late eighties, though, a girl disappeared. One of the Vernon girls."

"She disappeared?" I wish that had been suspicious enough for it to be investigated. But there's a long history of teens running away from this island. The last name sparks my memory. But I can't remember where I've heard it before.

"Everyone assumed she ran away," she explains, but the look on her face tells me she doesn't believe that.

"But you don't think so?"

She tilts her head and looks at the coffee table between us. "She's not someone I'd ever think would leave. She wasn't the first, though. Girls have gone missing before, and it's always been assumed they ran off," she says. "Sometimes we knew it was true; we'd hear things about them from time to time, they'd talk to family members, someone would go visit them, those sorts of things. Other times we never heard about them again—that's when it would make me wonder."

I grind my teeth together and clench my fists. In the old days, everyone assumed women from around the country were just running away. In reality, some of them were picked off by serial killers. Back then, apparently no one could fathom that anyone would murder all these women—or maybe no one cared. It boggles my mind now. Sometimes I wonder how anyone survived.

"How many girls do you know of that went missing?"

"Two. The other girl, that had to be in the eighties sometime," she says, her face tight, words strained. "Before that, I didn't pay much attention to it. In the seventies things were much different. People came and went a lot more. Some went to war; some moved out west."

If these girls who ran away weren't actually *runaways*, that would change things significantly. This killer had to get a start somewhere. Was one of those girls it? Did their bodies end up somewhere else? Did someone make sure no one found out the truth? "These weren't investigated at all?"

She shakes her head. "No—well, not really. The sheriff looked into it, but he never found anything other than signs pointing to the girls leaving." The details about Sheriff Dyer are all starting to click into place for me. He knew about the runaways, but the old ME, Barbara, also told him about the bodies of the Jane Does. He supposedly went to view the bodies but couldn't identify them. He lied to Butch Carver when he told him that Chloe made it to California safe, that she was fine. Something tells me that Sheriff Dyer knew what was going on but didn't want any of this linking back to Vinalhaven.

Something in her eyes tells me that she might have a history with the sheriff. "What do you know about Sheriff Dyer?" I ask.

"Jeb and I dated before I married your grandpa. He was older than me. I was a stupid girl," she says and then clicks her tongue. "He was sheriff, and his brother, Edmond, was the mayor."

I cross my arms and shift on the couch. She's never talked to me about this kind of stuff. "What happened?"

"He wasn't someone you could trust, and that's all I'm going to say," she says.

There's more to this story. I'm going to look into Edmond and Jebediah and see what I can find about them. Something tells me they might know where these girls really went. I know that Sheriff Dyer passed away, but I don't know about his brother. "Is Edmond still alive?"

She shakes her head. "No. Edmond had a heart attack and died a few years back after he left the island for good."

I purse my lips to keep my frustration from showing. Of course two of the three people who would really help me with this are dead.

My phone vibrates, and Jason's name flashes on the screen. I was hoping to hear from Noah to help break up the day.

"Hey, Jason."

"Hey, I need you to meet me at Lane Park."

Lane Park is a small park on Lane Island. It's a tiny island linked by a small bridge close to downtown. I sigh and hold up a hand to my grandma to excuse myself. "I'm in Calderwood Neck. What's up?"

"Jenna Arey called in a body. She and Cashton Carver were over there cutting class," he says with an edge to his voice.

"I'll be there as soon as possible," I say before hanging up the phone. "Grandma, I've got to go. Thank you for your help. I really wish I could stay," I say as I stand up and give her a quick kiss on the cheek and a hug.

"Don't be a stranger." She glides beside me to the door.

"I won't. I promise."

On my way to the car, I text Noah, See if you can find any info on Edmond and Jebediah Dyer. I'll update you later.

He texts back as I start the car. On it. See you tonight.

After texting a thank-you back, I make my way past the houses my family has occupied for the last seven or so generations and head to Lane Park.

I speed down the back roads toward Lane Island. Luckily, this time of day, there's no one on the road, so I don't have to worry about running into anyone. The park is toward the tip of the small island, close to the coast. It's about half a mile from the high school, so kids end up skipping here if they don't want to spend their afternoon in the cemetery. There are such *thrilling* options for teens in this town.

Like most of the rest of the island, the park is ringed with pine trees. There's a path that snakes through them in the back, a walking trail that sprinkles facts about the local wildlife on plaques. Along the right side, there's a huge wooden play area that looks like a castle. It's so old I'm pretty sure four generations have gotten splinters here. The wood is worn, cracked, like it might be made of the hulls of old ships.

"Where is she?" I mumble to myself as I walk toward the tree line.

Jason pulls up behind me and jogs up. He leads me to the body, which was dumped behind the stone structure housing the bathrooms that's set back in the woods a bit. From where we are, the hiss of the ocean cuts through the trees. Birds perch on the tree branches around us, chirping and fluttering. If it weren't for the body lying in front of us, it'd be beautiful.

"He's brought this one by boat too." I glance toward the tree line. There's a clear path cut through the trees from the beach; branches are broken, the underbrush disturbed. She wasn't dragged here, though. Our perp is careful with these girls after he kills them. There isn't so much as a leaf in this girl's blonde hair.

"Do you know her?" I ask him as we start roping off the scene.

"Piper Curtis," Jason says, wrapping crime scene tape around a tree.

I've heard the name. But Piper was so young when I was last here—she must have been one. She's laid down like the others, her long blonde braid draped over her shoulder. But this time, the killer didn't bother to clean up the wound on her arm. There's a strip of flesh cut from her wrist, and there's red smeared nearly to her elbow.

Jason photographs the body as I call in the ME and CSI teams. By the time I've got the scene roped off, we have several people lingering to see what's going on. I get statements from the two teens who found the body, neither of whom saw anything helpful. About an hour later, the CSI and ME teams arrive.

As I'm chatting with the CSI team, Jason waves me over. "Are we all set here? I've got to head home; the husband is sick."

"Of course, yes. Go. Tell him I hope he feels better."

He says thanks and starts to jog off but stops near the tree line. "Oh, Claire? Can you check out the tip line when you get back to the station? It rang a few times today, but none of us had a minute to grab it."

I nod. "Sure thing." I know what it's like to be so buried you barely have time to think about the tip line.

Once everything is wrapped up at the scene and the ME team has taken the body back to Augusta, I head back to the station, but I've got to talk to Sergeant Michaels before I check the tip line for Jason.

I knock at the edge of Sergeant Michaels's door. He's hunched over his desk, dark circles beneath his eyes. He glances up at me, and I swear it's like someone let all the air out of him. He looks defeated.

"I can't believe it," he says as he shakes his head. Like maybe this whole murder thing was going to blow over, and everything would go back to the way it was. There's no going back now.

"I need to talk to you about it for a minute," I say as I close his door and sit in the empty chair.

He steeples his fingers and rests his chin on them.

There's something I've been thinking about for a couple of days. We're not getting anywhere. The case is taking a turn, the kind of turn where the killer escalates. I can't stand the idea of more girls dying because I can't figure it out.

"I think we might be in over our heads here," I say, and I'm putting it mildly. I'm in so far over my head here that I'm drowning. "I think it's time we consider calling in the FBI."

He furrows his brow. "If we call them in on this, they're going to take the investigation from us. They don't know anything about this town, our people. It's hard enough to get things done as it is. No one is going to want to talk to the FBI."

"And what if we don't and more girls die?" Though I try to hold steady, frustration reaches my words.

"We're going to figure this out before anyone else gets hurt." I'm not sure if he's trying to convince me or himself.

"We need to at least do *something*, then. The patrols aren't helping, obviously." All they did was make him dump a body somewhere else, just as I suspected they would. "We need to institute a curfew for anyone under eighteen. They can't be out after dark anymore."

He nods. "That's a good idea."

"I think it's time we reach out to the media too. We need to get the attention of some of these parents. They need to realize how serious this is. If these kids are out of bed, they're at risk. They need to stay home."

"I'll make a statement about it to the media and see if it does any good. But, Claire, if these kids want to sneak out, that's what they're going to do," he warns. "They think it won't happen to them."

I wish he weren't right, but he is. But we can't just sit back and do nothing while these girls die.

After I finish up with Sergeant Michaels, I pull out my notebook and call the local dentist, Dr. Webster. While Sergeant Michaels and Vince notify the next of kin, I'm able to talk Dr. Webster into sending over the last dental records of the Vernon girls to the ME's office so I can match those against the Jane Does. Once I've got that scratched off my list, I dig into the tip line. Three calls in, and I'm getting nowhere. After two calls tattling on neighbors for nothing at all illegal, the next call is from a woman who's concerned someone downtown is *acting suspicious*. I delete them before the next message plays. For a moment, the line cracks, like tree branches being splintered. Far away, something rustles and groans. I straighten in my chair, and my heart pounds. Everything sounds so far off that it may as well be underwater. Excitement and fear mix inside me, making my stomach jump. I look at the screen. It's the fourth voice mail, one much longer than the others. The call came in at three a.m.

"I need to report . . ." a gravelly voice, splintered by static, cuts through on the other end of the line. "A body, in the—" The voice cuts out as a low moan echoes in the background. My heart pounds as I try to make out the sounds through the static on the line. "There's a body in the bay," he says, his voice finally coming through again. He groans, and something in the background grinds so loudly I pull the phone away from my ear. "In a crab crate." There's a final grunt and a splash.

My stomach clenches, and adrenaline pours into my blood. Is that the killer?

CHAPTER 21

My hands tremble as I dart across the hall to Sergeant Michaels's office. Though I take a deep breath to steady myself, it does absolutely nothing to calm the sense of dread rising inside me like the tide. In the few steps to his office, my mind speeds at a million miles an hour. He's taunting us. He wants us to know he's doing it. He wants to be chased.

"We need to call the coast guard," I say, and I'm amazed at how steady my voice comes out.

"What?" he asks, his eyes wide.

It takes me a minute to explain, to try and bundle up the information rolling around in my mind into a concise little package. I want him to listen to it, to tell me I'm wrong. I'd much rather there be any other explanation than this one. As Sergeant Michaels listens to the call, his face changes. His frown lines deepen; his eyes darken. It's clear he isn't coming to a different conclusion. Someone was killed on that call.

"I'm going to call the coast guard now. Do you know how to drive a boat?" he asks.

I cut him slack for talking to me like a mainlander. Here, you learn to drive a boat well before a car. "I do."

"Take the boat out, see if you find anything, and wait for the coast guard."

I nod. "Yes, sir." Though it's likely he cut the float for the trap—the big orange ball that floats on top of the water so the fishermen can find the trap. Then again, if he really wanted us to find it, he'd leave it. There are hundreds of traps in the bay; checking them will take all day.

"I'll text you when I hear from the coast guard. I'll have them bring in a dive team."

I nod, grab the keys to the Vinalhaven PD boat, and head toward the marina. As I make my way down Main Street, I pass Frank, and he offers me a little wave.

"Everything all right, Claire?" he asks.

I nod. "Yep, everything is just fine," I say, because I can't tell him the truth. I can't let anyone know there's a girl in the water just off the island right now. I continue toward the marina, Frank's eyes following me as I rush. Though I try to keep my face stoic and the rising panic inside me, I'm not sure I succeed.

My stomach is in knots when my feet echo against the worn wood of the dock. Water sloshes against the posts beneath me. I hop into the small police boat and steer it away from the dock. Cold mist stings my cheeks as I force the throttle forward. There's no way of knowing where the body was dropped. For now, I'll have to log every buoy that marks a crate location. That's the best way I can expedite this for the coast guard.

After circling the island for over an hour, I've marked the location of every floating red ball I can find. Beneath the waves, maybe a hundred feet down, she waits for us to find her. I hope we can find her today. Water will slowly strip away any remaining forensic evidence. The faster we get the body out, the better our chances are of finding something.

It takes hours for the team to arrive from Augusta, and around sunset, the dive team hauls the crate we've been looking for from the water. A woman is crumpled inside, in the fetal position. Her skin is pale, the color of a pearl. A dark-purple line blooms across her milky-white throat, making it obvious she was strangled, but there's no flesh cut from any visible area of her body. The girl is young, blonde, just like the others, just like the last one found in the water. She can't be older than sixteen, and I can tell from the reactions of the guys that she's not from the island. Before now, it seemed to me that these had to be different killers—no matter how I tried, I couldn't piece together the different MOs into a scenario where I felt confident it was the same killer. But now I'm questioning myself. Maybe he's chosen two different MOs just to throw us off, to keep us from connecting the dots.

All along, this killer has been saying to us, *Look at me; look what I can do right beneath your nose.* But this—calling us, telling us where the victim is—this screams to me that he's escalating, that he's reached what some of us call berserker mode. While this killer may have had a pattern that he stuck to in the past, something has changed that; something has shifted it. Either he's panicking because he knows we're getting close, or there's another big change in his life. A divorce, a separation, a job loss—something that made him deviate.

The pattern is alarming, and the rate at which this is accelerating puts serious pressure on me. If we don't solve this fast, I can't even imagine how many girls will die.

CHAPTER 22

The silence of my office is shattered by my phone vibrating on my desk. It's such a surprise I nearly jump out of my chair. I rub my eyes and stretch my neck. I've been hunched over a call log—trying to trace calls that came into the station today—so long my spine feels like it's fused into the shape of a question mark.

"Hey," I say as soon as the call connects. My voice is rougher, deeper than usual.

"You busy?" Noah asks. His voice is warm and as smooth as hot cocoa.

"Always."

He chuckles. "I shouldn't have even asked. I need to talk to you about the research you asked me to do on the old sheriff."

"What'd you find?"

"Have you eaten?" he asks. "I can bring you some dinner while we go over this."

"Not since lunch," I admit. I probably should have eaten a few hours ago, but I haven't been able to tear myself away.

"You in the mood for anything?"

"Surprise me."

While I wait for Noah to get to the station, I stand and stretch my legs. I head to the small break room to grab a fresh cup of coffee and realize for the first time how dark it's gotten outside.

"Shit, how is it already eight?" I mumble while I pour the coffee.

When the gravel crunches outside, I hop up and meet Noah at the door. He's got a few bags in his hands, all from the Haven.

"Did you buy one of everything?" I eye the bags.

"You didn't know what you wanted, and I couldn't decide, either, so I got a *few* things."

I give him a kiss and relieve him of a bag. "You're the best, you know that?"

"I try."

We head into my office and set up all the bags on top of my desk. Inside, I find a few orders of french fries, a couple of sandwiches, a burger, a wrap, and a salad. My stomach churns with hunger as the scent of the food fills the room.

"So?" I sit down and unwrap a turkey club sandwich.

He pulls his laptop out of his bag. Just as I pop a french fry in my mouth, he scoots closer so he can show me his screen. Sitting this close to him kicks my heart up a notch and threatens to drag my thoughts away from the case.

"So I found some records about the Dyer brothers."

"Go on."

"They both left the island in 2005, about four months after Rachel died. Mayor Dyer had a heart attack not long after and died. Sheriff Jeb Dyer went to work for a police department in Massachusetts." He clears his throat before continuing. "Jeb was only at the police station six months before he was fired."

I gape at him. In my time at the Detroit Police Department, I only heard of one officer getting fired. It took years and several suspensions. Being a cop is filled with red tape, for better or for worse.

Sometimes that red tape keeps departments from getting rid of assholes that shouldn't be cops. "For what?"

"Destroying evidence."

My eyes go wide at that. Destroying evidence is serious. "So he's likely the guy who took those pages out of Rachel's file, then."

"But why would he do that? Unless he's trying to cover up his involvement or maybe to cover for someone else," Noah says as if reading my mind.

Could he really have killed Rachel? He couldn't have killed Madeline, Emma, or any of the other recent victims; he's long dead. "It doesn't make any sense. What evidence did he destroy at the station in Mass?" Even though it's unlikely I'll be able to get anyone to breathe a word of it, as those things are confidential, I've got to start digging. "I'm going to find out why he was fired," I say as I pop another french fry in my mouth.

"If there's anyone who can, it's you." The way he looks at me lends me confidence—and also makes me want to rip his clothes off. But I don't have time for that.

I put in a call to the Salem Police Department. I'm passed around the station for twenty minutes until I finally reach a man with a low, rocky voice.

"Banks," he says when he answers. Even though I've only heard his voice, I can imagine him clearly by the misery in his tone. He must be a jowly, middle-aged man counting down the days until his pension kicks in. He probably hasn't worked the streets since the nineties. I've worked with men just like him.

I introduce myself and wait to see if there's a change in his tone so I can get a read on whether he's going to be helpful.

He clears his throat, and I imagine him straightening up in his seat. "What can I do you for, Calderwood?" His voice drops an octave and comes in clearer, like he's repositioned the phone.

"I'm looking for information on an officer who was fired from your station in 2005, Jeb Dyer," I say and hold my breath. If I still believed in God, I'd say a silent prayer. The long pause makes tension gather beneath my skin. In the background, the commotion of the station cuts into the line. There's a baby crying and two people arguing, but I can't make out enough words to figure out what it's over. He must be stuffed onto the floor, at a desk in the back, forgotten.

"You know I can—" he starts, but I interrupt him.

A thought has flickered from the back of my mind. I know someone who works in his station. Maybe it'll help me grease these gears a little. "You're in Salem, right? That must mean you work with Adam Gomez. He and I go way back." Gomez worked with me in Detroit before transferring a year ago. "Look, I don't need this for a case. It's completely off the record." The silence on the other end of the line is deafening. I'm not sure if he's hung up on me or if he's weighing his options. The background noise quiets, like he's muffled the receiver.

"You know Gomez?" he asks and pauses. "You didn't get this info from me, got it?" His voice is low, and I swear he's talking closer to the receiver now.

"Of course. We never even spoke."

"Someone caught him destroying files in disappearance cases," he says, and as soon as the words are out of his mouth, the line goes dead.

Disappearances here, disappearances there—what the hell did Sheriff Dyer get himself into?

CHAPTER 23

Gray morning light filters through the dingy striped hotel curtains. A glance at the clock warns me I needed to be out of bed fifteen minutes ago. It's not that I need to be in the office at a set time. It's that I need to get to the docks. A company name is etched on the side of every crab trap, and that's the best lead I have to go on right now. If someone saw who took it, maybe then I could make some headway in this. There's a good chance a fisherman might have seen something; they come and go at all hours.

I slide out of bed, and Noah groans while reaching for me. "Where are you going?"

"I've got to get to the docks. Interviews." I lean over and kiss him on the forehead. "Sleep. I'll see you later."

"Eh, I might as well get up. I've got to write an article on the situation in the Middle East." His voice falls, and he grimaces. He's clearly not looking forward to it. "I hate writing these. Half the time the situation changes before I'm even done writing the article, and then I've got to start over."

"I'm not sure if I'd rather investigate a murder or have to write that article," I say as I pull my clothes on.

"I'll see you tonight."

After I change, I head downtown. A thick fog rolls off the bay; it spreads slowly, like blood. There are only a few people on the streets: an older woman walking a small poodle that must be freezing in this weather and a man shuffling quickly toward the café. When I get down to the docks, I see a flurry of activity as people scramble on and off the boats.

"Where's the captain?" I ask a man in a thick leather coat as he stacks cages, a nub of a cigarette trapped between his chapped lips. He scratches his long gray beard and points down the docks. I nod my thanks and head in that direction.

My feet thud against the dock as I approach the captain. While everyone else is built wide, thick, this man is slender. If the boat shifted too hard in stormy seas, he'd be knocked overboard in an instant. He's like a palm tree growing in the middle of a forest of oaks.

"Captain?" I ask.

He nods as he turns to look at me. "Ah, the new detective," he says with a grin as he rubs his chin.

"I need to ask you a few questions, if you have a minute." I pull out my notebook.

He cocks his head before asking, "I don't need a lawyer, do I?"

I shake my head. "No, not at all. I have a few questions about your operation, your employees. I'm looking for some connections to evidence I found."

He nods. "Sure, let's step over here." He waves me away from the boat, toward Miller Ship Repair, the small shop Frank's got set up near the docks. Frank looks at us, wide eyed, when the door jingles. He doesn't get much foot traffic in here since he goes out to the docks to see the boats.

"We need to talk for a few minutes, if that's all right," the captain says to Frank.

"Of course. I'll be in the back if you need me," Frank says as he ambles out of the room.

"So what do you want to know?" the captain asks as he leans against the door. "I'm Adrian Hopkins, by the way." He holds his hand out. His skin is rough and calloused beneath my hand. Adrian has about a foot on me. He doesn't look like a fisherman. While the typical man at the docks is grizzly and a bit feral looking, Adrian is clean shaven and kempt.

"Good to meet you," I say as I pull out my notebook. "Have you had anything go missing from your boats recently?"

He crosses his arms and laughs. "There's always something going missing on my damn boats."

"Can you be more specific about what usually goes missing?" I ask as my eyebrow rises.

"Rope, tools, crab, lobster." He chuckles again. "That specific enough?"

"You have any traps go missing recently?"

"At least one a week," he says as he shrugs as if it's no big deal. I'm sure they're not expensive, but it's not like they're free. "It's the nature of the business. Some never come up when the traps are set."

"Have you seen anyone taking them? Or seen anyone suspicious around the boats?"

He shakes his head and shifts weight from one foot to the other. "I've heard from the guys once that they caught someone, but he ran onto a boat. They haven't seen him again after that."

"Is there anyone in particular you think might be taking the items?"

"For a while, I thought maybe it was Carver Fishing, but when I talked to Tom Carver about it, he'd had a few stolen too."

"Are there any employees you've both let go who might steal things to get back at both of you?"

He uncrosses his arms and walks across the room to peek out the window. "Most of the guys on the boats, they've got a criminal record. I don't have much of a choice. There aren't a whole lot of people who want to work on a boat anymore. So we work with whoever seems willing—but also remorseful for their past," he explains. "They're not bad guys, really."

It's not that surprising; I know about the history between fishing and criminal activity. At the very least I've got to ask if there could be any leads from this.

"Do you keep records of what each of the guys did before getting here?" I ask.

"I don't. I mostly have a 'Don't ask, don't tell' policy. I'd rather not know, you know? As long as they do the job and don't cause any problems, what business is it of mine?"

I know he's got a business to run, but that doesn't excuse it. The thought that there are criminals on these boats has always been in the back of my mind, but I hoped none of the guys were violent. Who knows at this point.

"One of the guys, though, I doubt he's going to stay for long. He's gotten locked up for beating his girlfriend a few times now," he explains and turns around to face me. "You're looking for who killed Madeline—that's what this is about, right?"

I nod. "Yes, it is." I glance over toward the boat, my eyes skimming the crew. "Who's the guy that assaulted his girlfriend? Do you think he could have done something to Madeline?"

"I don't think he'd do anything like that." He crosses his arms and takes a step closer. When he speaks again, his voice is much lower. "I saw Madeline talk to him a few times, though. She came down to talk to the guys a lot more often than she should have, but you didn't hear that from me. I called in a tip to your station about it."

It's not the first time I've heard about her trips to the docks; it's the first I've heard of his tip, though.

Vince didn't have any luck with his questioning, so I decide to ask, "What was she talking to them about?" Though I suppose the answer is Adderall, she could have also been looking for another boat to spend time on.

"She was flirting with them, like she was trying to find herself a boyfriend down here. The guys would talk to her—she's a pretty girl, after all—but everyone knew who she was. They knew how young."

"Can you point out the guy she interacted with the most?"

"Of course," he says. He motions toward a guy with shaggy brown hair and a coat that's so big on him I think he might have taken it from someone else.

"That's the guy who assaulted his girlfriend as well?" I confirm.

He nods and shifts away from me, like he can't wait to be rid of me.

I open the door, and he follows me back to the docks. "If you see anything else." I hand him my card.

"You'll be the first to know. Feel free to talk to the guys; maybe they can help you out. They see things that I don't."

"Thanks—I'll do that," I call back.

The docks creak beneath my feet, the boats are swimming with fishermen, and the gulls are circling above us, begging for scraps like winged hound dogs. This is a futile exercise, just like when I sent Vince out here. None of them are going to talk. If they've ever been to jail, they know the danger of blabbing. Then again, if I can't get a word out of them, I can always see if Noah has better luck.

I imagine myself at fifteen again, caution thrown to the wind, walking down these docks with my best friend at my side. When you're naive, these men are dangerously alluring. They're the key to an outside world that you can't touch otherwise. When you're looking through the lens of a homicide detective, they might as well be wrapped in warning signs.

"Excuse me," I call as I approach the first boat.

"Hey, sugar," a man calls in a singsong voice. He has shaggy brown hair and eyes so dark I'd swear they were black. Luckily, this is the guy the captain said I should talk to, the guy who thinks his girlfriend is a punching bag.

If I didn't need answers, I'd kick this asshat into the bay. I almost wish my jacket weren't covering my rig; that usually intimidates this type.

"I've got a few questions, if you have a minute."

"Shit, she's a cop," one of the guys mumbles under his breath.

"Hottest cop I've ever seen," the first guy says as he flashes his teeth at me. "You got cuffs?" He drags his tongue across his yellow teeth. "I *love* cuffs."

I sneer as I bite back the comment waiting on my tongue. It's as sharp as a barb.

When I don't respond to the cuffs comment, he takes a step toward me and crosses his arms. "What questions have you got, sugar?"

"Have you seen this girl recently?" I ask, pulling up a picture of Madeline on my phone.

He grins a little too wide for my liking. "She, uh, she came down here a lot." It's clear on his face that he's not lying. Chances are she wasn't just coming to the docks; she was coming here to see him.

"What was she coming here for?"

The other guys back off, thankfully. I'll take one person willing to give me info over the others.

He shrugs and looks back toward the bay. "The usual—vodka, cigarettes. She asked about Adderall a few times. But, of course, I don't give those kinds of things to underage girls. And I don't dabble in pharmaceuticals."

"Of course not," I say, not believing a word of it.

"There was something different, though. She asked if I could get her and a boy off the island without anyone knowing." He shakes his head and looks me dead in the eyes. "No one out here is going to be willing to commandeer their boss's boat to ferry kids off the island, especially not me. I've got kids of my own."

His voice is serious, firm. Every hint of the smile he had earlier is gone.

"Was there anyone around here you can think of who she might have asked, or who would have agreed to that arrangement?" I'd imagine most of the guys wouldn't be interested in helping a couple of sixteen-year-olds get off the island. That's more likely to get them locked up than weed.

He crosses his arms. "I've got no doubt she asked others. She was a determined, fiery thing. But no one would have taken her. That's a whole world of trouble none of us want. Some of us might have gotten in trouble before, but we don't mess with kids. We don't put them in danger. And we sure as hell wouldn't take them off the island."

I nod. "If you think of anything else, give me a call," I say as I slip him my card.

"Is that the only reason I can call?" he asks, his smirk returning.

"I'm not on the market, if that's what you're getting at," I say as I start to walk away.

"Sounds temporary to me," he calls back.

CHAPTER 24

The next day, a cold snap has gripped the island. I step outside my rental with my coat bundled around me, but it's so frigid that winter rips the breath from my lungs. My car offers little reprieve against it; though I turn the heat on, it doesn't do much more than circulate the cold air around. I back out of the driveway and steer toward the church. A few of the victims have come from outside of the church, but a majority have had some connection. I need to determine why this killer is so interested in the church and if Father Samuel has any new information for me. The streets of the city are nearly empty, thanks to the Thanksgiving holiday but I know Father Samuel will be here. I pull in to the church parking lot and walk toward the building.

Outside a hard freeze has seized the island, and I can almost imagine the cold grip of winter squeezing the town. Though I've got on one of my thickest jackets, it does little to shield me from the wind. Icicles nearly three feet long hang from the roofline of the church, and I try to keep a healthy distance from them. When I step through the double doors, it's only slightly warmer inside than it was out.

What seem like a thousand white candles flicker on the altar, casting a shifting light on the wall behind them. Father Samuel stands in front, backlit as if shrouded. He turns slowly when the door snaps shut behind me and takes a few steps from the altar. As he grows closer, it's as if a dark shroud is being lifted.

"Claire, it's so good to see you," he says with a warm smile.

"Could I steal a few minutes of your time, Father?" I ask as I reach him in the middle of the room.

He leads me to the front pew and motions at it. "Will this do, or would you rather speak in my office?"

"For now, this will work," I say. It doesn't seem like anyone else is coming in. If they do, then I'll suggest that we move.

"What can I help you with today?"

"I'm here because of the investigation. I'm deeply concerned about the continued safety of the girls that are members of this church," I say.

"I am as concerned as you are," he says gravely, his brown eyes shadowed with worry.

"Since our last conversation, I wanted to see if you have noticed anything here at the church that has troubled you."

He shakes his head. "No, though I did want to tell you that your mother has decided to step away from the choir group. She's no longer participating; Mrs. Miller has stepped in instead."

It's likely for the best that my mother stepped aside. Father Samuel smiles at me, deepening the lines on either side of his mouth. Though he doesn't look his age, with the lighting I suddenly notice the spiderweb of lines around his eyes. It occurs to me that he's been on the island as long as I can remember, and he may have some information on Sheriff Dyer that could help me.

"Did Edmond or Jeb Dyer attend church here?" I ask. I don't remember if they were ever at a service I attended; it was far too long ago.

He nods. "Yes, and their children—until their parents passed on, that is. Frank hasn't been since his father died."

"Frank is Edmond's son?" I ask, confused. I don't remember who Frank's parents were. He's in his early sixties, I'd guess. I'm not sure I ever saw him with any family.

"No, Frank is Jeb's son. The last names get confusing. When he was eighteen, he wanted his mother's surname. I suppose he had a falling-out with his dad. That poor family had a wealth of issues. I wish I had been able to help with some of them."

"When would you say Frank stopped attending?"

For a moment he's silent as he thinks. "I'm not sure. It's been at least ten years."

I nod. "And the other kids?"

"Edmond's daughter moved off the island about thirty years ago. And Jeb's daughter, Delilah, left in the seventies, though I can't really remember when it was exactly."

Did they really leave the island? With things as muddled as they are here, I can't help but wonder how many young women actually managed to escape this place. "Thank you for your help, Father. And happy Thanksgiving."

He holds up a hand to stop me as I start to stand. "There is something that I just remembered. It may be nothing, but a few nights I've seen a man hanging out behind the church. Each time I startle him and scare him off. But I haven't been able to tell who it was."

My stomach shifts with the knowledge. That could be our guy. I'll have Vince keep an eye on the rear of the church during patrols.

"Thank you. Until we figure out who that is, please don't let anyone use that exit."

I walk back through the church clutching my cell phone. I need to call Sergeant Michaels and tell him what I know. I push open the doors of the church and escape outside. The wind is frigid. What was a blue sky when I came in here has been swallowed by a blanket of gray. Tiny flakes of snow have just begun to fall from the clouds. The sun has been blotted out by the thick cloud cover darkening the sky toward the heart of the island. I find Sergeant Michaels's contact info and call him as I duck inside my car.

CHAPTER 25

No part of me wants to go back to the Lanes', but Margo might have met Sheriff Dyer while she was working at the hospital. I need to unravel the threads of the Dyers and figure out where they're leading me. She might not even talk to me again, but I have to try.

Low gray clouds have settled over the island, and small white flakes fall, twirled by the wind. An eerie silence always settles over us when it snows, and today is no exception. It's so quiet my blood whooshes in my ears as I walk up the path, and every crunch of acorns beneath my feet sets my teeth on edge.

Deep in the bowels of the house, I hear something shatter, and a man spits a curse. I stand outside the door, waiting to see if I can hear anything else. When no other sounds follow, I assume it was an accident. The stairs creak: someone climbing them slowly. Once the sound fades, I knock.

There's a window to the right of the door. Margo sweeps the curtains out of the way to peer at me. Her eyes tighten, and she glances over one shoulder. I'm not entirely sure she's going to open the door this time. Eventually, the lock clicks, and she slinks out onto the porch like a cat.

"You're back," she says, not quite surprised, and lights a cigarette. The smell of booze wafts off her like bad perfume. I'm not sure if she's drunk or if it's just bleeding from her pores. She doesn't waver on her feet; her eyes aren't glassy. To me, it doesn't look like she's been drinking at all, but she stinks like she bathed in gin.

"Can we talk for a few minutes?" I ask as I pull out my notebook.

"More questions about Jordan?" she asks in such a way that I expect her to roll her eyes, but she doesn't.

"No. I was hoping I could talk to you about your time at the memory hospital."

Her eyes go wide. "Can't say I expected that."

"You had Jebediah Dyer as a patient while you were there," I say, my words almost a question.

She nods slowly as she takes a drag from her cigarette. "Yeah, I saw him a lot while I worked there. He was there for about three years. He had taken a bottle of sleeping pills, and after that he was never quite the same. I'd say he was lucky that didn't kill him." She shakes her head. "They said he had early-onset dementia after that, but who knows if the pills just whacked him out of his gourd."

"What did you do there?"

"I was a geriatric nurse. Mostly, I did rounds, checked vitals, distributed medication—grunt work." She lets out a low, phlegmy laugh.

"Why'd you leave?" Grunt work or no, I imagine the pay would have been pretty good. Most people would kill for a job that pays really well around here.

She crosses her arms, the cigarette dangling between her bony fingers. "It's hard working somewhere where no one ever gets better. That's the kind of place it is. I went into it knowing that's what it was, but it still took a toll on me."

I can't imagine working day in and day out with people you get attached to, only to watch them fade away. I'd rather deal with murder. It's easier to be detached when you don't know the victim. It might just be me, though. Other cops take it differently, maybe because they've never lost anyone.

"Did he ever talk about any of the work he did?"

She grunts the way you would when your grandfather tries to tell you the same story for the four hundredth time. "He *loved* to talk about the good ol' days," she says as she takes another long drag.

"Anything in particular that sticks out to you?"

"Honestly? I tuned him out most of the time. That's what happens. These patients are so desperate to talk to anyone. They're abandoned in places they don't recognize, surrounded by strangers. They want to connect; they want you to *know* them. The problem is *we* know them, but they forget us. They learn your name, your job, and forget it all in the same day, the same hour.

"There were a few times he'd say things that would scare me, though." Her eyes are far off as she talks. "Out of nowhere, he'd grab me. His nails would dig into my arms. He'd nearly growl at me. I know by the way that he looked at me that he was talking to someone else," she says as she taps on the side of her head. "He'd scream at me that I had to stop. I tried to ask him to explain. His eyes were always wide, filled with terror, like someone had hurt him."

The way she says it makes my blood run cold. "Do you have any idea who he thought he was talking to?"

She shakes her head. "No. No one ever came to see him. I heard he had a bad falling-out with his wife, though. Some people said she went crazy. Other people said she left him and their son for some other guy. I assumed since he was yelling at me that he thought I looked like her." She flicks the ashes from her cigarette. "It was really sad. Three years there alone, and he died without even knowing who he was. No one ever came to visit him. He always mentioned his son should visit after everything he did for him." She sucks in air through her teeth and then lights a cigarette. "Toward the end, he thought his daughter was in the room with him. Though he always looked so sad; he never said anything to her. He'd just mention to me that she was there."

Why didn't Frank ever visit his father? Did he know anything about these cases? My mind spins as I try to piece it all together. From what I can gather, Sheriff Dyer knew that girls were going missing from the island, many of whom ended up dead. So why didn't he do anything about it? The killings couldn't have continued after Sheriff Dyer died if he'd had something to do with it—so should I be looking at Frank? Did he play a role in this or know something about it?

I finish up with Margo, but she hasn't got much else for me, and at the end of our talk, she makes it clear she doesn't want me to come back.

That's just fine with me.

CHAPTER 26

October 2004

She's on the phone again. There's a bathroom separating our rooms, but I can still hear her. If Rachel is home, she's on the phone. There's a constant droning from her end of the hall. When she's not here, when it's quiet, her absence is palpable—there's a silent void where Rachel should be. I set my book on the nightstand and creep down the hall.

What the hell is she even talking about? If you're always on the phone, how do you keep finding things to talk about?

I shouldn't be surprised. Rachel always has something to say. Mom has always said Rachel and I are opposites—she's a talker, and I'm a listener. While I'm sad, she's happy. Night and day.

I press my back to the cold wall as I creep down the hallway. I'm careful that she can't see me in the slit where her door is open. When she makes it this easy, it's like she wants me to overhear.

"It has to be sooner than that," Rachel says, her voice strained.

"We can't. Not yet. I need a few more weeks to get money together," a low voice replies. The voice startles me. I thought she was on the phone, but peeking through the slit shows me that Jacob is standing across the room from her. If our parents find out Jacob Warren is in our house, let alone in her room, they'll bury Rachel out back next to the willow tree.

"We may not have a few weeks," she argues.

"It's not like you're going to wake up and look nine months pregnant tomorrow. No one is going to have any idea."

"Please, it just has to be soon. I can't take it much longer," she says, and her mattress squeaks—she must have sat down.

"I'm doing everything I can. But my family can't know about this either."

"I don't understand why your family would have a problem with me," Rachel says with daggers in her words. It's just like Rachel. She can't imagine anyone not liking—no—loving her. She's the crown princess of Vinalhaven; everyone is supposed to adore her.

"It's not like your mother is going to be excited about us being together or this baby," he says, and there's an edge to his words.

"It just doesn't make any sense why your parents would have a problem with me."

"I've told you before. My dad told me the last time a Warren married someone from this island, two people ended up dead. And we lost half our business. That's when we had to start smuggling to survive."

"It's just so stupid," she says, her voice low. "Things have changed."

"It is. But it doesn't matter. No one will be able to separate us. We're in this together. It's you, me, and this baby," he says. "Shit, I've got to get home before they realize I'm gone."

"I wish you didn't have to go."

"I know. Me too," he says. "Meet me tomorrow night at the park?"

"Of course," she says.

I wait in the hall, listening for the window. Once I'm sure that he's left, I push the door open. Rachel's got her hair pulled up into a messy ponytail, and she has on a T-shirt so baggy it could double as a parachute.

"So you're leaving?" I ask as I sit on the end of her bed.

"You know I have to."

I knew it'd happen eventually. I always figured that she'd wait until she was eighteen before leaving. But her pregnancy changes everything. My parents wouldn't help her with college. She'd be on her own. And Rachel's not going to be any good at that.

"Don't worry. I'll wait until after your birthday," she says, as if that'll make me feel better. But it doesn't. My birthday is in three days. Is she leaving that fast?

"I really don't want you to leave," I say, and the truth of it surprises me. I don't want to lose her. I want her to be here, to be my sister again.

She shakes her head. "One day you'll understand, Claire-Bear."

CHAPTER 27

My thoughts are still raw when I wake up. In the few hours I've been asleep, I've had nightmare after nightmare. In every single one, I'm pushing Noah away. Off a cliff, down a river in a boat—in the last one I kicked him off a roof. It's enough to make my stomach turn. This time when I wake up, things are different; my heart is pounding, my skin sweaty, like I'm scared, not angry.

What woke me up?

I pull myself from bed, creeping across the ice-cold floorboards, and check my phone. There isn't a single notification waiting for me on the screen. A bad feeling, as heavy as a stone, sits in the pit of my stomach.

If it wasn't my phone that woke me up, what was it?

The sound of footsteps, loud and heavy, echoes from the living room. My heart creeps into my throat, and I grab my gun from the nightstand. With the cold metal pressed against my palm, I feel better. I throw the lights on and rush down the stairs—and find no one. The house is empty, silent.

Am I going crazy? Maybe my mom was right about getting a dog.

For good measure, I check the back door and the basement, but I find nothing and no one. Then I open the front door to check the porch—and my heart stops. A pink sweater is balled up right in front of the door. Someone left this for me.

I run to the kitchen to grab a plastic bag and use it as a glove to put the sweater inside without touching it. I don't know for sure, but my guess is the killer is taunting me. And this is from one of the victims. If that's the case, I can't afford to taint this evidence.

CHAPTER 28

A pinpoint of pain behind my eyes needles me. With every ebb, the dreams from last night fade away. Morning light edges around the curtains. Fear is still sharp in the back of my mind, but I push past it, because I have to. I don't have the time or energy to think about it. I drag myself downstairs to the kitchen and make myself a cup of coffee.

I should force myself to get into the office, throw myself into work. If I do that, I won't have time to think about how unnerved I am. I throw open the front door and search the porch, finding nothing this time, thankfully. I pull on my coat, my mug steaming in my hands. The frigid wind rushes around me, enveloping me as I take a seat on the porch step, mug in hand. Being outside helps me gather my thoughts, for some reason. For the first time in what seems like weeks, the sky is clear, bright.

Noah walks up the sidewalk as I sip my coffee. "You doing okay? You never called me last night." He leans against the porch railing.

"I'm fine. I just needed some time."

"Some time for . . . ?"

I sigh and clutch my coffee cup tighter. "It's just all a lot," I admit, though my brain begs me to keep the words bottled up inside. I feel like I'm getting so close to this killer, to figuring this out, but at the same time it could be so far away—and there are lives hanging in the balance.

I catch Noah up on some of the things I've found out about Sheriff Dyer. "I'm questioning all these connections to the sheriff. It seems he played a major role in all this, but I can't figure out if he helped commit any of the crimes or if he was covering for someone else."

"Well, he couldn't have committed any of the recent murders. So those would have to be a copycat."

"A copycat by someone who knew him well enough to know the details of the crimes that weren't ever released to the public," I say, finishing his thought.

I need to go talk to Frank and see if he can give me any information about his father. He has to know something. Or maybe he's involved.

A cold wind whips around me, but the warmth radiating from the cup keeps the chill at bay. Icicles sparkle, hanging from the roof of the station like crystal shivs. In the parking lot Noah and I say our goodbyes. From right outside the door, I hear commotion in the station. This time of day, it's normally dead. It's enough to make the hair rise on the back of my neck. I heave open the door and find the guys throwing on their jackets.

"What's going on?"

Sergeant Michaels emerges from his office. His plaid shirt is stretched tight over his broad chest, and his pants hang loose off his waist. His eyes are wide, far away, which is strange since he usually looks so focused. Something must have really gotten to him.

"Got a call that someone saw a body on the beach," Sergeant Michaels explains as he pulls on his coat.

"Where?" A lump forms in my throat as soon as I've gotten the word out.

"North of the school. Someone was walking their dog, stumbled on it," he explains.

Why the hell didn't anyone call me? I almost snap, but I decide better of it.

Jason, Sergeant Michaels, and I pile into a squad car just as the blanket of gray clouds rolls in and starts to spew sleet. Allen, thankfully, decides to stay put as we head for the beach. The car is thick with bad cologne, anxiety, and Jason's nervous words as he calls the CSI team in Augusta. Those guys have been here so often we're nearly on a first-name basis with them. We speed through downtown and past the school and pull off in front of the forest separating us from the stretch of beach where the body is.

I pull my hood up and throw the door of the patrol car open. Freezing rain pelts my coat until I reach the tree line. Between the rows of pine trees, I get a reprieve from the weather. Jason and Sergeant Michaels follow along a few feet behind me. Heavy fog hangs over the dark waves, and an ice-cold mist is carried by the wind, stinging my face. A few feet of sand sit at the edge of the tree line before the usual rocky shore of the island takes over. A hundred yards southeast of us, I see her.

My feet sink in the deep sand before I finally reach the rocks. The body isn't big enough to be a woman, but it isn't until I reach her that it really sets in that she's a girl. Water has soaked through her purple hoodie, and her jeans have flowers embroidered on the seams. It looks like if her hair were dry, it'd be blonde. Her skin is so pale, so translucent, it's unsettling. Around her jaw and neck there are bruises and small wounds, where the fish and crabs began eating her.

How long has she been in the water?

The hoodie she's wearing leads me to believe it's been a while. It's not thick enough for how cold it's been lately, but there's no telling until the ME takes a look. Even then, pinpointing this might be dicey. It's cold enough in the bay to preserve a body perfectly.

"She looks just like the other girls," Jason says as he stands over her crumpled body, the water slowly lapping against her cheek. She may look similar, but none of us know this victim.

Rachel, Madeline, Emma, Piper, all these girls—they all look exactly alike.

It takes a couple of hours for the CSI team to get the body. We take turns sitting in the car to warm ourselves up until they finally take her away. The CSI team warned me that there's likely no evidence left on the body, but the ME might be able to give us an estimated amount of time she was in the water. Jason and Sergeant Michaels seem to think there's no hope with this one, that there's no chance of recovering any clues—the case is starting to wear them down. But as their hope fades, the fury inside me grows. I won't give up.

I get a call from the CSI lab in Augusta. It's the analyst who's been assigned to the info about the Jane Does I sent over.

"I went through the dental records you sent over and looked at the database. We were able to match two."

I only sent over three sets: two of the missing girls my grandmother mentioned and another Carver girl. "Which girls matched?"

"Camille Norton and Vera Arey."

The dates they *left* the island were 1988 and 1980. Vera must have been related to Jenna's father. It's no wonder that no one really thought much of these girls running away in the eighties. Back then it happened all the time. I finish taking down the details from the analyst and ask him to email the data to me. Then I cross the hall to Sergeant Michaels's office.

"We need to talk." I shut the door.

"What's up?" he asks and takes a long sip of his coffee.

I need to be careful how I phrase this, because an accusation like this is pretty serious. But so far, there's no other conclusion I can draw. These girls had family, friends who checked up on them. And in every single case, Sheriff Dyer assured these families that the girls were fine.

"I've been looking into the Jane Doe database and the girls that seem to keep running away from the island."

He sits back and crosses his arms.

"We've had a few matches come up," I explain and read him off the names and dates I've got so far. "I've confirmed with the ME that she notified Sheriff Dyer of each of these Jane Does when they came in. He looked at each of the bodies, and every time he said they weren't from Vinalhaven. Several parents of these girls eventually came to the station and told him that their daughters had run away or disappeared. He relayed information to the families that the girls were fine." I pause to gather my thoughts.

"He went to see these Jane Does?"

I nod. "The old ME confirmed it."

"Were they in a state of advanced decomposition?"

"No. I've seen pictures of these women. If he knew them, there's no reason he shouldn't have been able to identify them."

If Sheriff Dyer were still alive, my hunch would be that he was involved in all these deaths. So are these new killings a copycat after all?

He looks down at the desk, as if grasping for what to say.

"Did you know anything about these girls back then?"

"I'm sure I did. But kids always leave the island. Some eventually come back. They need to get it out of their system," he explains. "There's an officer up in Belmont who used to work with Sheriff Dyer," he says as he writes an address down for me. "Mack Carver. You might want to talk to him, and if he doesn't give you anything, talk to Frank."

"Thank you." It means a lot that it's clear Sergeant Michaels sees this as my investigation. In Detroit, it was such a big force that sometimes people would get in your way, question your perp. If he wanted, Sergeant Michaels could step in and question this guy. But him trusting me to keep going when I could expose a much uglier side of this than we ever imagined—it boosts my confidence.

"I'll give him a heads-up you'll be calling."

I say my thanks. And before I leave, I remember the other thing I'd planned to talk to Sergeant Michaels about. "We need to start a nightly rotation of patrols on the water. We know this guy is out there on a boat, taking the girls out there. If we're patrolling the water, we might throw him off, keep him from killing for a while."

"That's a good idea," he says as he offers me a gruff smile. "I'm going to check with Frank to see if he can get us a couple more boats to use for a few weeks. It won't do us much good if there's only one of us on the water."

I finish up with Sergeant Michaels and head back to my office to call Mack. In a few minutes I introduce myself and set up a time to talk with him. He's got nothing going on, so I grab my stuff and head to my car. If I'm lucky, I'll be able to make it there by noon.

After I'm in the car, I pull up to the dock to wait for the next ferry. It takes nearly an hour for me to reach the old folks' home the officer lives at. Anxiety gnaws at me. This is the first person who might *really* have some answers about what happened when Rachel died and about the other girls. If he has nothing on Sheriff Dyer, this could lead me in a completely different direction. There have been so many dead ends lately—I just can't let myself get excited about this. It could easily lead me nowhere.

I check in at the front desk and wait for a nurse to lead me back. We weave down a long hallway, passing rooms with TV volumes so loud that the sounds all blur together in a dull roar in the hall. Each room looks like the typical hospital variety, but they're decorated to disguise them as little apartments.

"Mr. Carver, you've got a visitor," the nurse says.

"Thank God. If I have to watch one more minute of these damn house-hunting shows, I'm going to jump out the window," he says flatly.

"Mr. Carver, you can change the channel," she offers in a voice that hints she's probably already said this same phrase to him twelve times today.

"The batteries are dead."

"I'll find you some new ones," she says as she waves me in. "Let me know if you need anything."

"Thank you," I say as she disappears down the hall.

The room is decorated sparsely. A few family photos are arranged on a shelf on the right wall. Below that there's a love seat, and a twin bed sits in the corner next to the small window. All the furniture is arranged so that it faces the small TV. Mr. Carver is sitting on the edge of the bed in a plaid robe that's tied over pajamas.

"Claire?" he asks as he squints his eyes.

I nod. "Yes, Claire Calderwood. Are you still okay talking about your time with the Vinalhaven PD?"

"Of course," he says, a little laugh slipping out.

"How long did you work there?"

"About thirty years," he says. He pushes off from the bed to grab a small bottle of water from his nightstand.

"And why'd you leave?" According to what Sergeant Michaels told me, he quit a few years before Sheriff Dyer retired.

"Had some disagreements with the sheriff." He shakes his head. "That schmuck."

I raise a brow at that, and I can't deny the excitement rising at the back of my mind. "About?" I ask, sliding my notebook from my pocket. I want to be sure I write down all the details of this conversation.

"There were things I thought should be investigated, and he didn't. He let a lot of things go. He knew the Warrens were running drugs on the island, but he wouldn't do shit about it. His daughter was causing all kinds of trouble, and we couldn't do anything about that either. It just started feeling like all we could do was sit in the station all day."

So along with ignoring or covering up murders, he had a history of not investigating things that should have been investigated? *Someone get this guy a medal*, I want to growl.

"Was there anything else?"

He chuckles. "You'd need a week to hear all of it. If you knew what went on after Rachel died . . ." he says as he crosses his arms.

"What do you mean? What happened?"

"We had a list of suspects. We were doing interviews based on what we'd seen downtown around the time of Rachel's murder. He told us that the investigation was over."

Anger flares. "So he stopped the investigation?"

He nods. "That's exactly right."

That's not the way investigations work. Even if a case goes cold, it's not stopped. The only time an investigation should be halted is when it's closed because we've found the perp.

"What reason did he give you?" I ask, trying desperately to keep my frustration from reaching my words.

"He said that other girls had been murdered in Bangor and that the police department there informed him they had a killer who admitted to killing Rachel. But we needed to keep it quiet because he was pleading to two other murders in exchange for not being charged with Rachel's murder."

"Let me get this straight: he said they found Rachel's killer, but no one in town could know?"

"That's right. That was really the last straw for me. It didn't add up."

"Do you remember the suspects that you had for Rachel's murder?" I ask. That'd be a good place for me to pick back up.

"Sure do. Paul Clark, Jacob Warren, a couple of the fishermen who had domestic abuse problems in the past, Frank Miller, and your mother," he says.

Parents are always on the initial suspect list, but if they had no involvement, they get taken off pretty quickly.

"Why were Paul and Frank on your list?"

"Paul was her driver's ed teacher, and he'd been seen downtown the night she died. Frank was also downtown, but we determined he was just headed to his shop," he explains.

"Why was Paul downtown?"

"He was meeting someone for a drink."

I nod and make a mental note of that. I've got plenty of issues with Paul given his past, but I find it doubtful he killed his niece. So far, I've seen no motive. "And my mother? Is that because family is always on the suspect list? Or is there another reason?"

He shakes his head. "There were a few things that alarmed us about your mother. She didn't seem as upset, as rattled as we'd expect for a parent who just suffered a loss. She was very evasive in questioning, and she had a motive. She'd just found out that Rachel was dating Jacob Warren and was *very* upset about it. But we didn't have anything else on her. There was nothing to link her to the crime; no one saw her out that night."

"How did you find out that Rachel was dating Jacob Warren?"

"Your mother knew; she told us she'd overheard a conversation between them."

If she already knew about Jacob, why did she never say a word about it to me? That doesn't seem like the kind of thing my mother would let slide.

"Were you ever able to rule her out?"

He shakes his head. "Not fully, no."

"Was there anything else like this from Sheriff Dyer? Did he make a habit of ending investigations?"

"He told us we were to stay away from the Warrens, to never touch anyone in that family. That always made me wonder if they had something to do with her death."

Mr. Carver doesn't have much else for me, so I head back to Vinalhaven. By the time the ferry crosses the bay, the sun is hanging low in the sky. As I drive back toward the office, I see Frank heading into his shop near the docks. Instead of going to the station, I turn right and pull in to the small parking lot next to Frank's. The gray wood siding of the building is starting to peel toward the bottom. I eye the dirt caked in the frayed paint as I walk toward the door.

Instead of knocking, I head right in. There's no bell on the door to chime my arrival, just the yawn of the aged metal hinges. Frank is behind the counter when I walk in, looking over an engine part. He glances over his shoulder at me and offers me a smile. "Hello, Claire," he says, wiping the oil from his hands on his pants. They're already covered from top to bottom in stains.

"Evening, Frank. Do you have a few minutes? I was hoping to talk to you about your father."

The smile disappears from his face, and his eyes narrow with suspicion. "My father?" He croaks the words like his throat has shrunk around them. "Why?"

"I was wondering if he ever spoke to you about his work," I say, wanting to start out easy so I can gauge what he'll tell me. Questioning family members can be perilous.

He crosses his arms, his muscular forearms resting atop the bulge of his stomach. "No, he didn't talk about his job when he was at home."

"So you never heard anything about it, then?"

"Not anything that I can remember. It's been quite a long time."

"How would you classify your relationship with your father?" I ask. If he can't give me any details about his father's work life, I've got to try and get other information out of him.

"Strained," he says, his words more honest than I expect.

"And why would you say that?"

The muscles in his arms twitch. "We never saw eye to eye on anything. He was always disappointed in me, no matter what I did. My sister, though, he worshipped her." He glances toward the clock hung on the wall behind him. "Look, it's getting late. I need to close up for the night."

"I just have a few more questions—" I say, but he holds a hand up.

"Really, I need to close up. Maybe you can stop by another time, and we can talk more."

Reluctantly, I head toward the door, the blast of winter hitting me the moment I open it. I drive back to my rental, creating a list for myself in my mind. If I can't get answers from Frank about his father, I know exactly where to look next.

CHAPTER 29

With the killings escalating, we've ramped up the number of patrol boats on the water. Vince, Allen, Marshall, Jason, and the coast guard take turns keeping eyes on the water twenty-four seven. Noah and I stay late in the office digging into all the files about Sheriff Dyer after my conversation with Mr. Carver. My office is half-filled with old white cardboard boxes, the kind you'd imagine an accountant keeps tax records in. The air is thick with dust, but I find the scent comforting, like a library.

A few days ago, at my request, Sergeant Michaels dragged out boxes of case files from the seventies and eighties from an old storage facility in city hall. Noah and I have been slowly thumbing through the files, trying to see if we can find anything that mentions the missing girls. Deep in one of the boxes from the early eighties, a file from one of the old officers mentions Frank Miller aboard someone else's boat. The owner, Susan Woods, wanted to press charges, but Sheriff Dyer intervened, making sure his son wasn't charged.

"How many other times did you get him out of trouble?" I mutter to myself.

"What was that?" Noah asks.

I show him the files I've found so far.

"And I'm sure that's just the beginning," he says with his brows furrowed.

"My thoughts exactly."

In the files I find three similar incidents, all minor, but they establish an alarming precedent.

Noah clears his throat and catches my attention when I'm halfway through reading a file about a missing car on the island. "What's up?" I ask, glancing over my desk at the folder, though I can't see anything about it from where I sit.

"It looks like Kassie Mulholland was attacked in the late seventies. Someone tried to choke her. There are notes in here referencing parts of the file that are gone. There are several names blacked out." He pulls a sheet of paper from the file and sets it on my desk. "But you see right here," he says, pointing toward the bottom of the page.

I eye it, trying to determine what he's looking at—and I see it. A mention of Frank's name.

"It looks like he's been removed from the rest of the file, but they missed this one."

My heart pounds as I consider the evidence in front of me. I wish I had more to go on, but this is what I had a feeling we'd find eventually. Now I know what direction I have to go in. I've got to question Frank again.

After finding that last bit of evidence, Noah and I emerge from the station after midnight. The air is crisp, clear, and so cold it feels like my eyeballs are turning to ice cubes. We walk toward the parking lot, and I head to my car. "I'm going home. I'll see you in the morning, okay?" I say.

"Want me to come with, just to make sure you get home all right?"

I shake my head. "I appreciate the chivalry, but I'll pass. Thanks. Good night, Noah," I say, and he reaches for me as I start to walk away.

He folds me into his arms for just a moment, but I still feel the need to squirm away. Though I appreciate the sentiment, I can't help but think Noah wants this to go in a direction I don't. As I climb into my car and Noah walks back to the Tidewater, I worry that he deserves better than this. Better than someone who is going to keep shutting him out like I will. I've got more walls than a labyrinth, and every time he knocks one down, I know I'll just build another. They say that the heart is a muscle and that you can strengthen it. But what they don't tell you is that when your heart is broken by a loss as splintering as Rachel's, it never heals right. Some days I swear I can still feel the shards, the remnants of the pain woven into me the day I lost her forever.

As I drag myself back to my house, the whole city is swallowed by darkness, enveloped by the vacuum of night. I shove my key into the lock and turn, but it doesn't click open. It's like the lock is jammed. I jiggle the handle, trying to force it, but the door holds firm. It's too late for me to call Mrs. Peterson to get it fixed. I walk to the rear of the house, toward the basement door. The door has been a fickle thing since I moved in. If you nudge it and jiggle the handle just right, it can be slipped open. I'm glad I didn't ask Mrs. Peterson to fix it yet.

It takes a few minutes to finagle the door open. When I finally succeed, I breathe a sigh of relief. At least one thing can go right. The darkness in the basement is palpable, the kind of darkness you have to wade through. It doesn't help that the air down here is thick, moist, as if the night is pooling around me. I shut the door and reach for my phone to light the way. As I click the button on the side and try to tap on the flashlight, nothing happens. Of all the times for my phone to go dead.

I grumble as I shuffle across the concrete floor toward where I *think* the stairs are. A few feet in, lost in darkness, something clicks, hisses.

It's just the furnace.

I stop to listen, but the whoosh of blood in my ears is too loud. I can't hear anything else. I start to walk again, but that's when I hear it.

A footstep behind me. For a second, I hesitate, unsure if I heard it at all. Until I hear another. I run, hoping to God I find the stairs. Fabric rustles behind me. Fingers graze against my back. A scream bursts from me, so loud my throat aches. Large, rough hands twist into my hair and yank me back with a yelp.

"You kept me from killing tonight, cunt." His voice is rough, a snarl, edging on inhuman. "You aren't leaving me any choice."

He twists me around, and when I smell sugar on his breath, I know he's facing me. His hands smell like rum and grease. If there were any light down here, I'd be able to see him, to make out every line of his face.

I try to force myself backward, away from him, but his hands grip me too tightly. My arms come up automatically, and I try to wedge my elbows into his chest to free myself. He groans, and for a moment, I think I'm free. But his hands circle my throat, and his thumbs press hard into my windpipe. Pain spreads through my throat as he presses harder. My hands dig into his arms, and I kick, trying to force him to release me. An ache awakens deep inside my lungs as my body begs for air. If I can't breathe soon, I won't have the strength to fight much longer. Panic roars in the back of my mind. If I let him kill me, all those other girls will never get justice. He digs his thumbs deeper, and bile creeps up my throat in response. As I struggle, something primal fuels me. If I don't get free, if I don't get away from him, I'll die.

With fury and desperation giving me much-needed strength, I dig my nails into every bit of flesh I can reach. I kick and punch until finally his grip falters. I won't let this asshole kill me. I'm not going to die like this. I gasp, and my throat burns as I force a breath into my aching lungs. I turn away, hoping to get to the stairs, but it's too dark; I can't tell where in the basement I am.

There's a rush of movement, and his chest presses to my back. Large fingers lace into my hair, and I claw at them, praying I can do something, even if it just means getting DNA beneath my fingernails. My mind screams for me to get away, to fight. He holds me tighter, his huge arm wrapping around my throat. He's going to strangle me like he did the others.

I kick backward over and over, but he only holds me tighter in response. I bring my elbow back and hit him hard in the side, and his grip loosens enough for me to get away. I run from him, my arms outstretched as I search the darkness for the stairs. Though I'm tempted to reach for my gun, I can't shoot down here—I might hit the oil tank and blow us both to bits. He moves behind me, but thankfully he seems as lost in the darkness as I am. A cough sputters out of me, and my heart seizes. The noise will lead him right to me.

The brush of my fingertips against the banister is the most wonderful thing I've ever felt. I wrap my hand around the hard wooden handrail and pull myself toward the stairs, pounding up them to the first floor. I throw the door open, letting the light stream into the basement, before I unholster my gun. When I go back down to search, he's gone. All that's left is a set of keys in the middle of the floor.

CHAPTER 30

Once my hands stop shaking so much, I call the station. When Jason answers, I give him a brief rundown of everything that happened and ask him to get Vince and Allen sweeping the streets for my attacker. He tells me he's grabbing the equipment to swab my nails for DNA. After ending the call with Jason, knowing he'll be at my house in a few minutes, I call Sergeant Michaels. I explain the attack and let him know the guys will be looking for my attacker. Sergeant Michaels informs me that he's heading over to my place to look for evidence while Vince and Allen sweep the streets. After I hang up with Sergeant Michaels, I'm still on edge. Sitting on my porch, surrounded by the night, I'm nervous that my attacker might still be lurking. Out here, though, I'm not boxed in. Out here, I can run.

Before Jason or Sergeant Michaels can arrive, I dial Noah's number.

"Hey," he says groggily when he answers the phone. "Still awake?"

"Can you come over?" I ask, my voice strained, scratchy from being choked. A dull ache throbs where I was strangled, and the flesh stings, like it's been rubbed raw. There's going to be a hell of a bruise.

"Is everything all right?" he asks, and he's suddenly gone from half-asleep to completely awake.

"Yeah," I say, but my voice lacks the conviction it needs. "I just need you here." I don't want to tell him what happened over the phone. He'll be less worried if he can see me, see that I'm okay.

His mattress groans, and fabric rustles in the background. "I'm on my way," he says before ending the call.

Noah's out front in ten minutes, unfortunately before Jason. I stand on the porch and hold my hands up to keep him at bay. "I need you to not touch me until Jason gets here," I explain.

He stares at me, his brows knitting together. "What happened?" He takes a step closer, and his eyes tighten. "What the hell happened to your neck?" The protective anger in his voice makes me think he's going to hunt down the guy who did this and kill him himself.

Now that he's here, some of the tension in my shoulders drops. But I can still feel the panic lingering just beneath the surface. "When I got home from the station, someone was waiting for me in the house. He attacked me." We spooked the killer, and now he's going to focus on me. I'm the obstacle keeping him from killing again. The thought makes panic tighten around me, but at the same time, if he focuses on me, maybe it will distract him from killing anyone else. I should have gotten in his way sooner.

"Who was it? I'll fucking kill him," he growls, clenching his hands into tight fists. "It's not safe for you to be here alone."

I ignore his safety comment; he's just protective because of the shock. "I don't know. It happened in the basement. It was dark. I didn't see who it was," I explain. He must have been waiting in the house for me to get home. Was he going to come up while I was sleeping? The thought makes bile creep up my throat, but I swallow it down.

Jason walks up the path and calls out behind Noah. "Everything all right, Claire?"

"Yeah, it is." Noah turns to face him. "I'm Noah."

"Ah, yeah, I've seen you at the station. Good to see you, man," Jason says with a nod. "Wish it were under better circumstances, though."

Jason has a messenger bag slung over his shoulder as he walks up the steps. His eyes narrow on my neck, and I wave him inside. I sit on the couch, and Jason tosses the bag on the coffee table.

"I'm going to scrape beneath your fingernails, swab your cheek, and then check all the doors and windows for fingerprints, if that's all right," Jason says.

I nod.

"Can I get you anything?" Noah asks as he hovers near me.

I shake my head. "No, thank you."

Jason gets to work, gathering the DNA beneath my fingernails while Noah stands nearby, arms crossed, like a sentry. Normally I'd hate his hovering, his need to stand guard. I'm not a damsel in distress. But right now, I love that he's close. I love that he's *here*. Jason tries to make small talk, but I'm so drained after the long night that there's no way I could keep it up even if I wanted to.

"Did they take your fingerprints when you started?" he asks as he bags the evidence and swabs my cheek. After he's got that, I point him in the direction of the keys I found. Those will need to be fingerprinted too.

"I transferred them from Detroit." It's common to give DNA and fingerprints when starting at a new station. As careful as we are, shit happens; sometimes someone will inadvertently leave a print at the scene.

Sergeant Michaels pulls into the driveway, pops open his car door, and clicks on a flashlight. As he walks toward us, the beam of light bounces on the ground. Once he gives me a long appraising look, he says, "I'm going to check out back." I don't have a chance to say anything before he disappears along the side of the house.

"Good, I'm glad you had your fingerprints transferred," Jason says as he takes a step back and grimaces. I know he's going to deliver bad news. "Because of the backlog, it'll likely take us a bit to get the results back. There's only one lab, and they handle everything for the smaller towns. The only other lab is in Bangor. We've never been able to get them to process anything for us. They're too bogged down with their own shit." He shakes his head and turns his attention back to me. "You probably shouldn't stay here. You might want to stay at your mom's until we catch whoever did this. I'll prioritize this as much as I can, but they've got a rash of killings up there that's bogging everything down."

"She'll stay with me," Noah says automatically, and I bristle. While I appreciate his chivalry, I won't be ushered around and protected like the queen's jewels. And I certainly won't have my decisions made for me. I narrow my eyes at Noah.

"I'll see you later, Claire," Jason says. "Call me if you need anything."

"Thank you," I say as Jason heads toward the door. Once he's gone, I grab a bottle of water from the kitchen. Sipping the water, swallowing, awakens an ache in my neck, and moving my head doesn't feel much better.

"You can't seriously be considering staying here," Noah says as he follows me into the kitchen.

The cold granite bites through my shirt as I lean against the counter. "No, I'm not, but it feels like you're ordering me not to stay here," I say as I cross my arms. "I don't like being ordered to do anything."

"You know that's not how I meant it. It's not safe here. I just don't want you to get hurt." He takes a step toward me and rubs his hand along my arm. "I don't think it's sunk in yet. Claire, you could have died today."

The shock is still holding that thought at bay. Later today, maybe later this week, that thought will hit me like a ton of bricks, but I'm going to fight it off for as long as I can. I look at the floor as I gather my thoughts.

"My problem isn't that you want to keep me safe. I appreciate that, I really do. My problem is you making a decision for me without giving me any say in the matter. You may want what's best for me, but I get a say. This is *my* life." Frustration needles the back of my mind as I wait for him to tell me I'm overreacting or that I should be more reasonable. Maybe it's being on my own for so many years, maybe it's the stubbornness born into me, or maybe it's a combination. I've always depended on myself, made my own decisions. That isn't going to stop now. It makes my skin crawl that the killer knows where I live now, but I don't want to be ordered around.

"You're right. I'm sorry. I wasn't thinking clearly after everything," he says as he brushes his hand along my cheek. "It's hard to think straight around you. And seeing you like this . . ." He shakes his head as he takes a step closer, and butterflies flutter in my stomach.

Exhaustion sets in as my adrenaline crashes. I'm so tired I can feel it in my bones. "Are you really okay with me staying at the hotel with you?"

"Of course I am. The only other option would be staying at your mom's, right?"

I shudder at the thought. That or with my grandma. I don't want to impose on Noah or feel like I'm invading his space, but for the night I'm grateful just to have somewhere safe to stay.

CHAPTER 31

October 2004

My sister is sneaking out tonight. I know she's going to meet Jacob again. I heard her getting ready in the bathroom an hour ago. Outside her door, I wait until her window slides open. In the dark hallway, I count to one hundred and then creep into her room and out her window.

The gray sky above me showers the ground in a fresh blanket of snow. Even though I've got my thickest coat on, the cold creeps in, settling in my bones. The chill during the day is nothing compared to the night. It's like death is breathing down my neck.

Rachel cuts through the trees, tracing her way to the park near our house. She's got her arms wrapped tightly around herself, like she's cold. As I break through the tree line, light flashing through the slender tree trunks ahead guides me. A few of the light posts they put in the park a couple of years ago still burn bright. Rachel's silhouette climbs the hill in front of me. She glances over her shoulder when she breaches the tree line, and I know she's seen me. Rachel freezes and waves her hand as if to shoo me.

I'm not going anywhere.

A tall figure appears in front of Rachel, backlit by the streetlights. I can't make out who it is, but it has to be Jacob. The figure moves suddenly, grabbing Rachel, and I duck behind a tree, not wanting them to see me. I peek out as I hear Rachel try to say something. The man's got her by the hair, and I realize he's too tall to be Jacob, too big. Rachel moves fast, her tiny stature helping her wriggle free. She takes off into the woods toward me. I want to run. I want to grab my sister, but I swear my legs have grown roots.

Rachel reaches me faster than should be possible. The man lumbers after her, but he's slow. She grabs me by my shirt, the way our mom would. Her wide eyes search for mine in the darkness. She shoves me a bit, as if to wake me up, and pushes me toward the tree line.

"Claire, run."

"No, I'm not leaving you."

"You're not leaving me. Just hurry—get home. And don't you dare tell Mom and Dad what happened."

"Okay," I say automatically, and it's as if she has enough power over me to force my legs to work again. I take a step back, away from her, my heart pounding.

"Claire, promise. No matter what happens. You were never here," she urges as she takes off into the darkness. I run out of the woods, back toward our house. I run until my legs burn and my side splinters with pain.

Every day that I carry this secret in my heart, it gets a little heavier. I can't keep it forever. It's been two weeks. Two weeks without my sister. It still doesn't feel real. I still expect to hear her whisper in the next room. Every time I'm alone, I swear I can hear her say "Claire-Bear" in a singsong voice the way she always used to. My heart aches like it's being pulled from my chest. I can't do it anymore.

I've tiptoed around my mother's grief. I'm not walking on eggshells; I'm walking on broken glass. She's standing in front of the back door, a drink in her hand. Before Rachel died, she always wore pastels. Today, her clothes are as gray as the sky.

"Mom, can I talk to you for a minute?" I ask and flinch automatically. Half of the time she lashes out at me, and the other half, especially if someone is watching, she's saccharine.

"What do you want, Claire?" she asks, her voice halfway between annoyance and apathy.

"I need to talk to you about the night Rachel died," I say and cross my arms to keep my hands from shaking. I've already had this conversation with her a thousand times in my head.

She turns, and her expression is hollow, empty. But her eyes sharpen the moment they land on me. "We don't ever need to talk about that again. I don't want to hear a word about her. Not even her name." Though her words are soft, velvet smooth, her eyes are slits, like a snake's.

"I saw something," I say, a little firmer this time because I don't think she'll listen otherwise.

"It doesn't matter what you saw. We're not dredging any of this back up. I'm not going to bring embarrassment to our family."

"You think it's an embarrassment that Rachel died?" The last word gets stuck in my throat, and I have to force it out.

She moves her wrist, and the ice in her drink swirls. "Yes. I do. We're done talking about this. Go back to your room."

Two more times I try to talk to her about it. I try until she screams at me, until my heart breaks all over again. But there has to be something else I can do. I can't give up on Rachel.

Most girls skip school to hang out with boys, go shopping, smoke weed. I'm skipping school to tell the sheriff about what I saw the night Rachel died. My heart pounds as I slip out the back door. I've only skipped class once. My mom found out and grounded me for two months. I've wondered what she would have done if it were Rachel. Somehow I don't think she'd have gotten grounded.

I dart across the back parking lot. It's still filled with cars, as it will be for the next three hours. Though I glance back at the building several times as I cross, there's not a single person watching me. Under normal circumstances, I wouldn't be doing this. But normal went out the window the night Rachel died. I already tried telling my mom what I saw, and since she won't listen, the only other person I can tell is the sheriff. He'll be able to do something about it. Maybe if he knows what I saw, what I know, he'll be able to find the person who did this.

After I'm away from the school, it's a two-mile walk to downtown. I skirt the tree line the whole way, and my heart doesn't stop pounding until I cross the threshold of the station. The woman behind the counter tells me to take a seat. In a few minutes, Sheriff Dyer is peeking at me from behind the doorframe.

"What're you doing out of school, Claire?" he asks in what I imagine is his best dad voice. I've heard my friends' dads talk that way—mine, not so much.

"I really need to talk to you about Rachel."

"We already have your statement. You should go back to class." He motions toward the door with dismissal.

A lump forms in my throat, and though I try to swallow it down, it doesn't budge an inch. "There's something I didn't tell you."

CHAPTER 32

After what I've found on Frank and his father, all I can wonder is what else his father has covered up for him. I need to talk to Frank again. This time I need answers about his father and sister. Because it's possible that Frank was my attacker, I take Jason with me.

I glance at the clock in my car. It's a bit early to make our way to Frank's shop, but I'm too antsy to keep myself busy in town. Jason and I make small talk outside the shop rather than waiting in the car, because I'd rather catch Frank the moment he gets in. I've learned in all my time questioning suspects that people are more likely to tell the truth when they're frazzled or thrown off their routine.

Jason glances at the shop. "You really think Frank could have done this?"

Frank is my first *real* suspect for this, but I have nothing concrete. Though the past records point me in a pretty clear direction, that's all circumstantial. There's nothing tying him to the boat, the girls, the call to the station. If I talk to him, he might slip up; he might give me something. "I have suspicions, but nothing solid. We need to find direct evidence, and we've got to find it soon."

Frank's shop is in a small building that obviously used to be one of the smallest houses in Vinalhaven. It'd fit in perfectly with the tiny-house trend. From the porch of the shop, I've got a great view of the marina. Many of the boats pulled out of the harbor just as the sun crept up from the horizon. The docks are half-empty. From above, I'm sure it looks like a gap-toothed, jagged jack-o'-lantern. The boats that are getting a late start are small—probably people fishing for their families rather than company ships.

"How's your neck?" Jason asks, eyeing my bruise. It's an ugly eggplant color at the moment.

"Still tender but looks worse than it is."

Gulls circle above me, their chatter so loud it drowns out my thoughts. That's the good and the bad thing about the beach. You can't be alone with your thoughts, but the noise can help you take your mind off things. A shuffling inside the shop tells me that Frank is already here. His shop has a basement, and I imagine he's set it up so he can spend the night there if he wants.

"Good morning," Frank says as he cracks the door open. "I thought I saw someone on the porch."

There's a scratch on his cheek that sets my nerves on edge. I know I scratched my attacker. I'd guess on the face, but I can't be certain. My eyes travel down to his hands, where I know I did manage to do some damage, and there are matching scratches there too.

"What happened there?" I ask, motioning toward his face and hands.

"Damnedest thing—there was a stray cat on one of the boats I was working on. I tried to get it off of there, and it scratched me," he says without skipping a beat.

"You're lucky it didn't get you in the eye," I say, sharing a look with Jason.

The smell of strong coffee wafts from the house, warm and inviting. Even if I've had my fill of coffee, I'll never get sick of that smell or the way it envelops me.

"Do you have a minute?" I ask as I take a step toward the door. I could request that he come down to the station, but I've found that asking people questions at the station, even if they're not suspects, tends to shut them up and make them real careful about everything they say. Twitchy people ask for lawyers instead of giving answers.

"Of course. You're both probably freezing out there." He waves us inside. The cold this morning really isn't that bad. My cheeks may be numb, but the rest of me has managed to cling to the warmth from my car.

"Do either of you want some coffee?" He shuffles to the pot. "I just brewed it."

"No, thank you," we both say at the same time.

"What can I do you for?" he asks as he pours himself a cup.

"I was hoping I could talk to you about your father," I say, deciding to start with a subject that won't set him off immediately.

He presses his lips together and glances toward the floor as if saddened. "Again?"

I nod. "How would you describe him?"

He shrugs and sips his coffee. "He was quiet. He liked to keep to himself. Why the interest in my dad?"

"As I said before, just following up on some loose ends. He was the sheriff when Rachel died. I'm just trying to get a sense of him and how he investigated the case."

His eyes tighten, and I think I may have touched a nerve. "You already know that he and I weren't speaking when Rachel died."

"Is there anything else you can tell me about that?" Did the strain come from his father covering up his crimes? Or did they fight about something else?

He leans against the counter, his attention on the coffee cup. "After my mom died, things between us were never the same. He was never the same. Then after my sister died—it only got worse." He shakes his head. That'd be a lot for any family to bear; no wonder things became strained. Death either brings people together or forces them apart. If

Sheriff Dyer had been going through losses like that, his focus wouldn't have been on Rachel—or anything else, for that matter.

"When did your sister die? I thought she left the island." I didn't know that Frank's sister—Delilah Dyer—had died. All information I've seen or heard about her during this investigation stated that she left the island. A bad feeling coils inside me, and I'm glad I didn't come here alone.

"When I was sixteen." He glances at his coffee cup while he speaks. Though I expect to find some emotion behind his words, or a hint of it on his face—there's nothing. Frank sets his coffee down on the counter behind him and crosses his arms. "Are you asking about him because you think my dad had something to do with Rachel's death?"

"No, not at all." I try to keep my features in check. Usually I have a great poker face, but it's incredibly important that I don't show a hint of suspicion here.

He nods. "He didn't talk to me about cases, or anything, really. But I did notice that after Rachel died, he spent a lot of time in the park."

That's something interesting. Why would he be spending a lot of time in the park?

I circle back to his sister, needing more information about her. "How did your sister die?" Based on what I know now, it doesn't surprise me in the least that she ended up dead. But it does surprise me that he *knows* she's dead if everyone else thinks she moved, and that he either readily or accidentally supplied me with that information. Did he mean to say it? Or did it slip out?

His mouth twitches, and he scratches his neck, his thick fingernails clicking against the stubble there like it's high-grit sandpaper. "Why does that matter?"

"I've just never heard much about her." There was also no file on her at the station, and considering what I know about Sheriff Dyer's record-eliminating habits, a missing file makes me even more concerned.

Red creeps from Frank's collar, painting his neck and cheeks in crimson. "I don't like the cops in here asking questions about my family." There's an edge to his voice I've never heard before.

I know I've only got another question or two before he refuses to answer anything, so I'm going to take the opportunity to ask about the girl he attacked. "What can you tell me about Kassie Mulholland?"

His left eye quivers, and his hand tightens around his mug until his knuckles turn as white as pearls. All I can imagine is those hands around my neck.

"Get out."

"Maybe you should come back to the station," Jason suggests.

"Get the hell out of my shop. If you want me in that station, you'll have to arrest me."

Jason tugs on my arm, and we head out of the shop, back toward my car. It only takes a few minutes to get back to the station, and my hands tremble the entire drive.

"Thanks for coming with me," I say as the gravel parking lot crunches beneath the tires.

He nods. "How long until we can arrest him?"

"We don't have enough hard evidence yet. I might be able to press a warrant for DNA based on the scratches, but I'm not sure if we'll get it. I need to keep an eye on him so maybe we can get DNA on our own. I want someone watching him at all times."

"I'll head back over there in my car," Jason offers.

"Thank you. Stay out of sight, and please stay safe. We don't know what he's capable of."

"Yes, we do," Jason says, and he motions at my neck.

Jason gets out of my car and climbs into his. I yank my coat up around my neck and throw open the door. By the time I duck into the station, I'm chilled to the bone. Only Allen is in the bull pen, and he doesn't even glance at me as I pass. Sergeant Michaels is at his desk. I invite myself in and stand near the doorway. I catch him up on what happened with Frank and where my head is regarding his involvement.

"Is he the right build for your attacker?" he asks.

"It was too dark for me to tell. All I know is my attacker was much larger than I am. In that respect he fits."

"We need more for a warrant to get his DNA or prints."

"The guys are going to take turns watching him. Maybe he'll throw something away we can get prints or DNA from." We need something to test against the DNA from under my fingernails. I find it unlikely—based on all the cover-ups—that Frank's DNA will be in the system. And even if it is, it could take us a week or more to process a sample to submit for a database reference. Then who knows how long it will take to hear back about a database match. We don't have the time to spare.

He nods. "We'll have to keep an eye on him at all times. We can't afford another death or to have him attack you again."

Sergeant Michaels picks up his phone. As he makes sure to relay the message about Frank to the guys, I sit at my desk and glance at my computer without really seeing it. We're so close that there's a buzz in my blood as I nudge my mouse to the side, making the monitor come back to life. I force myself to focus and shoot Mrs. Peterson a quick email about the broken lock. The details of the case flood my mind again as soon as the email is sent. I want to tell Noah how close we are, that we might have our guy, but I can't tell him about this, not until I can bring Frank in.

CHAPTER 33

The next day, as I'm reading an email on my phone—Mrs. Peterson has fixed both of the locks on my rental and dropped the new key in the mailbox—with a fresh cup of coffee in hand, I head out of the café and am nearly run over by a large man. Blinking, forcing my eyes to adjust to the sunshine, I realize it's Madeline's dad who nearly ran into me. He looks the worse for wear. He's got on a stained T-shirt under his open coat, and his stubble has grown into a shaggy beard. His eyes are somehow dim and feral at the same time.

"Mayor Clark," I say, and he grabs my arm, yanking me into the café.

As soon as we're inside, I step away from him, out of reach. Under any other circumstances, I'd be angry. But I'm determined to remember everything he's been through. I'm not sure I'd act any better in these circumstances. He glances behind the counter at Morgan. "You, go outside," he orders her.

Her body goes rigid for a moment. I think she's going to argue. Instead, she walks past us and hangs out just outside the doors.

"Not surprised to see you here, Calderwood," he says, his words laced with venom.

"Mayor Clark, how are you doing?" I ask, choosing to let the malice behind his words roll right off.

His brows furrow, and he clenches his fists at his sides. I swear there's a vein pulsing at the side of his head that makes me want to back away, but I don't. I stand my ground. "Obviously not as well as you. Parading around downtown with your *boyfriend* without a care in the world." He throws every syllable at me like a dagger.

There's a snide remark already waiting on my tongue. But I bite it back. He's hurting. If there's anyone who deserves to be cut some slack, it's a grieving parent. Arguing with him or hurling an insult isn't going to make this situation any better.

"I'm very sorry that you feel that way. We're doing everything that we can," I say as calmly as I can manage.

"Everything you can? Your *everything* is going to get every girl on this island killed."

My heart pounds in my ears, and I glance out the window in the direction of the station. About a hundred yards separate me from it. Though I should probably say something else comforting, I know if I open my mouth again, the words that come out are going to be anything but. I try to move past him toward the door, but he sidesteps to block me. Isabelle Arey enters the café just as I'm trying to slip past Mayor Clark. Her eyes sharpen when she sees me.

"Excuse me," I say forcefully as I step to the side. This time he lets me pass. But as I leave the coffee shop, Mayor Clark and Isabelle make it clear with their matching scowls what a shitty job they think I'm doing.

Fuming anger boils beneath my skin. Though I was planning to go back to the station, I need to vent some of my frustration, or I'll blow up at one of the guys. I head to the hotel. With each step I climb to Noah's room, I feel a little bit better, as if being one step closer to him can help set my mood right. I knock lightly, and Noah calls back, "It's open."

I open the door and look at him with a raised eyebrow. He's got his laptop resting on his legs as he leans back on the couch.

"It's open? There's a killer out there, and *it's open*?" I ask, trying to see the humor in it. He's obviously not at all concerned.

He shrugs. I catch sight of his grin, and the hold the anger has on me lessens.

"I need to get something off my chest," I say as I walk over and sit next to him on the couch. "Am I interrupting anything super important?"

"No," he says as he snaps his laptop closed.

"The mayor just stopped me in town to tell me what a shitty job I'm doing."

"You know—" he starts.

But I hold my hand up. Anger seizes me, choking off the words I'm desperate to vent. Fear flickers in the back of my mind, sweeping the rancor from my tongue. What if he's right? What if I'm not doing enough? This isn't like the cases I worked back in Detroit. Every moment I've spent with Noah, the times I didn't stay at the station until the early hours of the morning—if I had sacrificed more, would I have solved this sooner? Would lives have been saved?

Emotion rushes to the surface, hitting me so hard I'm afraid it may actually bowl me over. I stand up and pace the small room. I may not have done any of the killing, but if I dragged my feet, I am just as guilty—just as responsible in this. Noah stands and reaches for me. But I back away, desperate to build a wall between us. I feel myself coming apart at the edges, as if I'm moments away from shattering all over the floor.

"You're killing yourself over this," he says. "You're doing everything you can." I take a moment to breathe, to wait for the vise around me to loosen its grip. But when the wave doesn't pass, I know I need to get out of here. The walls seem to press in on me from all sides. And though Noah's presence is normally comforting, right now I just feel like I need to justify how I feel to him, and how can I if I can't even make sense of it myself?

I step toward the door, hearing the mayor's words in my mind all over again. "I've got to run home and grab some things," I say, and Noah reaches for me again, but I take off out the door before he can convince me to stay. I take a deep breath, sucking in the cold air as soon as I throw open the door. A cloud escapes, shaping my breath on the wind. I turn right and walk down Main Street toward my rental, hoping that with every step I take I can shed the words that have built up in my mind.

CHAPTER 34

I walk slowly up the walkway toward my house and grab the key from the mailbox. I've nearly shaken off the emotions that bubbled up inside me after the confrontation with the mayor. Just as I reach the porch, my phone vibrates in my pocket. I glance at the number on the screen. It's a Bangor area code.

"Detective Calderwood," I say as I accept the call.

"This is Ethan from the CSI team in Bangor. I wanted to update you about the items that your team sent up for fingerprinting."

My heart pounds. "What'd you find?"

"There were no fingerprints on the screwdriver. The keys had a portion of a print, but it won't be enough to match it against anything," he says, his voice flat.

"Thank you for the call," I say as my stomach twists.

Fishing my key from my pocket, I shove it into the lock and open the door.

As I head to the kitchen to grab a bottle of water, the sound of the boards creaking on my back porch draws my attention. I open the door, ready to draw my gun, but find Ryder leaning back on a patio chair. His long black hair falls behind him. Though he's got on a thick hoodie, the gauze binding his wrists peeks out from his sleeves. He has to be cold in that.

"What are you doing here?" I ask. The last thing I expected was to find him on my porch.

"I need to talk to you."

I narrow my eyes. "They released you already?"

He lets out a low laugh and scratches his eyebrow. I've wanted to stop by to talk to him, but his doctors wouldn't let me anywhere near him. Something about questioning him leading to further mental trauma.

"Can we go inside? No one can know I'm here."

My backyard is ringed with trees. Unless someone walks back here, no one will know. Even my neighbors can't see onto the back porch. I'm not going to stand here and argue that point to him, though, so I wave him into the house.

Clearly they didn't let him out. He must have snuck out of the hospital. I'm going to have to make a call once we're done here. Ryder hovers near the door with his hands in his pockets until I motion toward the couch.

"Why are you here, Ryder?"

"I need to talk to you about her," he says as he leans over, resting his elbows on his knees.

"All right. What about *her*?"

"I'm sure you've heard all kinds of rumors. It's hard to keep things quiet in this town. But I want to be sure you have the right information before I leave."

"Whose idea was it to keep the relationship secret?"

"Mine. Madeline didn't want it to be a secret at all. But I didn't want anyone knowing about us."

That surprises me. Why would he want to keep her a secret? Did she not fit into the persona he'd built?

"My family has a reputation, you know. The people we love suffer because of that. I knew her dad would just think she was dating me to get back at him." He sighs. "I didn't want her life to be harder because of me, and honestly it'd end up harder for me at home. My parents won't let us date anyone from the island."

It's a sweet sentiment, and he's right—most girls on this island would suffer if they dated a Warren.

"How long had you two been dating?"

"Almost a year."

They were able to keep a lid on it for a year? No one seems to have any clue they were that serious.

"Recently, things changed, though. Madeline was trying to finish up high school a year early so she could go to college. She really wanted the hell out of this town." He laughs to himself, but there's no humor behind it. "She wanted to get her GED so we could leave last August. But I told her to stick it out for one more year. I wasn't ready to leave yet. I didn't think I could support us."

"Did anyone else know that was her plan?"

He offers me a one-shouldered shrug. "Madeline had a lot of friends, friends I didn't talk to." He looks down and grimaces, his hand rubbing the back of his neck.

Ryder doesn't seem as fragile as he did a couple of weeks ago. But I'm still hesitant to ask. "Ryder, did you know she was pregnant?"

His eyes go wide and well with tears. "No," he finally manages to choke out. "Is that why she was rushing me to find a way out?" He buries his head in his hands, and a strangled growl slips from him.

I reach over to try and comfort him.

"Why didn't she just tell me?" His shoulders shake as his body is racked by sobs.

"I don't know, Ryder. We won't ever know."

Tears pool in his eyes when he looks up at me again. "All she wanted was to move on with our lives, to get the hell out of here, and I couldn't give her that." His lips twist, and he stares off into the distance.

"Ryder, it's not your fault that she's dead. I know it doesn't help now, but I hope one day you realize it," I say. I'm not the kind of person that tries to fix people. The career path I followed wasn't about fixing but about closure. But I desperately want to fix this kid. He doesn't deserve to suffer through this.

"That's easy for you to say. She was meeting *me* in the park, because I didn't want us to be seen together having a date. I knew how bad that'd be for her. Her dad would have flipped." There's an edge to his voice; it's close to cracking. Years of this, and it doesn't get any easier to sit across from someone who's upset. I steady my thoughts so what I'm going to say doesn't come out sharper than I want it to.

"Believe me. I've been very close to where you are. It's the same place I was in with Rachel. Looking back, there are things I could have done to save her. If I had told someone what I knew . . ." I trail off, unsure what else I want to say to this kid. And the burden is doubled, because my future niece or nephew died right along with her. Two lives I'll never be able to make amends for, no matter how many killers I find.

"How do you live with yourself? How have you convinced yourself that you deserve anything? That you deserve to be happy again?"

"For a long time, I didn't think I did. But I realized Rachel wouldn't want me to spend the rest of my life punishing myself." It was something that took me years to process. When you break it down, Rachel was a much better person than I was. She did what she could to save me. And all I did was keep my mouth shut. Rachel had to know. There's no way she didn't know that something terrible was about to happen to her, and the only reason I got away was because she wanted me to. "Someone told me something that helped after Rachel died."

"Oh?"

"You're never going to be the same again. But one day, you'll be okay. Maybe not tomorrow, maybe not next week, but one day you will be."

"So don't aim for happy; just aim for not wanting to die every moment that I'm awake. Got it," he says as he rubs his eye into his palm.

"It does get easier."

He shakes his head and lets out a strained laugh. "You don't get it. I don't want to be okay. I don't want to get over this. I *deserve* to feel like this."

I don't argue with him, because the conviction in his voice tells me that there's no point. It will take years for him to come out of this fog. I can only hope that he makes it through.

"Even if you find who did this, it's not going to bring her back," he says, but I think he's saying it more for himself.

"I know. But it will stop someone else from going through the same thing. Whoever did this isn't going to stop with Madeline, Emma, Piper, or Rachel. They'll take someone else's daughter, sister, girlfriend."

He nods, and my cell phone vibrates.

"Sergeant," I say as I answer the phone.

Ryder pulls out a pack of cigarettes from his pocket and points to them, as if to ask me for permission to smoke one. I wave my hand for him to go ahead, and he lights one.

"Ryder Warren escaped from the hospital. We need to keep an eye out for him on the island. They were sure he'd come back," Sergeant Michaels informs me.

"How'd he escape?" I ask, and Ryder raises an eyebrow in response. He stands, but I motion for him to sit back down.

"He took someone's badge while they were on the shitter. If you see him, grab him and let me know so we can get him back to the hospital," he says and ends the call.

"They figured out I'm gone already?" Ryder asks as he takes a drag from his cigarette.

I nod. "Yep. I'm supposed to be looking for you."

"Are you going to take me back to the hospital?"

"That depends. Are you going to hurt yourself again?" I ask, because I'm pretty sure he won't. This kid reeks of guilt—it comes off him in waves—but I don't think he's going to hurt himself because of it. There's a part of me that doesn't want to turn him in—because I don't know who to trust in this. My fear is that someone is going to try to pin something on this kid, and that will push him over the bit of ledge he's got left.

He shakes his head. "No. It all just got to be too much, you know?"

I nod. I do know. I know what he's feeling—or pretty close, anyway. There were days I thought the grief and guilt would swallow me whole. With my emotions as raw as they were, I didn't think I could ever be okay again. Everyone told me it'd get easier day by day—it didn't. It took good days, and it took bad days, but eventually I realized somewhere beneath all of this, I was still there. "Madeline would want you to live, to be happy."

A thin, lifeless smile curves his lips. "I know. Even if I had killed her myself, she'd still want me to be happy. That's just who she was."

"What are you going to do?"

"I'm going to Bangor. I can't stay here; everything reminds me of her."

"As long as you promise that you'll call me if you think about hurting yourself again, I never saw you. But you'll have to figure out how to get yourself off the island." There's only so much of a risk I'm willing to take for this kid.

"Thank you."

Ryder hangs out in the living room until dark and then disappears into the night. I wait until he's gone before I head back to the hotel. The next morning, with no word or sightings of him, all I can hope is that he made it to Bangor okay.

CHAPTER 35

Early Saturday morning, my phone vibrates on the nightstand, pulling me from what feels like less than two hours of sleep. My eyes burn, raw with exhaustion. Noah and I stayed up too late looking through more case files with details on Frank, trying to find answers about his sister, but everything we've found has pointed to her leaving the island—and though I've asked around, the only responses I've gotten match that story. Though I blink over and over, trying to make out the words on the phone's screen, it takes me what feels like five minutes to read them.

"You want me to handle that? You've barely slept," Noah offers.

"Thank you, but I've got it," I say as I unlock the phone. "Mom," I say as soon as the call connects.

"Hi, darling. What time are you getting to the church tonight? I thought it'd be good if we arrived at the same time," she says, her voice so chipper I'm sure it's an octave from shattering glass.

"Church?" I have no idea why she thinks I'd be going there tonight.

"There's a memorial for all the victims."

"I'm not sure," I start to say, but she clears her throat, interrupting me.

"Everyone is expecting you to be there," she says, and the undercurrent in her voice tells me everyone expects it because she told them to.

If the whole town is expecting me, I can't bail. I can't dodge something like this.

"I'll be there at seven," I say.

"Is everything okay?" Noah asks.

"I've got to go to the memorial at the church tonight, if you want to come with me," I offer.

Noah nods. "Of course. I'll be there if you want me to be."

I settle in the hotel room, a box of files at my feet. As Noah types away on his laptop, I dig back into Frank's history.

—

The edge of the bed dipping from Noah's weight pulls me from my nearly unblinking gaze on my laptop. He brushes hair away from his face and says, "You should probably find a stopping point so we can head to the church."

I nod and close the laptop. Shifting on the bed toward the edge, I groan. After the constant rush of adrenaline and stress lately, my whole body aches. I try to stretch my sore muscles and groan again when a sharp pain radiates from my bruise.

"You all right?" Noah asks as he rubs my neck.

I nod. "Everything hurts right now. I'm sure it will be fine once I get moving," I say, and I'm not sure if I'm trying to convince him or myself. But I need to do this. I have to be there. Most of the town will be, and I'm curious to see if Frank will show up.

The bruise on my neck has only gotten worse since the attack. Purple, blue, and green handprints are etched on my skin. The last thing I need is for everyone in town to see it. After I get dressed, I call Sergeant Michaels.

"Claire," he says as soon as the call connects.

"I'm going to the memorial tonight." The idea of Frank being out there, possibly attacking someone else, while I'm at the memorial makes me want to second-guess the whole thing. "Who has eyes on Frank?"

"Allen is watching Frank tonight. He's staked out there now. Jason is in town as well, keeping watch. He's sweeping between the church and park."

"Sounds like we're all set, then. Call me if they see anything," I say.

"You know I will."

The reality of going to the memorial hits me, and I turn to face Noah again. "Are you sure you want to go to this?" He's going to be diving headfirst into being picked apart by this entire island. No matter why he might be going with me, to everyone there, he will be my date.

"If you want me there, I want to be there."

I know what he's really thinking, what he won't say—I shouldn't go anywhere by myself right now. "You're throwing yourself to the wolves," I warn him.

He grins. "Then I hope I taste good."

I roll my eyes at him. "They're going to ask you a million questions."

"Good thing I have a million answers." Though I didn't think it was possible, his grin widens. I smack his arm. "You wound me!" he cries dramatically before falling back on the bed.

It takes me a few minutes to finish getting ready, and then we head to the church. My mother is leaning against her Jag outside when we walk up. Her eyes narrow, and I know she's seen my neck. I adjust my shirt to cover it, realizing that during the drive it shifted to reveal my bruise.

"What on earth happened?" she asks, her eyes still on my neck long after it's covered.

"Problem with a suspect," I say as if it doesn't bother me a bit. If I show that it scared me, that it was at all an issue, she'll panic. And the more I talk about it, the more likely it is to upset me again. I can't deal with her panic and my own.

"You shouldn't be doing that job. I keep telling you that," she says as she clicks her tongue and crosses her arms. I've had this argument with her a million times. Police work is a man's job, I don't even need to work, our family money will take care of me—we've been through all her points so many times I could make her arguments for her. But I've never wanted the family money; that's not the life for me. I've always wanted to make my own money, to be my own person.

"We should go inside," I say to change the subject. Hopefully the moment we step inside she'll stop questioning my life choices.

"It's lovely to see you again, Noah," she says, ignoring me as she kisses him on the cheek. Great—maybe he can be her new favorite.

"You too, Mrs. Calderwood," he says, offering her a forced smile.

"Evelyn! Over here!" Jan, one of my mom's friends, calls from right outside the doors to the church. Her black hair is pulled up in a french twist. She's wearing a short black dress, the kind most would find inappropriate for an occasion like this. According to my mother, though, Jan is in the market for a new husband, and that excuses all.

"Let's go. There's no reason to dawdle out here," she says as if it were her idea.

We trail behind my mother, her sleek black dress swaying back and forth as she walks in front of us. As usual, she's got on impossibly high heels. They've always been her trademark. She tried to pass the tradition on to me, but I was hopeless. I'm just not a high heel kind of woman, and I'm fine with that. It's not like I can chase down a suspect in stilettos anyhow.

"Where's your dad?" Noah leans closer to me, his voice low.

"He doesn't like getting out much. He's always been a bit of a shut-in." Hell, I don't think my dad has ever even left the island. He's lived in the same house his entire life. My dad may as well be a hermit. I've always been surprised he left the house long enough to meet my mom.

The church is packed. From the looks of it, nearly every person in town came. Pews line the room all the way to the altar. With night falling outside, the stained glass windows are dim, lifeless.

Being in the church again makes my stomach sour and my heart clench. The air is thick, heavy, like everyone in here collectively let out the breaths they've held for too long. Family units clot together, swarming from one group to another. I can read them. They think their togetherness will save them from the same fate. I wish there were something that would save them from this. But deep down, I know none of these girls are safe.

My mother ushers us around like we're a collection plate. She looks at me as if waiting for me to ask questions, but here, in a situation like this, listening has much more value than questions. As we move to our seventh group, my phone vibrates, and I'm thankful for a reprieve.

"Excuse me, I've got to take this," I say, glancing to the rest of the group as apologetically as I can manage.

"Want me to come with you?" Noah asks.

"I'll just be a minute."

Sergeant Michaels's name pops up on the screen, and I answer it as soon as I step through the back door. Darkness blankets the island, and back here, I blend into the shadows. Above me, a sliver of a moon stands out against a twinkling sky.

"Hey, Sarge—" I start to say, but the sound of scuffed footsteps forces me to turn around. In the darkness, I see nothing. But I feel it, a presence so close the hairs on the back of my neck stand on end. Something cracks hard. Lights explode behind my eyes; then darkness claims me.

The ocean rocks me awake. A slow, pulsing throb, like the waves, starts at the back of my head and radiates through the rest of me. Pain splits me in two as my consciousness returns. My eyes flicker open, and I look out over the ocean lit only by the sliver of a moon. It takes too long for my mind to register that I shouldn't be here—right around the time I realize I can't move my wrists, my legs. I'm bound to a chair, ropes so tight around my arms and legs that my feet and hands have gone numb.

Panic swells inside me, and my heart beats with a frenzy. My breaths come so quickly my head swims. Though I try to look for the shore, to see how far from the coast I am, the lights glitter so far in the distance that for all I know it could be fifty miles.

"You're awake," a rough voice calls behind me. Though I try to turn my head, whoever it is, is too far behind me for me to see. But I recognize the voice now. Though it doesn't match the voice of my attacker—he was too feral, too raw then—now that he's calm, I'd know it anywhere.

"Frank, untie me," I say, my voice steadier than I feel.

He chuckles, low, and my blood chills.

"Come on—if you're going to kill me, at least be a man about it," I growl as I struggle against the restraints.

His feet thud against the wooden deck of the boat behind me. "Don't act like this is my fault, sweetheart. You had to get in my way. You had to keep me from what I have to do," he scolds.

"What do you have to do? You have to kill?" I ask, trying to coax him into talking to me more.

"These Christ-cunts are all alike," he spits. "They go in there to sing their hymns and beg for forgiveness, and then they come out to lead their double lives." He stalks closer.

"What's your problem with church?" I ask, curiosity vanquishing the fear from my voice. I knew the killer had an issue with the church, because he cut off the tattoos. But what caused it?

"They're all guilty of something. They try to use God to absolve themselves. But I know the darkness in their hearts. He can't help them. Only I can," he says.

The boat rocks, water lapping at the hull. Though there's not much of a breeze, the water is choppier than I would expect on a night as clear as this.

"How can you help them?" I twist my wrist against the rope, hoping to find a weakness, but there's none.

"By killing them so they can't hurt anyone else," he explains, and he starts to slam something hard into the hull of the boat until water hisses and sputters onto the deck. "I can't choke you—that's a punishment for them. And you're not guilty of their crimes. But the sea, the sea will take you," he says, and all the adrenaline in my blood gives way to ice. He's going to let me drown. I'm not sure if that's a worse fate than being strangled. "You weren't like the others. You didn't act like her. I thought you were different," he mumbles.

"Who?" I ask. But he doesn't answer me; he just keeps banging something hard into the hull of the boat. "Please, stop this now. We can talk this out," I plead.

"I didn't want to kill you. I want you to know that. You're making me do this."

"What about the others? Did they make you do it too?"

He's silent for a long time. Then he says, "I had to kill them. If I didn't, my sister came back. She was the first I punished. After that, she cursed me."

"Wha—" I start to ask, but he cuts me off.

"It's too late," he says as he steps in front of me.

"Frank, please," I plead, and my voice cracks.

He grabs onto a line, pulling a tethered boat closer, and steps out onto the deck. A few seconds and a roar of an engine later, he disappears into the darkness. Cold water laps at my feet, and I struggle against the ropes and the chair he's bound me to. No matter how much I struggle, it doesn't budge. With every rapid beat of my heart, the water rises higher. My head swims as panic takes over.

The sea rises higher, like cold fingers tightening around my legs. I struggle, and my chair topples to the side. Water rushes around my side, shoulder. My head lolls against the deck. The more adrenaline pours into my blood, the more I realize I can't stop this. The more I move, the more my skin burns. Fibers from the ropes dig into my flesh, and I know if I get out of this, I'll be rubbed raw. The water laps against my side, rising higher. Reflexively, I suck in a sharp breath as the icy water bites into my flesh.

I lurch hard against the restraints on my ankles, and I'm able to pull out a bit of slack. My heart races, and hope rises in the back of my mind. I can do this. I can get out. My wrists ache as I tug at them, but with each movement, I'm getting more room to move. I kick hard again, the water splashing inside the boat.

With the cold of the water and the way it's rising, I've got only minutes before hypothermia kills me. A wave of adrenaline hits me, and I pull hard enough to free my right hand. With my hand free, I pull on the ropes holding my left. I get free just as the water lapping against the left side of my face floods my mouth. Realization hits me all at once. We're at least one hundred yards from the shore. In normal conditions, I could swim that with no problem, but in freezing water it's another story. With the boat halfway submerged, I force myself forward and out, throwing my body fully into the water. Goose bumps dot my arms, my legs. The more I try to propel myself through the icy water, the heavier my limbs become. I flop onto my back, floating and kicking myself toward the beach. I alternate between front and back as I try desperately to fight the cold and stay afloat. By the time I reach the shore, my body is as stiff as stone.

I crawl up the beach near the park, and a wave of hope hits me, propelling me. If I can go a little further, I can reach Jason. He's on patrol there tonight. When I make it through the tree line, the beam of his flashlight cuts through the dark night 150 yards in front of me.

"Jason," I call.

The light moves toward me, and he jogs, the beam bouncing. He stops dead in his tracks when he sees me. A second later Noah jogs up beside him and helps me to my feet.

"It's Frank," is all I can manage to say through the waves of shivers racking my body, though Jason already knows. With his help, I climb in the patrol car. When he slides in, he starts the car and turns the heat off. As desperate as I am to warm up, I know why he's doing it. If a person with hypothermia is heated too quickly, they can go into shock and die.

"I'm going to take you to the hospital, and then—"

"The hell you are. We're going to get Frank *now*," I growl and explain the situation fully, even though I'm overcome by spasms. This perp isn't getting away from me. The asshole killed my sister and then tried to kill me. I'm taking him down now.

"We need to at least call for backup," he says.

I agree, and after we're done calling Sergeant Michaels, I send Noah to get me dry clothes so I don't end up with pneumonia—not to mention it wouldn't be comfortable to start an interrogation soaking wet.

When we pull up to Frank's shop, Sergeant Michaels and Marshall drive in behind us. Though Jason has been slowly cranking up the heat for the last ten minutes, I don't feel any warmer. My muscles are seized with shivers, and my damp clothes cling to me like a second skin. My heart pounds, and I reach for the car door. I take a deep breath to ready myself.

As a group, we move to the front of Sergeant Michaels's squad car. It takes a few seconds for us to coordinate. Though I want to pull my gun, kick in the door, and clock Frank across the face, that's not going to happen. Sergeant Michaels is determined to go in first. We all draw our rigs.

"Claire, you watch around back in case he goes out there," Sergeant Michaels says.

Frustration ripples through me. I want to be in the front, cuffing him. Not waiting around back. And though I try to fight him on it, he won't listen.

Sergeant Michaels's knocks resonate through the house, and the scuffs inside warn me of movement. I strain my ears as I try to listen over the pounding. My pulse skyrockets as anticipation boils inside me. He should have answered the door by now. I have half a mind to barge in the back. Just as I take a step forward, the door flies open. I jump back, the door whizzing by so fast the air hisses against my cheek.

Frank barrels into my side, knocking the wind from me. But I'm able to regain my footing, barely. I raise my gun.

"Stop, Frank. I'll shoot," I warn. My finger presses against the cold trigger. With my heart pounding and the adrenaline burning in my veins, all I want to do is shoot him. I want to put this asshole down. But I can't. Because as much as I want to bury a bullet in his brain, that'll erase the answers I need, the answers the other families need, and this isn't just about me.

He turns and faces me. Even in the low light, his eyes are wild, feral. There's a war being waged on his face. His feet are planted firmly, his fists clenched. *Run or fight.* From the way his lips twist, I think he's going to choose fight. But he turns, taking off toward downtown.

"Guys!" I shout as I run after him.

Frank is faster than I imagined he'd be—or maybe he just seems fast, as my joints are so seized from the cold that I can hardly move. He jogs down an alley in front of me, and I grab the flashlight from my belt. I won't let him get away. My heart pounds as I turn, chasing after him. We weave through the alley, dodging dumpsters and stacks of pallets. My chest tightens, as if I've strapped my vest too tight. The alley spits us out on Main Street, beside the café. My feet pound against the pavement, and I gain on him, closing the twenty-foot gap between us. I push myself harder. I have to catch him. I have to take this asshole down. Once I'm close enough, I jump, tackling Frank.

His body hits the ground with a hollow smack, the impact so hard it knocks the air from my own lungs. Though I expect the fall to knock him out, he thrashes, his elbows coming at me the moment he hits the ground. I dodge to the left just as he nearly hits me square in the jaw. Wind hisses past my face as I dodge to the right now. I punch him hard in the kidney, my knuckles throbbing just seconds after they make contact. Adrenaline burns in my veins, taking away the kiss of pain shortly after I register it.

"Stay down, goddamn it," I growl as I struggle to pin him to the ground.

He rocks backward again, his whole body shifting, and he nearly bucks me off like an unbroken stallion. Though I try to avoid it again, his elbow connects with my jaw. Lights explode behind my eyes, and my mouth floods with copper.

I hit him hard in the spine with my knee, so hard a bolt of pain shoots up my leg. I clench my teeth against it. The moment I slap the cuff on his left hand, all the fight goes out of him, like he's deflated. The sound of the guys running up behind me assures me this is over. We got him.

CHAPTER 36

Sergeant Michaels and Allen drag him off the ground as I read him his Miranda rights. They take him back to the station, and when Jason and I pull in, I find Noah waiting in the parking lot, a bundle of clothes under his arm.

"Did you get him?" he asks as he hands over the clothes to me.

"We got him. Thank you," I say, out of breath, as I give him a quick kiss. "I'll catch you up later."

Once inside I head into the bathroom of the station, peel off my wet clothes, put on the dry ones Noah brought me, and grab a cup of coffee. I'm still so cold that I feel like my soul has frostbite. It's going to be a couple of hours before I can start questioning Frank. We've got to get him processed first.

Sergeant Michaels pulls me into his office while Allen and Marshall are processing Frank. "Are you going to be okay in there?" he asks, concern thick on his words.

"I'll be fine," I say quickly and turn back to the door.

"You can't pretend this isn't personal to you."

"This is personal for *all* of us. We're all involved," I say, because while it may not be blood, everyone on this island feels like extended family. We know these people. We all lost people we knew and loved.

He nods. "I want Jason in there with you, just in case."

"Fine." I grab Jason and pull him into my office so we can get on the same page.

"What'd you find at his place?" I ask. While I got changed and Frank was processed, Jason spent a couple of hours at Frank's place to start executing the search warrant with Vince. I can't believe that Sergeant Michaels was able to get a judge to sign off on it so quickly. But apparently, he had some favors to call in.

"Several pieces of dried flesh. Tattooed flesh," he says as he wrinkles his nose. "And two purses of victims."

Checkmate.

We head into the interrogation room. Frank is slumped at the table, his wide shoulders hunched. Jason and I take seats at the table across from him. I've got a legal pad in front of me so I can take notes and have him write a statement in his own words after he confesses. Because he *will* confess.

"So, Frank. When did you kill for the first time?" I ask as I take a sip of my coffee.

He glares at the table and glances up at me for just a moment. I can't tell if he's going to cooperate or if it's just now sinking in that he got caught.

When he doesn't speak, I add. "We searched your house. We know." As if the things he said on the boat—or him trying to kill me—weren't enough.

He twists his head from side to side, popping his neck. A low, cold laugh rolls out of him. "When I was sixteen."

Frank is in his sixties now. Over forty years of killing. The pieces all click into place for me. So I was right: Sheriff Dyer didn't do any of the killing. He just covered for Frank. And Rachel was the first kill he couldn't clean up. Someone found her first.

"Who was it?" With the disappearance of his sister and the missing details about her, I knew something had to have happened to her; otherwise we would have been able to find details about where she'd gone.

"My sister," he says, and a sinister, joyless smile spreads across his face.

"And why did you murder your sister, Frank?"

"My mother left us when I was six and my sister was ten. Delilah thought it was my fault that she left. It changed her. Made her so angry. When my dad would leave us alone, she'd beat me. Eventually, I felt like I deserved it, like I really did make Mom leave. As I got older, though, it got harder to stomach. I watched her go to church, be nice to everyone else, and then come home and beat me. I couldn't take her double life. And in my teens I finally fought back. When I was sixteen, I strangled her. When Dad got home, he saw what I'd done. We took her body into our boat and dropped it in the water."

I write down a few notes and do my best to remain stoic, though the details turn my stomach. "How many others have you killed?"

He shrugs and laces his fingers together atop the table. "I don't know."

"How many murders did your father cover up for you?" I ask, hoping if I'm more specific, he'll answer me.

"Six or seven."

"What were their names?" I ask, writing the possible number of victims down on the paper.

"Figure it out yourself." He spits the words at me and then smirks like he's pleased with himself.

"How often did you kill?" Jason asks.

"There wasn't any timeline—just whenever my sister's voice started screaming in my head again." As he says this, he motions toward his left ear.

"Why did you start killing more often?" I ask. All serial killers escalate, but typically there is a reason, and it seems his kills were very spaced out for a long time.

"Cancer. My time is running out."

I'm not sure whether to be happy or pissed. Even after he does get locked up, the punishment will only last so long if he's sick.

Anticipation boils beneath my skin. I know the answer already. I'm sitting across the table from the person who killed my sister. But I still have to ask. I need to hear him say it.

"Did you kill Rachel?"

He nods. "Things changed when I killed Rachel. Dad couldn't hide what I'd done anymore." His fingers steeple on the table in front of him. "He said he wouldn't cover for me anymore. That's when I started dumping them in the water. But it didn't feel the same—I didn't like it. They belong in the park. For years, though, I didn't have many options. I had to make my sister's voice stop. But after my diagnosis, I wasn't as worried anymore; I could put them wherever I wanted. Either way I'm going to die." His eyes meet mine, and the look in them is so foreign I don't even recognize him.

"Why, Frank? Why?"

"They deserved it. They were just like my sister. That's the last question I'm answering. I want a lawyer."

CHAPTER 37

Noah and I have gone around and around in circles for weeks. Half of me wants to leave the island and pray that I never have to see it again. The other half of me doesn't dare leave until Frank's trial is over. Things have been slow, almost painfully slow, since we caught Frank three weeks ago.

We're back in Noah's hotel room. He's got his laptop open, typing away on a deadline. Every day I wonder how much longer he's going to stick around—or how much longer I want him to stick around. At some point he's got to get back to his real life. And I've got to figure out what I'm going to do. I'll end up dead from boredom in a few months if I stick around here.

"I think we should move in together," Noah says out of nowhere. It takes me so off guard that I nearly choke on my coffee.

"I'm sorry, what?"

"I think we should move in together, whether that's here or South Carolina or wherever else you want to go."

It's the first time he's mentioned moving in together. The other conversations led me to believe we'd both still have our own space—which is what I've wanted.

"I'm not ready for that. I don't think *we're* ready for that," I say, worried the honesty will give too much bite to my words.

"Why? We spend almost every night together anyway. It just makes sense, unless you don't see this going anywhere."

I open my mouth to argue, to tell him all the reasons I'm not ready, that maybe I *don't* see this going anywhere, that maybe it's better for both of us if it doesn't, but my phone interrupts me. Worried it might be about my case, I grab it. "Hold that thought," I say as I accept the call. "Detective Claire Calderwood."

"This is Sergeant Pelletier from the Camden Police Department."

Camden is right across the bay, about fifteen minutes north of Rockland after the ferry. "How can I help you, Sergeant?"

"You solved those murders down in Vinalhaven, right?" As he talks, I can hear seagulls cawing in the background.

"Word already got out about that? Yes, I did."

He clears his throat. "Yeah. I was hoping I could get your help with something here. We found a body, a young girl. She was dumped in a motel."

My heart races the more he talks. A million questions pop into my head at once and fight their way to my tongue.

"What was the state of decomp?"

"There isn't any. The body was barely cold when we found her."

I look across the table. Noah eyes me curiously. "Yeah, I can help you with this. I'll be over there as soon as I can." After Rachel, with Frank's trial coming up—it's time to move on. It's time to see what else the world holds for me beyond this island. Noah smiles at me, the dimple on the left side of his mouth quirking.

I push up from the small table in the kitchen of Noah's room and walk across it. The blinds in the window are open, snow swirling from the clouds in a curtain of white. But it's not the scene outside I'm looking for. Instead I angle myself to see my reflection—and for once, I don't see Rachel standing there but myself with Noah framed behind me. For the first time it's not the specter of the past I see; it's the future ahead of me.

ACKNOWLEDGMENTS

Thank you to the incredible editors who helped me with this book. Megha Parekh—thank you for seeing what *Next Girl to Die* could become. And Charlotte Herscher, thank you for helping me take this story to the next level. And of course—to the rest of the Thomas & Mercer team and everyone at Amazon Publishing, your work and support on this project are so very appreciated. Thank you for everything that you do.

Thank you to my amazing literary agent, Laura Bradford, for believing in me and always being there. Without you, this book would not have been possible.

To the best critique partner on the planet and one of the best friends I have ever had, Elesha Teskey—without you NONE of my books would have been possible. Thank you for listening, reading, and helping me make sense of every dumpster-fire draft.

Thank you to Stephen J. Nelson, MD, medical examiner for Polk County, Florida, for answering my questions about autopsies and investigations—your expertise was invaluable.

To Jodi Gallegos, thank you for answering my weird medical questions and for being a beta reader for this book.

To my other beta readers, Layla Reyne and Sarah K. Stephens, thank you so much for reading *Next Girl to Die* and helping me on my way to publishing it.

To my husband, thank you for everything.

To my mom, kiss noise. Please rip out the sex scenes before you let anyone else in the family read this.

ABOUT THE AUTHOR

Dea Poirier was raised in Edmond, Oklahoma, where she found her passion during a creative writing course. She studied computer science and political science at the University of Central Oklahoma. She later spent time living on both coasts and traveling the United States before finally putting down roots in central Florida. She now resides somewhere between Disney and the swamp with her husband, son, two dogs, and two cats.